# DEADLY CONNECTIONS

## PLAIN JANE

**Plain Jane Stories**

Plain Jane is a British author.
'Deadly Connections' is her first murder mystery novel.

For more information about the author and her upcoming novels visit www.plainjanestories.com

# 1

*Last night, I heard the scream of a dying man. And I ignored it. I ignored his cry.*

Perched on the edge of a leather armchair, I glanced across at the detective inspector who had made himself comfortable on my sofa, and then at the young female constable standing in the doorway, her pen poised against a pocket notebook.

A damp film broke out on my brow.

The detective waited for me to respond to the news he'd just delivered: a man had been found dead on the public footpath that runs alongside the bottom of my garden.

An invisible hand wrapped round my throat and clenched. It was an effort to say a meagre, 'Oh God. How awful.'

'I need to ask you some questions, Mrs Jarvis,' the detective said.

'It's Miss.' The lie was accompanied by a blush. I prayed they didn't notice. 'And it's Jen – Jennifer.'

He asked of my whereabouts the previous evening.

'I was here, at home,' I said. 'All night.'

'And did you see or hear anything unusual? Anything at all?'

Guilt stung me all over as I remembered the man's last cry.

'Yes,' I said faintly. 'But I didn't realise what was happening, you know, what … ' Unable to complete the thought I put my face in my hands.

'Are you all right?' I heard the police detective say.

To my ear, his voice was distorted – a deep, drawn out drone. My head felt heavy. I had to fight to stop it lolling. It made straight thinking a gruelling task.

The detective gave a short cough. The constable tapped her pen against her notebook. The sound reminded me of the pelting raindrops that had fallen in last night's thunderstorm.

I took a moment to pull myself together, then sat up and faced them. 'Sorry. I'm really struggling to take it in. I can't believe something like this has happened round here … so close to home.'

'A very unpleasant business,' the police detective agreed. 'Which is why it's important you tell me everything you know.'

'Yes, of course,' I muttered, allowing myself to be distracted by a cobweb elegantly draped from the corner ceiling cornice.

'Why don't you start by telling us what you did yesterday?' the detective prompted.

Looking back, I encountered two expectant, watchful faces.

'Well,' I said, swallowing and thinking carefully, 'I was working for most of the day, in the shop – the candle shop on the High Street. I own it. And my mother helps out. She usually stays all day on a Saturday, but it was much quieter than usual, because of the heat. A heatwave doesn't do any favours for a candle shop.' I managed a limp smile. The detective gave a slight nod in response. The constable scribbled in her notebook.

'Saturday's normally our busiest day,' I said, building a steady rhythm to my words. 'We get a lot of tourists passing, mostly walkers and cyclists following the National Ridgeway Trail. It runs close to the town and people often stop off to visit. But by lunchtime it was sweltering and the place was deserted. Mum decided to take the afternoon off. I stayed on to keep an eye on things and sort some paperwork, then closed up at around five o'clock.' Along with my glistening brow I could feel damp under my armpits and in the crease behind my knees. I squirmed on the edge of the armchair.

'And then …?' the detective said.

'Then I went for a walk with the dog.'

The policeman scanned the room.

'He's in the kitchen.' I jutted my chin in the general direction.

'I see. And where did you go for your walk?'

The recollection evoked a deep longing. It had been such a lovely evening – the sort that lifts your spirits. I'd strolled out of Ridgelow into freshly cut hay meadows and lush cow pastures that hemmed the town, smiling to myself as I contemplated a quiet, relaxing Saturday night, followed by a lazy Sunday just mooching around. Digby had sauntered behind, nose grazing the ground until an interesting smell in the grass compelled him to dart off and investigate. A glorious sun commanded the sky, sending hazy heat beating down. It wasn't long before the dog had started to pant and my shoulders started to burn, so we'd headed for the comfort of shade and of home. Following a grassy trail into cool woodland, we joined the narrow public footpath that winds along the fence line at the bottom of my garden. I let myself in through the back gate I'd recently had installed and made my way up to the house.

'And what sort of time would that have been?' the detective said.

'Around six o'clock.'

'I see. And then what did you do?'

'I had a night in. Ethan, my boyfriend, is away for

the weekend.'

The detective leant forward, elbows on knees, hands clasped together. 'And what happened last night? What was it you saw or heard?'

An inward groan rattled my bones. For the umpteenth time I wished I'd called the police as soon as I'd heard the argument.

*He'd still be alive if I'd picked up the phone. Why didn't I pick up the damn phone?*

Buried under a thick blanket of remorse, I struggled to breathe.

'It's really important that you tell us everything,' pressed the policeman.

Images, smells and sounds tumbled round my head like pieces of a jigsaw puzzle flung up in the air. This was serious stuff. I knew it was vital to give the police a clear picture and get my version of events absolutely right. Carefully sifting through the pieces, I began to assemble together the final moments leading up to the man's death.

'I sat outside on the terrace for most of the evening reading a book,' I told the police officers through a tight throat. 'Then at around 10 o'clock I went inside and locked up for the night. I know it was about ten, because the church bells had just tolled the hour. It was still hot – really sticky and close – so I opened some of the upstairs windows, then ran a bath.'

*The water was a cool and refreshing tonic against my clammy skin. Eyes closed, I lay back and soaked up the peace and quiet, lost in a comforting daydream about Ethan.*

'Then I heard a voice outside. A male voice. It came from the direction of the footpath. He sounded angry.'

*My eyes snapped open. I sat up. Water lapped back and*

*forth around my waist.*

'It's not the first time there've been people out on the footpath late at night. A bunch of kids sometimes hang around the bench near my back gate, chatting, drinking and smoking. They don't realise how far their voices travel. When I've got the windows open and the wind is in the right direction, I can hear whole conversations. Once, they got so rowdy that my neighbour, Izzy, called the police, but by the time they arrived all the kids had scarpered, leaving a pile of cider cans and takeaway boxes behind for us to clear up the next day.'

*More voices – all male.*

*One in particular stood out.*

'His tone was more urgent than the others. I tried to hear what they were saying. There wasn't any wind, so the words were muffled, but they started arguing and in the next minute things turned nasty and a fight broke out. It all happened so quickly.' I looked at the detective. He said nothing, but gave a small nod to encourage me on. 'Digby, my dog, started barking at the noise, so I got out of the bath, put on a robe and went downstairs to shut him up.'

*Someone cried out; the sound a nasty tear in the hush of night. A chill of foreboding washed over me.*

'I ran to the phone, ready to dial 999, but then I heard sirens. I assumed Izzy had heard the fight too and had already called the police, so I didn't. Digby was going mad, spinning round and jumping up at the back door and I decided to let him out. I thought he might see off the kids, if they were still hanging around.'

*The dog bombed off, disappearing into black.*

*Sirens and voices were replaced by incessant, sharp barks.*

'After a minute or two I called for him, but he

ignored me. I haven't had him long and we're still getting to know each other. Sometimes he's a bit disobedient. I had to go and fetch him.'

*Bare feet slipped into flip flops.*
*A hand reached for a torch.*
*The light was dim, the battery ready to give up the ghost.*

'I followed the path down to the bottom of the garden and could hear Digby chasing about somewhere close by.'

*The weak beam traced the wooden fence.*
*The yellow glow came to rest on the back gate.*

'All of a sudden I was very aware of being alone in the dark,' I told the police officers, shivering as I remembered the moment. 'Something wasn't right and I had a really strong urge to get back inside.'

The picture I'd assembled for the police with the jumbled pieces was almost complete, but not quite. The young constable was doing well to keep up. A trail of blue ink filled another page as she scrawled away, biro scratching against paper, fingers stained as she lightly smudged some of the words.

*My ears pounded with the sound of my own heartbeat.*
*Nervous fingers tightened the cord of my thin cotton robe.*

Trying to tame all the chaos in my head and keep things simple, I took a long, deep breath before saying, 'I managed to grab Digby by the collar and took him back to the house. But he wouldn't settle and kept whining and staring at the back door. It made me wonder if someone was still out there. So I was extra-careful to lock everything up before I went to bed, but I still didn't sleep very well. It was too hot and a storm passed over at some point. The sound of the rain hammering on these old windows kept me awake. Then this morning I got up and took the dog for a walk by the canal – we were out for quite a while – and not long after I got home you knocked on the door.'

The constable was still scribbling furiously. Beads of sweat lined her nose and upper lip. I felt sorry for her for having to wear a thick protective vest in the height of summer.

'Thank you, Miss Jarvis. You've been very helpful,' said the detective. He settled into the leather sofa. Cushions creaked beneath his weight.

As he took a moment to reflect, I sneaked a look at him. He was rather ordinary – middle aged – average height – slight paunch – wispy, unkempt greying hair. No particularly interesting features stood out. His cheap charcoal suit and sombre navy tie gave the impression that he wasn't remotely interested in his appearance. He could be anyone. While most people would probably be offended by such a description, I could see it was a useful look for a police detective, because he would just blend into the background. I could also see from the narrowing of his eyes there was much more to him on the inside than the outside. He'd taken in everything I'd told him and was succinctly processing and filing the information.

'I need to confirm a few things,' he said, giving me a penetrating stare. 'You were here alone all night?'

'Yes, that's right.'

'You had no visitors? No one at all came to this house?' He raised an untrimmed grey eyebrow.

'No one.' There was a pause – a long one. So long that I felt compelled to break the silence, and then the words tumbled out in a rush. 'Look, I feel terrible about what happened out there, I really do. I know I should have rung the police as soon as I heard them arguing, but as I said, I assumed – wrongly – that it was that bunch of kids messing around again. And then I heard sirens and thought that Izzy had already made the call.'

'We all make mistakes,' said the detective, still staring at me. 'I've got a few more questions, if you don't mind.' He didn't wait for my permission to continue. 'Your partner – Ethan. You said that he's away at the moment?'

'Yes. In Wales.'

'Do you live here together?'

'No. This is my house. He's got his own place on Brook Street. Number 32.'

'What's his full name, please?'

'Wells. Ethan Wells.'

The constable wrote down the details.

'And when are you expecting him back?'

'Some time tonight. I'm not sure exactly when. It'll depend on the traffic.'

*Why all the questions about Ethan?*

'Does anyone else live here – parents, children, lodgers …?'

'No. Other than the dog, I live alone.'

That seemed to satisfy him. 'Thank you. You've been most obliging.' He stood up, smoothing out the creases in his trousers as he righted himself.

'No problem.' I rose to my feet too.

In silence, we walked single file into the hallway – me, the detective, then the young police constable. The dead man came too, his last cry lodged in my mind, along with a question that I had tried to swallow away during the police visit, but to no avail – it had to come out.

As I opened the front door I dared to ask, 'Do you know who he is?'

The detective, who was halfway over the threshold,

froze, then completed a slow pivot. As he faced me a speck of interest flickered in his eyes. 'His name is Robert Ashmere,' he said, watching me closely.

*Robert Ashmere?*

'Did you know him?' the detective said, quite casually.

It didn't ring any bells. 'I don't think so.' But the hairs on the back of my neck stood to attention. 'Was he local?'

'He was from Oxford.'

'Oh. So what was he doing in Ridgelow? And why was he on the footpath in the dark?'

'That's what we're trying to establish,' the detective said.

'Of course. Sorry, that was a stupid thing to say.' I bit on my lower lip then added, 'I'm a bit all over the place at the moment, what with knowing a man died out there,' I glanced back over my shoulder, towards the garden, 'and then being interviewed by you.'

'This is just an informal chat, nothing more. At this stage, anyway.'

It was my turn to freeze.

'Well,' I said, wishing he would hurry up and leave, 'it's a horrible thing to happen. Everyone round here will be shocked when they find out.'

To my relief the police officers stepped outside.

'Why don't you see if anyone's home next door,' the detective said to the constable. 'I'll be with you in a minute.'

With an obedient nod, she headed off, sensible shoes scrunching on the gravel driveway.

The police detective turned back to me. 'We've had to seal off your back gate, to secure the investigation area. You won't be able to use it for a while, I'm afraid.'

'That's fine. I understand.'

'There is something else I'd like to ask …'

He grappled around inside one of his suit pockets and pulled out a small, clear plastic bag containing a creased photograph. He handed it to me. It was a head and shoulder shot of a couple on their wedding day. She was all platinum waves, hypnotic green eyes and amethyst lips. He was older, with dark, receding hair, designer stubble and a brooding, arrogant stare.

'Do you know this man?'

'No,' I said while experiencing a slow sinking feeling.

'It's the deceased – Robert Ashmere. Take a good look.'

As I stared at the man's face, my ears began to fill with the sound of his last cry.

My next question was almost a whisper. 'Do you know what happened to him, how he died?'

'We're not sure of the exact cause of death at this stage, but the man suffered serious head injuries.' The detective was quite matter of fact about it.

A gory image of a bludgeoned body lying in the bushes sprang to mind.

'Are you absolutely sure you don't know him?'

'Yes,' I forced myself to say firmly. 'And I've never heard the name Robert Ashmere before either.'

The detective fumbled around in another pocket and drew out a second clear bag. This one contained a piece of paper. With a steady hand, he held it up, right in my face.

'If that's the case,' he said, pulling an empty smile, 'can you please explain to me why Mr Ashmere had your name and address with him on a note in his pocket?'

2

Scrawled on the crumpled piece of paper were the words, *Jennifer Jarvis, Corner Cottage, Summer Lane, Ridgelow.*

Well, I had no idea how my name and address came to be in the dead man's pocket and I told the police detective exactly that.

*What the hell's going on?*

I could now see why he'd been so persistent with his questions and a wave of nausea rolled in my stomach.

He pocketed the note. 'I assume your business interests mean you've no plans to leave Ridgelow over the next few days?' he said, looking me right in the eye, but with no obvious emotion in his.

Lost for words, I hugged the front door, wishing I had Ethan to cling to instead, and gave a weak nod.

'Good. You're going to be an important witness in this enquiry, given the fact that you appear to have heard the incident taking place and the strange coincidence that Mr Ashmere had your name and address with him.' His tone shifted to a self-important nasal clip and he seemed to grow in height. 'We'll need to take a formal statement. Come to the station first thing tomorrow. Ask for me, Detective Inspector Pitts.' He handed over a business card and strode away, leaving me wilting on the doorstep.

The policeman turned into Izzy's driveway. I knew she was out – her car was gone – and the constable was walking back, shaking her head. I shut, locked and bolted the door, then fled to the kitchen and sat at the scrubbed pine table staring through the open French doors, down the long length of garden, wondering who the dead man was, how he knew me, and what the hell the police were thinking. Then, overcome by an urge to call Ethan, just to hear his voice, I jumped up, grabbed my phone from my handbag and dialled his number. But it went straight to voicemail.

*Why did he have to pick this weekend to go and climb a sodding mountain?*

I hung up without leaving a message, because I had no idea what to say.

My legs were both weak and fidgety. I paced the length of the kitchen then sat down again, drumming my fingers on the table top then rubbing my face with my hands. I wanted to cry. But even though a hard lump hurt my throat I couldn't drop a single tear. Yet again, the man's last cry began to pinball round my ear canals like a terrible tinnitus.

*Why didn't I pick up the phone? Why didn't I pick up the damn phone and report the fight?*

The fact that I'd left a man to die out there was more than enough to contemplate, but that he might be someone I knew?

The walls of my cottage started closing in. There was no air. I had to get out. I had to talk to someone. With Ethan dangling from a rope somewhere in Wales, I decided to ring Lisa. I knew I could trust her with my life and was relieved when she answered and agreed to meet. Scooping up my handbag and the dog's lead, I called for Digby, who was sunning himself on the terrace, oblivious to the drama unfolding around him. Dodging potholes in the rough, dusty surface of Summer Lane, I hurried on foot towards the centre of the town, passing the police as they knocked on a neighbouring front door. I gave a false smile and was sure I could feel the detective's stare boring into my departing back.

It was a good fifteen minutes' walk to the High Street. Even on a Sunday Ridgelow was alive with activity. Nestled at the foot of a dramatic, dark green, leafy ridge, the old market town attracts thousands of tourists each year who come to admire the historic buildings, soak up the heritage and explore the surrounding rolling Chiltern Hills. Many shops, including mine, were closed for the day, but people were content to mill around and soak up the charm. The town looked particularly pretty in summer time. A local community group created glorious hanging baskets, window containers and bedding displays, and this year they had secured Ridgelow a finalist place in the coveted Britain in Bloom Awards. The High Street was a riot of colour, and a sweet, heady, floral perfume danced in the air, dulling the acrid smell of traffic fumes.

I skirted round a group of teenage backpackers huddled over a map and brushed past couples lingering by estate agents' and jeweller's shop windows. A christening party streamed across the road from the imposing medieval flint and stone church, babbling over a peal of bells. As they gathered in the entrance to the Chequers Inn, a hostelry dating back to Tudor times, some of the children made a beeline for Digby as I weaved through the crowd. But, desperate to talk to Lisa, I didn't hang about.

Like most places, Ridgelow has succumbed to the expansion of bland chain coffee shops, but Lisa and I prefer a family run tea room called Betsy's. Tucked away down a cobbled alleyway, I've happily whiled away many a Sunday afternoon there. I like the simplicity of the place; the mismatched crockery and furniture; the old-fashioned touches like the quaint little tea cosies and the nostalgic Big Band background music.

I bagged a table in the shady courtyard. Digby went to ground under my chair. As I waited for Lisa to arrive some comforting baking smells wafted through an open window. Normally, the thought of a fruit scone with raspberry jam and clotted cream, and a steaming pot of strong breakfast tea, put an expectant smile on my face, but the stench of death hanging in the country air quelled my appetite.

A few minutes passed before Lisa came strolling towards me, long blonde hair bouncing in a high ponytail and a broad beam wrapped around her face, oblivious to surreptitious admiring glances from men hiding behind their sunglasses, newspapers and wives.

'You look chirpy,' I said.

Lisa kissed me on the cheek and sat down. 'I am,' she said, still beaming. 'The sun is shining, I've got tomorrow off work and I'm about to stuff my face full of cake. I can't think of a better way to spend a Sunday afternoon.' She stretched out her bare, slim arms and yawned. 'Actually, I'm bloody shattered. This week's been an absolute killer.' I winced, but Lisa didn't notice and carried on chatting. 'I was up half the night with a poor old pony who had a bout of colic.'

Lisa is a highly respected vet with a specialisation in equine reproduction. Unfortunately, I'm allergic to horses, but that didn't prevent us from forming a strong friendship at school. We remained close during our university years, despite me being in Leeds and Lisa in London, and I was gutted when, on a whim, she jetted off across the Atlantic, hot on the heels of a fellow veterinarian student called Hamish. She spent two years working in the Californian racing scene before heading home with a brilliant CV, bronzed glow, gleaming smile and broken heart. It turned out that Hamish definitely preferred blondes, and unfortunately for Lisa, there was plenty of choice on the Golden Coast while she was immersed, literally up to the arms, in the intricacies of thoroughbred breeding. Lisa jokes that Hamish was jealous of her relationship with a particularly handsome stallion, ironically called Dark Deeds, but inside I could see she was in pieces about his betrayal. And despite setting me up with the two men in my life, Ethan, and more recently, Digby the dog, she hasn't had a serious relationship for quite a while, although I know she gets plenty of offers.

'Anyway …' Lisa stifled another lion-sized yawn, '… enough about work. What was it you wanted to talk about? You sounded a bit upset on the phone. Is everything okay?'

'No. Not really.' I toyed with a paper napkin, unsure of where to begin.

Sensing something important was coming Lisa straightened up. 'What is it? What's up? You haven't fallen out with Ethan, have you?'

'No. We're fine. It's nothing like that.'

'Then what?' She put a reassuring hand over mine.

The obstinate ball of sobs that had refused to budge now threatened to freefall. I blinked back the bitter tears and lowered my voice. 'I've got mixed up in something horrible – really horrible.'

The waitress came over and Lisa had to wait in suspense as she took our order, which gave me time to get a tighter grip on myself.

After a couple of deep breaths I said, 'Right, here it is … Last night, a man died on the footpath that runs along the bottom of my garden … '

'Died? How?'

'The police said he was found with head injuries.'

As I spoke, an artic chill grazed my left side by an empty chair at our table. As the dead man's face invaded my mind, my skin erupted in goose bumps.

'You mean he was *murdered?*'

'The police didn't actually say they're treating it as *murder.*' I flinched at the word and at the wave of cold that had settled beside me. 'It could have been an accident.'

'Well, they'll know soon enough after the post mortem. Oh, how awful. And so close to your house too.'

'I know. I've had to answer all sorts of questions about it. The police came round this morning. They wanted to know if I saw or heard anything.'

'And did you?'

I dropped my gaze. 'Yes. I did.'

The icy chill next to me intensified and I was consumed by a run of trickling shivers. Again, Lisa had to wait for me to continue as the waitress returned with our cake and carefully poured out the tea.

'I heard a fight and a man cry out,' I told her a few seconds later. My hand shook as I reached for my teacup and took a sip.

'Jeez! What did you do?'

'Nothing.' Concentrating, I managed to return the cup to the safety of its saucer.

'Nothing? Didn't you call the police?'

'Shh! Keep your voice down.' I shot a furtive look around the courtyard, but everyone appeared to be minding their own business. 'No, I didn't. I didn't realise what was going on. And it all happened so quickly. I thought it was those bloody kids messing around again, then I heard a siren and assumed Izzy had already made the call, but it must have been an ambulance on the way to the hospital. The man was found this morning. His name is Robert Ashmere. He was from Oxford.'

Lisa had devoured most of her cake as she listened. Mine remained untouched and I pushed the plate towards her.

'Oh, Jen.' She threw me a pitiful look as she picked up my fork. 'You must feel terrible.'

The sobs attempted a second escape, but I battled them back and avoided a public meltdown. Sensing my anguish, Digby appeared from beneath my chair, jumped onto my lap and delicately nibbled my earlobe. His timing was perfect. I hid my face in his fur and breathed in his biscuit smell until I was back in control.

'It shouldn't have happened,' I said. 'I should have called the police as soon as I heard them arguing. Things would have been different. I know it. He wouldn't have died.'

'It's not your fault,' Lisa said through a mouthful of chocolate cake.

I couldn't speak for a moment. Digby took advantage and repeatedly licked my nose in an attempt to cheer me up.

'Jen, it's not your fault,' Lisa said again, after swallowing with a large gulp.

I returned the dog to the floor. 'It gets worse. I haven't told you everything.' My voice began to wobble. 'It turns out the man who died had my name and address written down on a note in his pocket.'

Lisa slopped Earl Grey tea over the red gingham oilcloth. 'You knew him?' She dabbed chocolate crumbs from her mouth with a paper napkin before mopping up the spillage.

'No. The police showed me a photo, but I didn't

recognise him.'

'How come he had your name and address then?'

'I don't know. That's what the police were trying to find out.'

'But he must have been coming to see you?'

'That's how it looks, but I wasn't expecting anyone. I've no idea who he is.'

We talked in low voices about possible connections.

'Are you sure he wasn't someone you knew at university, or from your old job at the bank?' Lisa suggested.

'I don't think so. And anyway, why would he turn up unannounced at my house? Why wouldn't he send me an email through Facebook or something?'

Lisa pondered some more, weaving the end of her ponytail through her fingers as she tried to come up with a good answer. 'Maybe it was something to do with the newspaper feature about your workshop and business award?' she said. 'Lots of people will have read it by now. Maybe this Robert chap saw it and wanted to talk to you about making some candles?'

'Then why didn't he come to the shop? The address isn't a secret – it was printed as part of the publicity. Why did he have my home address? And how the hell did he get hold of it?'

'And why he was out on the footpath late at night fighting with someone?' Lisa added, tossing the blonde ponytail back over her shoulder.

Despite racking our brains, we couldn't think of any logical explanation. After a while we gave up and I offered to pay the bill. I went inside to settle up and joined a short queue at the till. As I stood waiting I couldn't help overhearing the conversation at a nearby table, where a rotund woman with badly dyed red hair, an overly painted face and braying voice was holding court.

'... he found a dead man on the footpath behind Summer Lane. Lying in the bushes he was. Looked a terrible mess ... ' The narrator was Shirley Langham, unofficial chief of the local grapevine. '... been beaten up!' There were a few shocked murmurs and a collective drawing of breath. 'A man murdered right on our doorsteps, what is the world coming to? And there's poor old Roger, jogging along on a Sunday morning, then would you believe it, he comes across a body. You don't expect that round here, do you? I bet the house prices take even more of a tumble.' Glancing up, she noticed me standing in the queue. 'Hello, Jennifer. How are you dear? And your mother?' It took a fraction of a second for her to twig. 'Doesn't your house back onto that footpath? We were just talking about this dreadful murder. Do you know about it? Did you hear anything?'

The noise level in the tea room subsided and I became the centre of attention. Mumbling something about being a deep sleeper, I slapped some cash on the counter and hurried out. As the door closed behind me, I heard Shirley say to her audience,

'Do you know Jennifer? She owns the candle shop, you know – JJ's? Runs it with her mother – Mary. She's the woman who lost her husband a couple of years ago. To the Big C, remember? Now that was another sorry business ...'

I stumbled into the courtyard with a heaving chest and heart-rush.

Lisa looked up from her mobile phone – she'd been texting someone – with a look of concern. 'Jen?'

I sank into a chair and explained that the gossips were already tucking into the death fodder with relish.

She put her phone away. 'Will you be all right on your own at your place? You can always come and stay with me if you like?'

'Thanks, but Ethan will be back soon. He'll stay with me. And I've got Digby.' I bent over to pet the dog and was rewarded with a wagging tail and another lick.

'Maybe I should walk you home then? You don't look too good. I don't mind hanging around if you want a bit of company to take your mind off things?'

I told her I would be fine. She gave me a hug and said to call if I changed my mind and we parted company.

But I didn't go straight home.

The police visit and the dead man's note were eating away at me. I was torn between trying to distance myself from the whole horrid business, yet at the same time desperate to know what was happening. After a quick mental wrestling match I made a decision and headed at pace towards Beckett Close and the entrance to the public footpath.

There was a strong police presence in the small cul-de-sac. Five marked police cars and a police van were parked up around the opening of the woodland trail. Bright yellow tape had been wound round a lamp post and two tree trunks to make a cordon. A baby-faced police officer stood silent and bored as he guarded the scene. A group of onlookers stood back behind the police line watching investigators combing the ground. I joined the rubbernecking pack to watch the proceedings, but was rudely elbowed out of the way by a thickset man with a gelled rockabilly quiff and black suede creeper sneakers, brandishing a professional digital camera.

'*Chiltern Messenger*, local press,' he said, puffing his chest and flashing a press card at the young officer, who was unimpressed and warned him to keep back with a surprisingly deep growl. Leaning over the yellow tape, the man started taking photographs.

'They'll find the footprints of half the town on that path,' said one woman loudly and to no one in particular. 'I walked down there myself yesterday. And what about the tourists? I know they've got all sorts of clever technology and gadgets and things, but I don't see how they'll be able to track everyone down.'

It was a good point. Ridgelow is a very popular destination for ramblers and cyclists, because it's so close to the prehistoric Ridgeway track. Public footpaths and bridleways criss-cross the parish and most are well used. The footpath behind my house is no exception. It gives easy access from the town to the top of the ridge and is in regular use, although not usually at night.

The woman added, 'I bet that storm we had last night won't help them. Hell of a downpour, wasn't it?'

There was a general murmur of agreement from the gathering.

I assumed from the lack of an ambulance or mortuary vehicle that the body had been removed. And thankfully, there was no sign of Detective Inspector Pitts either, but the business card tucked in the pocket of my denim shorts was a grim reminder that another conversation with him was only hours away.

There wasn't much to see, so the journalist got out a notebook and started picking out people in the crowd, asking if anyone knew who had died, or what had happened. I slipped away before he got to me and made my way home the long way round.

Back on Summer Lane, I noticed my neighbour's car parked back in her driveway and wondered if she had heard last night's commotion. Rapping the brass

Moroccan knocker, one of many artefacts shipped back from her globe-trotting jaunts, I stood back and waited.

'Just coming . . .' a rich voice sing-songed.

Izzy Wilder opened up, barefoot and in loose linen gardening clothes. A coloured scarf tied in an arty knot on top of her head swept a long, wavy silver mane back from startling blue-violet eyes.

'Jennifer! Digby! What a lovely surprise!' she welcomed with open arms. Her tanned, lived-in face oozed worldly experiences and broke into a supersized smile. 'Have you come for those strawberries I promised? Excellent timing. I've just been down to the veggie patch and they're perfectly ripe. They'll do very well in a nice flan or fruit salad.'

From the moment I moved in three years ago, Izzy and I have got on famously, initially over the garden fence, then she started leaving fruit and veg parcels on my doorstep, which progressed into 'pop-ins' and cups of tea, which developed into rather raucous evenings full of backgammon, mojitos and putting the world to rights. In her seventies – she's cagey about her age – Izzy always beats me at scrabble, knows some very rude jokes and is learning how to tap dance. And occasionally, she smokes a cigar.

I explained there had been a disturbance the previous night and asked if she'd heard anything. But it turned out that Izzy had been in London watching *War Horse* at the theatre with her daughter and grandchildren and had driven back that afternoon.

'Sounds exciting,' she said, her smile perking up another notch and bare feet jigging on the spot. 'Come in and tell me what's been going on.'

Izzy's home, Plum Cottage, is a traditional Chilterns brick-and-flint build with leaded windows. Dating back to the 17th Century, it's older than Corner Cottage and bigger, having been extended at the rear to create a beautiful bespoke kitchen dining space – of which I am very envious – and above, a vaulted master bedroom.

She led me outside to the large patio area at the rear, offered up my usual chair, and listened as I filled her in.

'A man killed?' she cried. 'While you were home alone? Oh, how dreadful for you.'

'I didn't realise what was going on,' I said. 'It all happened so quickly.'

Talking it through, we established it was quite likely that I was the only one who'd heard the fight, given that she'd been away overnight, the Barringtons were on holiday in Madeira, and the only other cottage on Summer Lane was currently vacant and awaiting the arrival of new tenants.

'I did wonder if something was afoot,' Izzy said. 'I heard voices coming from the footpath earlier, when I was picking some peas. It must have been the police searching the area.'

'They've sealed off the entrance in Beckett Close. I went down and had a quick look earlier, to keep an eye on things. It's all cordoned off.'

'Well, let's hope they do a thorough job and find something that'll help catch the culprit quickly. It's not nice to think that someone capable of killing a man is walking around, free as a bird, in our lovely little neighbourhood.'

'We don't know for sure what happened yet,' I said, suddenly feeling lightheaded. 'The police didn't actually say he was murdered. It might have been a terrible accident.'

'But you heard them fighting. And he'd been

beaten up. Sounds pretty nasty and violent to me. Anyway, I'm sure we'll hear all about it soon enough. Shirley Langham seems to have a bat phone to a number of well-nourished sources. She'll be all over this like an outbreak of measles.'

A pounding heart joined my spinning head as I wondered how long it would be before news of the note in the dead man's pocket came to light and Shirley came knocking on my door, inviting herself in for a cuppa and deep-filled gossip sandwich.

'Jennifer, are you all right?' I heard Izzy say, seemingly from a distance.

Refocusing, I discovered a pair of blue-violet eyes, etched with concern, looking at me.

'You drifted off. And ...' Hesitating, she cocked her head and wrinkled her brow into accordion pleats, '... and, well, for a moment you looked positively ill – all pale and shivery. If you'd been abroad recently I'd have put money on you having malaria.' The pleats deepened. 'Is everything okay?' When I didn't answer, unabashed she delved further. 'Has something happened between you and Ethan?' Her face dropped at the thought.

Izzy has a soft spot for Ethan. She says he reminds her of her late husband, Archibald, that he has the same sort of calm authority about him that makes you feel safe and protected and in capable hands.

I shook my head, which made the spinning worse. 'Ethan and I are fine.'

'Then it must be the shop?' she said, speaking more to herself than to me. 'I suppose this heat wave is affecting business and you're worrying about it?'

'It's not the shop.'

The urge to confide in my neighbour was of tidal

wave proportions. She's such an open book that it's hard not to be the same around her. On a couple of occasions I've even come close to telling her about something else I'm ashamed of, but so far I've managed to rein myself in, just in time. I know I would regret telling her. She might pressure me into telling Ethan, which I really don't want to do, because I'm not sure how he would react. And he means the world to me. I really don't want to upset him.

'Maybe I can help?' Izzy gave me an encouraging smile that lit up her eyes.

'Can you turn back time?'

She arched a refined silver eyebrow and cleverly said nothing.

I gave a heavy sigh, then filled the silence: 'When the police came round this morning they showed me something strange. One of them had a note. He said it was found in the dead man's pocket … Oh Izzy, the note … well, it had my name and address on it.'

She caught her breath. 'Good God, you knew him?'

'No. The police showed me a photo, but I didn't recognise him. And I don't know anyone called Robert Ashmere either.'

'That's his name? Well, he was obviously coming to see you.'

'It looks that way. The detective asked if anyone came to the house last night. I told him I'd been in on my own, but I'm not sure he believed me.'

'Why on earth not?' Izzy snorted.

'I don't know, because it's the truth. But he stared at me a lot, like he was trying to see right inside me, and I could tell he didn't believe what I'd said.' A searing heat flowed over me from head to toe like bubbling lava. 'And then he told me to go to the police station tomorrow morning to make a statement.'

'That's perfectly normal,' she reassured soothingly. 'You did hear the fight and they'll want to record it officially.'

Still feeling hot and woozy, I asked Izzy for some water. She hurried off to her kitchen, returning with a full glass.

'Here you are, love. Try not to worry about it too much.'

I took the drink, and a small sip. 'I can't help it. I mean, it's bad enough knowing a stranger died out there, but what if he is someone I know?'

Izzy leant over and patted my forearm. 'Poor you. What an awful thing to get mixed up in.'

'And now I've seen that photo I can't stop picturing the dead man's face.'

Sympathy switched to curiosity. 'What did he look like?'

'A bit cold-looking, you know, in a moody James Dean kind of way – dark hair, dark eyes and designer stubble. I suppose he was in his mid to late thirties, but I don't know how long ago it was taken. It was a wedding photo.'

'His wife must be devastated. I wonder if they have any children?'

I felt utterly wretched. 'It's my fault. I should have called the police when it happened.'

'Oh, come now. You mustn't blame yourself. I'm sure if I'd been at home I'd have thought exactly the same as you. If it helps, I'll tell the police about the pesky, loitering teenagers to back you up. At least this horrid business might stop them hanging around. Perhaps we ought to make up a rumour that we've seen his ghost to scare them off?' She smiled wickedly.

I didn't find the quip funny. The dead man was following me everywhere. I'd felt him all day, chilling me to the bone in thirty degrees, his piercing scream ringing in my ears.

'Back to this note,' Izzy said. 'Are you absolutely sure you don't know the man?'

'Well, Lisa and I spent ages this afternoon trying to work out who he was, but we couldn't come up with anything.'

'Tell me again what you know.'

'Not much. His name is Robert Ashmere. He was from Oxford. I assume there's a Mrs Ashmere because of the wedding photo. That's about it.'

'And all the voices you heard arguing were definitely male?'

'Yes.'

'And how many were there, do you think?'

'I'm not sure.' I inwardly replayed the scene again. 'But I'd say at least three. Digby was barking so much it was hard to tell. Not a lot to go on, is it?'

'No, not really …' Her lilac-coated eyelids drooped as she drifted into thought then a few seconds later, pinged wide open again. 'Have you searched him?'

'Sorry?'

'Have you searched for him online? It's the first thing I do if I don't have the answer to something that's bothering me. I've conquered many a *Daily Telegraph* crossword that way. I do hate leaving them unfinished – it keeps me up at night – so, if I'm really stumped, I cheat a tiny bit by logging onto a crossword solver. It's no worse than using a dictionary.' Excitement radiated from her like a nuclear glow. 'I think we should Google this Robert Ashmere and see what comes up. He might be on one of those social networking sites like Twiddle.'

'Twitter,' I said, kicking myself for not thinking of it first.

We hurried into Izzy's study and she switched on her computer. I knew she kept in touch with her son in Australia via Skype, and that she ordered her groceries online, but I hadn't realised how adept she was with technology.

'I like to keep busy,' she said, fingers deftly typing in her password. 'As soon as I've done my chores in the house and garden, and the crossword, I switch on and surf the web. And I've told you all about compiling my family tree – fascinating stuff – some skeletons in that closet, I can tell you. But that's a story for another day. This is far more exciting.' She was really enjoying herself, despite the morbidity of the situation. Typing the name into the search engine, she reached for her half-moon glasses and examined the screen. A few listings appeared, but didn't reveal anything useful. Izzy scrolled down the page and said, 'Ah ha! Here we go. Look – Robert Ashmere Photography.' She clicked on a link and a face emerged.

A cold hand gripped my spine.

Izzy took one look at me and knew she'd unearthed the dead man.

It was a black and white image. He looked older. His dark hair was cropped short and his face was etched with faint lines and creases, but the eyes held the same brooding stare.

'I see what you mean about the James Dean thing,' Izzy said admiringly. 'And there's something a little Mediterranean about him too. Bit of a looker, wasn't he?'

I gave her a withering stare. She reddened and

apologised for her lack of respect, then got up so I could take her place and navigate round the site. Most of the content was a gallery of his photographic work and there was a small introduction about his passion for photography and a price guide. Despite sucking in every trace of information I could find, in the end it didn't amount to much.

Disappointed, I said, 'I still have no idea why this man would want to contact me.'

Izzy, who'd been scrutinizing the website over my shoulder, was more positive. 'At least you know what he did for a living. And look, there's a contact number. Maybe you should ring it?'

'Oh, I don't know about that.'

'Why on earth not? I would.'

'Really?'

'Of course.'

'I'll think about it.'

I made a note of the number on a scrap of paper and retreated back to Corner Cottage. Taking my place at the kitchen table, I trawled over my memories of the previous night, trying to make sense of what had happened, deeply aware of the contents of my pockets: Detective Inspector Pitts' card on one side, Robert Ashmere's phone number on the other. I understood Izzy's frustration at not knowing all her crossword answers. The questions in my own mind were bellowing at me, demanding attention. They hammered against my skull, determined to get out. The noise was deafening.

I had to do something.

Reaching for the scrap of paper, I picked up the phone and dialled.

3

Holding my breath, I inwardly counted the rings – one, two, three – before the call connected and a voice picked up.

'Hi there ...'

Held in twitchy fingers, the handset trembled against my ear.

'... thanks for calling Robert Ashmere Photography ...'

My heart skipped a few beats.

'... I can't take your call at the moment, but please leave a message after the tone and I'll get back to you as soon as I can.'

I heard a beep, immediately hung up, discarded my phone on the table and bent over double, breath roaring like a champion sprinter. One hand located the back of a wooden chair and dragged it behind me. I sank onto the seat. As my breathing steadied, the dead man's answerphone message tore around my mind, which was now as chaotic and overcrowded as Piccadilly Circus. A sickening truth emerged from all the noise.

*I know that voice.*

*I know that man's voice.*

*I've heard it before.*

The abandoned phone, idling on the table, sprang to life, jangling crazily and vibrating against scrubbed wood. My respiratory rate rocketed all over again. I tried to catch the name on the display as the handset jived to its own Latino ringtone.

*Caller unknown.*

A pulse throbbed in my neck.

*What if it's his wife ringing back?*

Thinking on my feet, I composed a story about

wanting a quote for some wedding photography and then, heart in mouth, took the call.

'Hello?'

'Dydd da,' boomed a deep voice.

Every muscle in my body went rigid. 'Hello?'

'Dydd da,' the voice said again. 'It means *hello* or *good day* in Welsh.'

I relaxed. 'Ethan, you sod. You scared the living daylights out of me. Where are you?'

'At home, idiot.'

A waterfall of relief gushed over me. 'I'm so glad you're back.'

Ethan chuckled. 'Hey, you sound like you've really missed me – perhaps I should go away more often?'

I could hear the smile in his voice and feel its affection – an instant pick me up. For a lovely moment I felt like the person I used to be, before death had darkened my world.

'Your phone number came up as unknown,' I said.

'Yeah, I lost my mobile. It's lying out in the rain, slowly dying somewhere in the Senni Valley. I've bought a cheap pay-as-you-go to tide me over until I can sort it out with the phone company. So, what's new in the riveting world of Ridgelow? Wait – don't tell me; the vicar's bicycle's got a puncture, moles have mutilated the cricket pitch and the WI have had another bun fight? Jen …? Jen …? Are you still there?'

Trying not to cry, I told him about the fight on the footpath, the police visit and the note in the dead man's pocket.

Ethan was horrified. 'Oh, I'm so sorry you've had to deal with this all on your own.' He said he'd come straight over, and ten minutes later I was enveloped in the safe haven of a reassuring hug.

'I've missed you.' My choked words muffled against his broad chest as I clung on to him for dear life.

He buried his face in my hair. 'Ditto,' he murmured then stifled a yawn. 'Sorry, it was a long drive back. I'm shattered.'

I met his gaze and lost myself in his dark, chocolate eyes – then noticed one was ringed with blue, purple and black. With the small scar above his lip, a memento from his school field hockey days, he looked more brute than affable vet.

I caressed the bruise. 'That's not tiredness.'

'Ah, yes.' He rubbed his Roman nose with a forefinger then pulled a boyish, rueful smile. 'I'm afraid I had a bit of a tussle with a tree bough. The stupid thing got in the way of me and my bike. If you think I look bad, you should see the tree …' He broke off, winced and then added, '… and the bike.'

'Boys and their toys,' I sighed. 'That'll cost you.'

His face folded as he told me it was a write-off, but he perked up again as he described the rest of his weekend.

'The climbing was excellent,' he said, giving me a squeeze. 'You should come next time. You and Digby could go for some great walks. The scenery was amazing.'

As we exchanged smiles a blissful warmth encased my heart. Thank God Lisa had had the foresight to introduce us. Ethan joined the vet practice just over a year ago and she thought we might get on. She was right. The moment we met we clicked. It was completely unexpected and lovely. Izzy says he's an old soul. Lisa calls him a good egg. Even my mother, who can be hard to please, has grown fond of him. He ticks most of the boxes on the list I suspect she has actually drawn up on my behalf: tall, dark – albeit prematurely greying, handsome and well-mannered. Although I'm sure she would prefer him to be a doctor rather than a vet. All I know is that the love I have for him is beautiful and fierce and that I want us to spend the rest of our lives together. It's hard to live with the fact that I'm already married to someone else: a man I don't even know, let alone love, and a man who I haven't set eyes on since the day we wed.

Ethan has no idea. No one in Ridgelow does. It's a secret I've been hiding for years. The truth is, in the eyes of the law, I am not Miss Jennifer Jarvis at all.

'You look exhausted.' Ethan brushed a stray strand of hair from my cheek.

'I feel it. You will stay tonight, won't you?' I said, wishing I could be cocooned in his arms forever, safe and protected by his bubble-wrap hug.

He kissed my forehead. 'Course I will. You don't think I'd leave you alone after all this?'

We wandered into the kitchen. Ethan opened the bottle of wine he had brought round, poured two glasses, offered me one, then took his over to the open French windows and stood in the frame. The balmy summer evening and birdsong belied the horror and violence of the preceding night.

'I can't believe something so hideous has happened round here,' he said with a grimace.

I was still struggling to believe it too. Moving to his side, I put my arm around his waist and pulled him close again. He reciprocated with a consoling arm round my shoulders. Together, we peered down the sprawling garden, which, thanks to Ethan's green fingers and my regular watering, looked a picture of health. The lawn was soft and springy and the borders were brimming with cottage garden plants. The stone patio area, which he'd recently rescued and re-laid, was cluttered with terracotta pots and wooden buckets full of lavender, geraniums, snapdragons and aromatic herbs. It was a shame my gaze blanked out the abundant charms of Mother Nature and was lured down to the fence line where an ugly scene had taken place only hours before. Remnants of fear still hung in the air and I couldn't help picturing the dead man lying in the rain.

Ethan must have been having similar thoughts. He put down his wine and gathered me back into his chest, resting his chin on top of my head. 'I don't want you walking Digby on your own,' he said. 'Not until the police have caught who did it.'

I was touched by his concern. For a short moment a ray of pleasure overcame the cloud of guilt that hung over me. 'Don't worry. I'll be fine. I've got a personal alarm I can take and Digby won't let anyone lay a finger on me.'

'At least stick to places where other people are around.' His tone was firm.

Keen to change the subject and keep things as normal as possible, I asked if he'd taken any photos on his trip to Wales. He needed little encouragement to whip out his camera and present a slide show of mountainous landscapes and what looked like some riotous beer drinking as I baked a pizza and tossed together a salad. After dinner, Ethan watered the garden – I couldn't face it – and then we curled up on the sofa and watched mindless TV before heading off to bed. But morning was a long time coming. Piercing screams and brooding eyes tormented me throughout the night and I got up feeling groggy and heavy with dread at the thought of making a statement at the police station.

As soon as Ethan headed off to the vet practice I called my mother to tell her I'd be late for work. I didn't want to explain where I was going, or why, so I lied and said I needed to pick up some supplies for the shop.

After a quick shower, I scanned my wardrobe for something suitable to wear. Having never been to a police station before I had no idea what to expect, or what was expected of me. This made me nervous. I tried on various outfits, settling on my usual uniform of straight legged jeans and T-shirt, but added a poppy-coloured silk jacket to smarten things up, hoping I looked like a respectable, reliable witness. A generous squirt of serum tamed my choppy bob, but did nothing to disguise the roots sprouting at the base of my highlights. A smidge of pink blush on the cheeks gave my pallid skin a luminous lift, but even my most expensive concealer failed to combat the dark under my eyes. When I took a final glance in the hall mirror as I rushed out the door, I found my usual fresh face had morphed into a stranger's, and I didn't like the look of the person staring back.

I arrived at the police station on time, but Detective Inspector Pitts kept me waiting for a long twenty minutes in a small, stark interview room with only a watery coffee in a plastic cup for company. When he swept in and blessed me with his presence, trailed by another officer, I was reminded of my old school headmaster and stood to attention. The policeman's smirk left me feeling foolish and I awkwardly bumped back down again.

Detective Inspector Pitts sat at the table directly opposite, cleared his throat and in monotone said, 'Thank you for coming, Miss Jarvis. You've been asked here to give a witness statement in relation to the death of Mr Robert Ashmere. I need to tell you that it is a legal document and may be used as evidence in court.' He indicated to the policeman sitting beside him. 'This is Detective Constable Sams. He'll be making a note of everything you say. Then you will be asked to read and sign the statement to confirm that it's a fair and accurate record.' There was a short pause during which he eyeballed me. I shrank from his spotlight stare, wishing I could evaporate like my watery coffee. 'Right then, let's get started, shall we?' Having dealt with the formalities, there was a sudden change in his voice, which became sharp, active and pronounced. 'I'd like you to tell me *everything* you can remember about your movements on Saturday 5th July and explain *exactly* what you heard during the course of the evening.'

My account was the same one I'd given him at the house, except this time he probed me about the voices I'd heard.

'How many were there?'

'Three, I think, but I couldn't say for sure.'

'Can you describe each voice? Did you notice any type of accent, for example?'

I reminded him that the dog had been barking at the time.

'Did you hear any specific words, Miss Jarvis?'

'No, they were muffled. It was the tone that stood out. One voice sounded quite aggressive.'

Again he pressed me on my relationship with Robert Ashmere and again I told him that I didn't know the man, but again I sensed that he didn't believe me. Half an hour later, he was still asking me the same questions. My posture had weakened and I slumped in my chair, but my resolve was still strong and I answered everything he asked with a great deal of thought and care, but gave an audible sigh of relief as I signed the final statement.

But the ordeal wasn't over.

The detective had one more request.

'It would help our enquiry if you would consent to providing a DNA sample,' he said. 'It would be voluntary, and of course, you have the right to refuse, but it will assist us in the elimination process.' Quick to take my stunned silence as agreement, he stood up. 'Good, I'll let the duty officer know.'

Panic ran riot in my veins. 'Wait. I'm not sure. I don't want my DNA details stored on your files.'

'It's purely for the purpose of assisting our enquiry,' he countered, looking down on me. 'It wouldn't be added to the police database.' One of his untrimmed eyebrows twitched and he began to rock, ever so slightly, back and forth on his heels.

I knew that refusing might make it look like I had something to hide. The detective remained silent, gently rocking, as I struggled with indecision. After a long moment I decided not to refuse, but not to agree to it either.

'I need a bit more time to think about it,' I said. 'I'll give you a call when I've made up my mind.'

Detective Inspector Pitts accepted my response with a courteous nod then thanked me for my time, but my inner alarm bell, reverberating in the depths of my being, warned me that he was hiding his displeasure.

I don't remember the drive back to Ridgelow, or parking my Mini in a space on the High Street, or walking the short distance to the shop. But seeing my troubled reflection in the shop window jolted me back to earth. I quickly straightened my sagging shoulders and rearranged my tight features before stepping inside and facing my mother.

The old-fashioned bell over the door jangled, and the familiar waft of mingling candle scent encased me: calming rose, lavender and chamomile mixed with uplifting zesty orange, lemon and lime, chased by heady, spicy, ginger, cinnamon and cedar wood.

'Ah, good, you're back.' My mother slipped out from behind the mahogany serving counter. 'I was wondering how much longer you'd be.'

I noticed she had swapped her usual shop uniform of black trousers and a plain blouse for a pretty floral shift dress. It was a good choice. The brightness lifted her complexion, flattered her figure and softened her raven crop cut. Before I could offer a compliment, she brandished a piece of paper at me. I knew exactly what it was: a list of jobs she wanted to discharge.

Lists are her comfort blanket. She writes a new one each day and methodically works her way through, ticking off chores and reminders, smiling with satisfaction as she completes the tasks, or more often than not, passes them on to me. It's a source of much amusement between Ethan and myself that my mother refuses to acknowledge that I'm the boss and should be the one doing the delegating. And as she works voluntarily, I can't pull her up on it. I know she'd be upset and I need to keep her onside. Without her, I'd have to pay for help, which, right now, I can't afford. Besides, she's good with the customers and puts money in the till, so for that, I can forgive her pretentions of grandeur.

My footsteps echoed as I crossed oak boards, past display units filled with candles of all shapes, sizes, smells and colours, to a door at the rear concealing the workshop. My mother followed on my heels. I hung up my jacket and handbag and switched on my laptop, aware of her presence hovering around like a mosquito waiting for a moment of stillness.

'Now then,' she began, as I sat down, her natural efficiency verging on brusque. 'We've run out of packing boxes again, so I couldn't finish the Internet orders. And the till's low on change; we're completely out of pound coins. Didn't you say you were going to get some on Saturday, or did I imagine that? Oh, and a man called in – Oliver Harper. He left his business card. He wants you to call him. He said he has a proposition to put to you. I tried asking for more information, but he wasn't very forthcoming. Were you expecting him and forgot to tell me?' She ran the tip of her pen down the list, tapping it against the paper when she caught up with herself. 'I've restocked the greetings card rack with those lovely handmade cards Daphne Swift dropped off for us. I think they'll sell really well, don't you?' She looked up. 'By the way, how did it go at the wholesalers? What was it you went for again?'

My mother has a habit of asking question after question without waiting for a response. It's just her way, but even though I'm used to it sometimes she can be a little tiring. Battered and bruised by Detective Inspector Pitts' interrogation, I found myself fighting back a curt response. I began counting to ten in my head, and as I reached number four, was rescued by the jangle of the bell. My mother rushed out and by the time she returned my short fuse had been snuffed out.

'If you're desperate for change I'll pop to the bank in a minute,' I said.

She gave a dismissive flick of the wrist. 'Oh, don't worry. I'll do it at lunchtime. You haven't forgotten I'm going out for lunch, have you? With a friend?' For a brief moment a glimmer of pink grazed her cheeks before she recovered her poise.

*A friend my eye.*

It was the fourth time in two weeks' that she'd made plans to take an extended lunch with a *friend*.

'No, I haven't forgotten. Take as long as you like. I can manage.'

I debated with myself when and what to tell her about the awful events of the weekend. I didn't want to cause my mother any unnecessary concern, but Ridgelow is a small town and I knew that if I didn't mention it, she would hear it from someone else.

I needn't have worried.

She came over, pulled a fretful face and said, 'Jennifer, I don't know if you've heard, but apparently a man was killed on the footpath behind your house on Saturday night. Penny Bolton popped by earlier and told me all about it.'

I tried to sound casual. 'Yes, I know. I've been to the police station this morning to make a statement.'

I had my mother's full attention.

As her face drained of colour, her eyes filled with questions. 'The police?' She pulled up a chair. 'I thought you said you were at the wholesaler?'

I admitted I'd told a lie. 'But only because I wanted to tell you in person – I knew you'd worry while I was gone.'

'Why on earth did you have to make a statement?'

The temperature in the warm workshop seemed to plummet as I said, 'Because I overheard an argument which turned into a fight and the police wanted to know all about it.'

My mother stifled a moan with her fingertips.

I thought it best to get it over with. 'And weirdly,

the man who died had a note with my name and address on it in his pocket.'

My mother was beside herself. Her face contorted into strange angles with each question she fired off. 'What? Why? Did you know him? Was he a friend of yours?'

I waited for the volley to subside before telling her the story. It took ages to explain, because my mother constantly interrupted and swung me off track.

'I thought you weren't quite yourself when you came in,' she said. 'I could sense it. And you look like you haven't slept for a week – those bags could hold sand. Oh, Jennifer, what a terrible thing to get mixed up in. Do you think you should get some legal advice? Shall I contact Brian Rotherford and make an appointment?'

Calling the family solicitor was a thought I'd sweated over during my interrogation at the police station, but I'd decided that it might look like an overreaction and that I should sit tight and see which direction the investigation headed in first.

'No, Mum. There's no need for that,' I said, dearly hoping I was right.

'But the police think you're involved.'

Patience waning, I gritted my teeth. 'That's. Not. What. I. Said.'

'But you've been questioned – at a police station!' Her voice threatened to shrill. 'Why didn't you call Brian? You should have called him. He should have been there with you. Why didn't the police let you call him?'

'Because I wasn't arrested,' I said, trying not to catch her mounting hysteria. 'You only have a solicitor present if you're arrested. I went voluntarily, to give a witness statement. It's normal police procedure. It doesn't mean anything.'

I didn't think it wise to tell her they had asked for my DNA.

She huffed. 'Well, I think you're silly not to check your rights. It sounds like a very serious situation.' Rolling her eyes, she turned and gave me a cold shoulder, but unable to stay quiet for long, was soon back on my case. 'And why did the man have your name and address with him? How did he know you?'

I stared at the computer screen wondering the same thing. 'I don't know,' I said. 'But there must be a logical explanation. Don't worry, I'll work it out.'

'For heaven's sake, Jennifer, don't get even more involved.' My mother proceeded to rebuke me about the need to be vigilant and lock all the doors and windows at night. Echoing Ethan's concerns, she warned me about traipsing around the countryside alone.

For the rest of the morning she was uptight and distracted, cleaning the same glass cabinet three times and getting in a tizzy when she misplaced her list. When lunchtime came and she went off to meet her friend, I breathed a sigh of relief, turned on the radio and tried to immerse myself in my outstanding paperwork. But my head was all over the place and the numbers on the spread-sheet refused to add up, so I pushed back my chair and headed for my workbench instead, the thought of creating a batch of new candles forcing my spirit out of the gutter. Putting on my old leather apron was almost as comforting as being ensconced in Ethan's arms. The familiar, soft hide was a gift from my father, presented on my thirtieth birthday, only weeks before he died. It's a proper handmade utility apron and it's been with me every step and knock of the journey from home hobby to acclaimed candle emporium. The more I wear it, soil it and scold it, the better it looks.

Fumbling the waist cord into a crude double knot, I tried to shut out all thought of Robert Ashmere and his curtailed life and turned my attention to candles, first lighting a handful of fragranced tea lights to induce a creative mood, then retuning the radio to a classical station, before switching on the melting vats and cutting a block of wax from a vast slab. Soon the scent of sweet orange and geranium, and the sound of Elgar's *Land of Hope and Glory*, filled the workshop. The tips of my fingers tingled with anticipation as I poured hot wax into tins and moulds, and concentration became satisfaction as an ensemble of newborn candles flowed onto the worktop.

My mother returned all too soon and she wasn't alone. On hearing voices, I went through to the shop and she introduced me to her visitor.

'Jennifer, I'd like you to meet Spencer Lewis, a good friend of mine. We've just had a lovely lunch at the new Italian restaurant.'

*Odd.*

We'd already agreed it was overpriced rubbish. The company had obviously eclipsed the poor food and service.

'Pleased to meet you.' I held out my hand then retracted it again when I realised it was crusted with wax.

The man guffawed, but it at least broke the ice.

It was a peculiar pairing. I'd have never picked him out for my mother, because he completely swamped her petite frame. But when I imagined the list she must have drawn up for herself setting out her requirements in a man, I could see how he might fit the bill. He had a pleasant enough face, like a large English apple – round, rosy and with a waxy sheen – plus a good thatch of gunmetal grey hair and a full, neat, moustache. His sage chinos and navy blazer were well cut and I noticed an expensive watch strapped to his wrist. My interest travelled down to his shoes – polished chestnut city brogues. All in all, Spencer Lewis seemed very well-heeled indeed.

'Nice place you've got here,' he said. Keen eyes roved over full shelves and displays. The appraisal felt personal, as though he was actually looking me up and down. I let it go: after all, I'd just been doing the same to him.

'There's a workshop out the back,' said my mother, 'where Jennifer makes the candles. It's all done naturally: no nasty chemicals or ingredients involved. And I'm in charge –' I gave her a pointed look, ' – of the shop.' She threw me the same quick glare she used to give when I was six years old and tugging on her sleeve, and proceeded to lead Spencer into my workshop. I kept out of the way, pretending to restack a display in the window. Screened by a mountain of candles, I overheard her explaining the production process and showing off the award I'd recently won. Then they ambled into the kitchen area where she made a brew.

Spencer was the first to return, bearing a loaded tray, his cumbersome frame looking more Igor than society butler. He bit his tongue in concentration as he placed the tray on the counter and looked pleased with himself when he managed to do so without slopping a drop of tea. My mother scuttled in soon after, shooed him out of the way then clucked about, pouring into cups and offering up home baked shortbread. I accepted a cup and a wedge of sugary biscuit and slid back to my workbench, spying on them through the open door as they sat by the till, chatting in chummy, low voices and smothering trills of laughter. I saw the loneliness that had hardened my mother's face and sharpened her tongue in recent years dissolve in his company, and I wasn't sure if the pang in my heart was of happiness for her, or sadness that my father was fading away.

Digby also kept a close watch on Spencer from his basket in the corner, cocking an ear at each bout of laughter. When I sauntered out with my cup for a refill, he was glued to my heel, then had a good sniff of Spencer's before trotting off, seemingly uninterested, back to his bed and burying himself under his blanket. I hung around the greetings card rack, pretending to appreciate the new batch of cards that had been delivered.

Spencer was telling my mother about his first grandchild. 'Look,' he said proudly, 'here he is, the little tyke.' He flipped open his wallet and thrust a photo of a startled looking baby at her and then me. My mother came over all gooey while I couldn't help thinking that Digby was much cuter. 'He's getting quite mobile now – almost burnt a hole in the carpet with all his bottom shuffling!' He guffawed. My mother trilled. I took a swig of tea and decided I needed to know more about this man.

As he seemed so well acquainted with my mother, I assumed he would be familiar with the direct approach, but thought it best to keep my questions light, polite and humdrum.

'Do you live locally, Spencer?' I ventured.

He shook his head. 'Not in Ridgelow. I'm in Bellsden, just outside Chartley-on-the-Hill, so not too far away.'

'A lovely spot,' said my mother, who then quickly added, 'not that I've been there recently. It's just what I've heard.' She gathered the dirty teacups onto the tray and returned them to the kitchen in a hurry, saying she was going to wash up.

Left to our own devices, Spencer and I openly assessed each other over the counter, like chess opponents considering our moves. He was quick to play.

'I hear you've been renovating a ruin on Summer Lane?' There was a heap of genuine surprise in his voice. 'That's a hefty project for a young lady to take on.'

*Ruin?* I bristled at his description of my tumbledown cottage, and at his amazement that a *young lady* like me was capable of building her own home.

'Yes, I have. And I've really enjoyed the experience,' I lied. At times I'd wanted to knock my head against the crumbling walls and throttle the builders.

'Quite the little business woman.' Spencer seemed unaware of his patronising tone. 'And I really love this place. I've never seen anything like it. It's got the look of an old-fashioned sweet shop and smells like heaven. And your mother was telling me that the online business is going great guns?'

Even though my back was up, for my mother's sake, I tried not to be defensive and cagey.

'That's right. The website will be making more than the shop soon. We might even need to consider some extra storage space at this rate.'

Spencer manned up to his full height. 'Well, if you do, maybe I can help you out.'

'Oh. Thanks very much. Is that your line of work then – warehousing and logistics?'

He guffawed again as though I'd told a great joke. 'Oh no, but I've got a very full little black book, if you know what I mean.' He tapped his nose and winked. 'There'll be someone in it who'll be able to do you a deal.'

I noticed that when he spoke his moustache took on a life of its own, undulating on top of his lip like a thick, fuzzy slug. It was very off-putting, and I tried not to look.

'So, what exactly do you do?' I said, peeling dried wax off my hands.

'This and that. You know, a bit of property here and there, home improvement services and a small retail investment, that sort of thing. If it'll make money, it's got my name on it.'

I arranged my face to look suitably impressed.

'I like to describe myself as a local businessman,' he said, encouraged by my acting. 'It keeps options open. And what about your plans for this place, Jennifer? If you're thinking of expansion and need an investor, I hope you'll consider me in the running?'

'I'm happy to keep JJ's small and select,' I said, pleased that even if he seemed a wheeler-dealer sort, it at least sounded like he had an income and his own funds and wasn't after my mother's.

Spencer pulled up his cuff to look at his watch. I tried to catch the brand name, but he was too quick.

'Right then,' he said, 'I better make a move. It's been a pleasure to finally meet you, Jennifer. Heard a lot about you.'

'Likewise,' I said, even though I hadn't known of his existence until less than an hour before.

As he shook my hand, my mother hurried out to say goodbye and escorted Spencer outside, where they lingered on the doorstep. Uncomfortable at the possibility of them … I bolted into the workshop.

An air of awkwardness descended and my mother and I skirted round each other for the rest of the afternoon. I was dying to know more about Spencer – where they'd met and how serious it was – but dared not ask. My mother has a secretive side. Ethan says I'm much more like her than I realise. Fortunately, this doesn't seem to have put him off. At least Spencer had been a decent distraction. After the horrendous weekend, and the grilling I'd had at the police station, and also from my mother, I was wholly drained. It was a real relief to divert my tangled thoughts of the dead man back to the here and now, and lose myself in candle making and my mother's budding love life. But when I closed up and headed home later that afternoon, I found an unknown car parked outside my house.

Reluctance gripped me by the soles of the feet and stopped me dead at the top of the driveway. The driver's door opened and Detective Inspector Pitts stepped out. I'm not sure I did enough to hide my displeasure, because Digby sensed my unease and growled.

The detective was amused. 'Sparky, isn't he?' It was the first time he'd raised a genuine smile. 'It's always the small ones you've got to watch.'

I apologised for the dog's behaviour and asked what I could do for him.

'I've got a few more questions,' he said. 'Won't take long. Shall we go inside?'

As it wasn't a choice, I let him follow me in, but didn't show him into the sitting room and made him stand in the hallway, where he questioned me all over again about the voices I'd heard on the footpath, then retrieved the photo of the dead man from his pocket and asked me to study it again. Once more, I told him I didn't know Robert Ashmere, or have any idea why he had my name and address with him, and then the detective played his hand.

'Put yourself in my shoes for a moment, if you will. Mr Ashmere died in suspicious circumstances on the footpath behind your house, close to your perimeter fence. You claim to have heard the incident take place – an argument followed by a fight. So far from the enquiries we've made, no one else appears to have heard anything at all. Mr Ashmere also had a note with your name and address written on it in his pocket. It therefore follows that he either visited you, or was planning to. According to your account, it's the latter, but there's no one else who can confirm this. And finally, you have consistently denied knowing Mr Ashmere, yet yesterday evening, at precisely 6.47pm, you telephoned his photographic studio, a fact you omitted to tell me this morning when you made your witness statement, and again tonight when I asked if there were any further details you could remember. Now, you tell me, Miss Jarvis, if you were standing in my shoes, what would you be thinking right now?'

4

I couldn't believe I'd been so stupid, but it hadn't crossed my mind to mention the phone call. I was quick to explain I'd been curious about Robert Ashmere and wanted to find out more about him, to see if I could work out why he had my name and address with him.

'I suggest you leave the investigative work to the police in the future,' the detective warned. Straightening his tie, he made for the front door and stepped outside without saying goodbye, then strode up the driveway, past his car, and turned towards Plum Cottage.

*He's going to check with Izzy, to see if our stories match up.*

Sure enough, fifteen minutes later, an engine turned over, tyres crunched on gravel and Izzy came streaming round, blooming with excitement, silver mane breaking loose from a casual chignon.

'I've just been interviewed by the police,' she said, thrilled. 'That detective asked how you got hold of the murdered man's phone number, so I showed him the website and explained it was all very innocent and that we were just trying to find out more about him, to see if we could work out who he was.' Izzy plonked herself down at the kitchen table while I flicked on the kettle. 'I gather you rang the number?' she said, hungry for more murder fodder.

'Yes, but it went through to an answering machine.'

'Oh. So you didn't find out anything new?' She visibly sank.

'No. And I wish I'd never rung it. I've just had another grilling. That detective thinks I know the man and that I'm not telling him everything.' The kettle boiled and as I picked it up and began to pour I slopped scolding water over my other hand. 'Ouch. Bloody ouch.'

'Quick, under the tap.' Izzy sprang from her chair with a liveliness that defied her years. She guided me towards the sink and ran cold water over my burn. 'What makes you think that? What did he say?'

'That no one else heard anything, that I've got no alibi to confirm that the man didn't come to my house, and that because I phoned his studio and didn't mention it, it looks suspicious. That was the general gist of it.'

Izzy handed me a cotton tea towel. 'I see.' She let out a pitying sigh. 'Come and sit down. Forget the tea. I'll make us a nice strong coffee with a dash of something even nicer and stronger.'

I dried my hand and sat at the table. Beneath the surface my legs trembled like jelly. Izzy made herself at home in my kitchen, and soon a large steaming mug of coffee was placed in front of me, to which she added a generous splash from a dusty bottle of Baileys she'd unearthed from my pantry.

'Don't worry,' she said, tipping an extra shot of liqueur into her own mug. 'The police will get to the bottom of it soon enough. I suppose they've got to explore every avenue so they can eliminate people from the enquiry. I expect that's what they're doing with you.'

I sincerely hoped so. 'He might be right though, about me knowing Robert,' I said. 'I recognised the voice on the answer machine, but I can't think when or where I've heard it.'

Izzy pulled a face. 'Silly sod. Of course you recognised him. You heard him on Saturday night when he was arguing with someone on the footpath.'

Terrier ears pricked up at the sound of a key turning in the front door and a ball of black, white and tan fur dashed into the hallway barking manically, claws scrabbling on the tiled floors. Ethan came in, cuddling and fussing Digby in his arms.

'Ah, jolly good. Perhaps you can talk some sense into her?' Izzy said.

'What?' He released the dog, came over and kissed me on the cheek.

'She's worried about the police,' Izzy told him on my behalf. 'She thinks the detective in charge of the case thinks she's hiding something.'

Ethan ruffled my hair. 'That's ridiculous.'

'Well, why else would he keep turning up and asking me so many questions?' I said.

'What do you mean?' He joined us at the table.

'The detective came round again tonight,' Izzy enlightened.

'Oh. Didn't you go and make a statement first thing?' he said, looking to me.

'Yes, but when I came home tonight he was waiting for me.'

'Wasn't he happy with what you told him?'

'Apparently not.' I hesitated, knowing that Ethan was going to think me incredibly dim for what I was about to tell him. 'The thing is, last night I did something stupid … The dead man was a photographer and I found out his number and rang it …'

'It was my fault,' interjected Izzy. 'I egged her on. I thought someone might answer and be able to explain why the man had Jennifer's name and address with him.'

'But I got an answering machine and hung up. Then you came round and I got distracted and forgot about it. When I made the statement this morning I didn't mention it and now the police have found out and think I'm hiding something.' Ethan tried to suppress a groan. 'I know it was a silly thing to do,' I said before he did. 'I just wanted to find out why the man was coming to see me. Oh, this is all such a mess.' I rubbed my eyes and saw stars for a second.

'Now, now. Don't panic or get in a pickle,' said Izzy brightly. 'The police are just doing their job. If they seriously thought you had something to do with it they would have arrested you by now.'

'Exactly,' said Ethan, reaching for one of my hands and giving it a squeeze. 'It's just going to take a bit of time for them to work it out, that's all.'

An abrupt rap on the front door stalled the conversation.

'I'm not expecting anyone,' I said, looking up, fear racing through my veins. 'Oh God, what if he has come back to arrest me?'

Ethan was up and out of his chair as though the seat had caught fire. 'You two stay here,' he said. 'I'll deal with whoever it is.'

Izzy strained to overhear his conversation with the visitor while I hid my face in my hands and prayed.

'It can't be the police,' she whispered from her stakeout position by the doorway, 'or he'd have invited them in.'

Ethan's voice began to escalate from measured and polite to openly hostile.

I looked up. Izzy had her back up against the wall and was leaning into the frame, ear trained on the doorstep discussion. She caught my eye and made a face that said, *unlike Ethan*, then stage whispered, 'It's definitely not the police.'

Finding my feet and some courage, I went to Ethan's aid, shadowed by my neighbour. His frame packed the low cottage doorway, blocking most of the view and the light, but I could see the top of someone's head – a brown quiff – over his shoulder and a pair of black suede thick-rimmed shoes below.

'Is everything all right?' I said.

The Ethan who turned round was not a man I knew. His face was ablaze, twisted with rage, and his body was taut and trembling. The source of antagonism pushed his head over the threshold.

'Jennifer Jarvis?' he said, ducking and diving to dodge Ethan's body blocks. 'Matt Pearson, Chiltern Messenger. I'd like a word.'

'What about?' I replied, the air thick with a bad feeling that had descended like a sudden sea fog.

'Robert Ashmere.' Before I could protest, he threw a hand grenade question at me. 'I understand you heard the fight and the man being killed. What was that like?'

His loaded ammunition hit me straight in the guts.

'I've told you she's not answering any questions,' Ethan growled. He attempted to manhandle the journalist away from the house, but although shorter than he, Matt Pearson was stocky and robust and wedged himself into the doorway.

'We'll be covering the story in tomorrow's edition,' he said, dropping his gaze down his right hand side. I followed his eye-line and noticed a tiny Dictaphone clutched in his palm. 'It'll probably make the front page. I just want to give you the chance to have your say about what happened, so you can explain why you didn't call the police. Why was that?'

I gasped and buckled.

Ethan's hand reached out and cupped my left elbow. 'Don't say anything, Jen,' he said. The sneer he gave the reporter plainly said, *you pond life.*

Izzy, who had been observing the exchange behind folded arms and pursed lips, had heard enough. Taking matters into her own hands, she squeezed past Ethan, charged at Matt Pearson, grabbed his Dictaphone and tossed it in a nearby leylandii hedge.

'Hey!' The reporter spun round and leapt onto the front lawn, almost tripping over his suede creepers. 'You'll have to pay for that,' he said, recovering his balance and looking irked.

'Make me!' Izzy stamped her foot and shook her silver mane like a cantankerous little pony. 'If I were you, I'd get off this property this very instant. Call yourself a journalist? You're nothing but a bully. I'm sure the Press Complaints Commission will be very interested to know how you conduct your business. Don't they have strict rules about doorstepping? You should be ashamed of yourself. Go on, sod off, you nasty little hack.'

Recognising that arguing with a pensioner – or at least this particular pensioner – wasn't going to lead anywhere, Matt Pearson scowled, rummaged around in the hedge for his recorder then strutted off with a false air of nonchalance towards a flame-red vintage Triumph motorbike, parked up on Summer Lane.

'Nice one, Izzy,' Ethan said with a grin, looking more like his old self.

'My Archie would never have behaved like that,' she said, hands on hips as she watched the motorbike snake through the potholes. 'He didn't need to harass people to get to the truth. Balls of steel and bones of integrity – that was Archibald. They don't make them like they used to.' She looked to the sky and mouthed something to her late husband. 'Righty-o, now that's all done and dusted, time for my hot toddy and foot soak, methinks. Jennifer, I shall leave you in Ethan's capable hands. Cheery-bye.'

Back inside, we hunkered down on the sofa. As Ethan chuckled at a Monty Python rerun, I mulled over the spat, wondering where the reporter had got his information and how much he knew. I couldn't imagine the police releasing the details, but having never been involved in a criminal investigation before, I didn't know the form. And, if it wasn't the police, it meant that someone I knew, someone I'd confided in, had let slip.

I did a mental tally of everyone I'd talked to:

*The man I love.*

*My best friend.*

*My next-door neighbour.*

*My mother.*

Who in my time of need had proven untrustworthy?

At my feet, Digby yawned, stood up, stretched then sprung onto the sofa and nestled between us. The feel of his warm body snuggled against my thigh ignited a flame in my heart. He had been such a lucky find. Almost always by my side, he's become my closest confidant, my partner-in-crime. I petted his shaggy, fox-like head and he stared at me through dark, worldly eyes.

*At least I can count on you, Diggers*, I told him through mine.

**5**

'Jennifer … JENNNIFERR …' My mother's cries climbed from a pinched bark to an aggrieved wail that reverberated around the shop.

Leaping out of my chair, I ran to her aid. 'Mum?'

My first impression was that she had been taken ill. Her shoulders were hunched over the serving counter and her arms wrapped across her abdomen as though in immense pain.

'Mum?' I said again, thinking it looked bad and that I might need to call for an ambulance.

She looked up. Her face was a sickly grey and she was struggling to speak. She jabbed a forefinger at the newspaper on the counter top and pushed it towards me. I eyed the blue and white masthead of the *Chiltern Messenger* with my heart in my mouth. The moment reminded me of opening my first exam results, only this time my mother had viewed the contents first and it obviously wasn't good news. Bracing myself, I scanned the front page. My heart plummeted from the roof of my mouth into the pit of my stomach when Robert Ashmere glowered back. I slammed my eyes shut. Too late. Once again, the dead man settled himself at the front of my mind, bringing with him a series of snapshot memories that flickered like an old cine film on a never-ending reel.

*Voices on the footpath.*

*A fight breaking out.*

*Standing alone in the dark garden, consumed by a feeling that something was horribly wrong.*

Remembering my mother was in the room I hastily composed myself, opened my eyes and braved another look at the image dominating my thoughts and the page. It was the same black and white photograph the detective had insisted I study over and over again, only this time the dead man's wife had been trimmed out and Robert was featured alone. I devoured the accompanying story. It was a sensational splash that implied I had ignored the man's cries for help and left him to die out in the rain. The article was cleverly worded and entirely true. And it left no doubt in readers' minds that there was a big question mark hanging over my head.

My mother gasped, 'Where did they get all this rubbish? Surely not from the police?'

'I doubt it,' I said, scrunching the newspaper into a ball and pounding it into the waste bin. 'Anyway, knowing who it was won't make any difference. The damage is done.'

My mother clucked about, insisting I call the family solicitor, and after a lengthy discussion with Brian Rotherford, during which I retrieved the paper from the bin, read out the article and told him about the fight on the footpath and the note in the dead man's pocket, he advised that there wasn't anything libellous in the newspaper report, and that as no official allegation had been made towards me, the police were acting within their normal powers.

He did have some words of caution. 'If they ask you to go back to the police station, call me, so I can be present,' he said. 'It's one thing to make a witness statement, but things may step into different territory if it comes down to further questioning. I'm not saying this to worry you, Jennifer, but this is a murder enquiry and given the connection you have to the deceased – this note – you must be prudent.' He ended the call by telling me to contact him if I had any further concerns, or if the police asked to see me again.

It felt good to have someone knowledgeable on my side, so that if things did take a turn for the worst I would be more prepared.

News of my association with Ridgelow's most notorious crime spread like poison ivy and the shop was chock-a-block with people dropping in for a browse, hoping to be the first to discover a juicy piece of gossip that no one else knew. I presented the same deadpan response to everyone: that I'd overheard an argument on the footpath and was helping the police with their enquiry, and refused to be drawn any further. Most of them left with empty hands and full imaginations.

By mid-morning I'd had enough of the freak show treatment and desperately needed some space and air. Leaving my mother to fend off the locals, Digby and I got in the car and headed for Haven Woods, a forest estate on the edge of the rolling Chiltern Hills. Parking up under a shady beech tree, I locked my handbag in the car boot and set off towards a stone trail. Digby hurtled doggedly after squirrels as I followed the serpentine path down a steady incline. Overhead, an airplane droned through an azure sky. As it passed, two red kites spiralled high above performing circle displays and calling to each other through eerie screeches that reminded me of Robert's last cry.

The ground flattened as the woods opened into a wide avenue. Row upon row of Scots pines and Norway spruce stood to attention either side of the wide pathway, which was edged with deep verges filled with long grasses and wild flowers. Butterflies and bees flitted and hummed, here and there, going about their daily business, and yards ahead a muntjac deer trotted across the track and disappeared into undergrowth. I walked at a steady pace with the weight of the dead man on my shoulders, trying to calm the chaos in my head and quell the potent cocktail of feelings his death, the note and now the front-page slur had induced. I still had no idea who Robert might be, or why he was coming to see me. But of one thing I was certain – Detective Inspector Pitts didn't believe me. And if I couldn't convince him I was telling the truth, he would continue poking and digging around. This thought made me highly anxious and I completed the circular woodland walk without noticing much of it.

Back at the car park I clipped a lead on Digby's collar and headed towards my Mini, still lost in dark thoughts, only to discover the car had been broken into and my handbag stolen from the boot.

'Oh no,' I groaned to Digby, examining the mess they'd made of the rear window.

Shards of glass glinted and glistened all over the interior. I couldn't put Digby inside, so I tied him to a nearby picnic bench and stood wondering what to do. My brain struggled to cope with the latest challenge I'd been thrown. It was hard to construct even a simple plan.

*Call Ethan …*
*Ask him to collect Digby …*
*Get the car to the garage …*

At least I'd had the foresight to take my phone on the walk. I rang the vet practice, but Ethan was in surgery, so they put Lisa on instead and she immediately said she would come and help. Then I called the bank to cancel my debit cards, and the police to report the theft. The officer on the end of the line took all the details, but wouldn't send anyone out, instead suggesting I check nearby rubbish bins and bushes in case the thief had pocketed the cash and dumped the bag. Digby and I scoured the ground around the car park as we waited for Lisa, me seeking the handbag, Digby looking for more squirrels. I was grateful for his companionship, if not his search skills. But there was no sign of the bag, or my purse which had contained a single ten pound note.

*Ten measly pounds.*

It was going to cost a small fortune to deal with the damage. Worst of all, the bag had been a gift from Ethan.

'Oh, what bad luck,' Lisa said through a half-opened window as she pulled up in her battered, dusty Land Rover. 'As if you've not got enough on your plate. Don't worry about Digby. I'll take him back to the practice. Come and get him when you're ready.'

With Digby safe and sound, I sat on a picnic bench at the side of the car park and rang my mother.

'Jennifer, you're a walking disaster,' she chided. 'Why didn't you take your handbag with you?'

It wasn't the best of moments to have a debate – I really wasn't in the mood. I cut her short, then used a dog towel to brush away the glass on the driver side, got in the damaged Mini and pulled off, imploring the remains of the shattered rear window not to cave in or out as I trundled along at twenty miles per hour to the local garage, hazard lights flashing. Leaving the car in capable hands, I headed home to freshen up before collecting Digby en route to the shop. It was only when I got to the top of Summer Lane that I remembered my house keys had been in my handbag. The long groan that threatened to surface was plugged by the comforting realisation that Izzy had a spare. I trudged up her drive and rapped on the Moroccan knocker.

'Be with you in a jiffy.' Izzy's fruity, theatrical

voice was muffled.

Peering round the side of her entrance porch I noticed the sitting room window was ajar. Through the gap I spied my neighbour, clad in a lilac velour lounge suit, on the floor, on all fours, with her rump poking straight up to heaven.

'It's only me. Are you okay?' I called.

'Perfectly,' she shouted back, crumpled pink face peeking out from under her armpit. 'I'm doing the downward-facing dog. Can't rush out of the move. Bear with …' At snail pace, she lowered herself out of the manoeuvre then rolled upright and came to the door. 'Howdy, stranger,' she said, adjusting the crooked towelling sweatband that attempted to tame her mane.

'Sorry to bother you,' I said wearily, 'but can I have my spare key? My handbag's been stolen and I'm locked out.'

Izzy ushered me inside. 'My dear girl, what on earth happened?'

I explained I'd left my bag in the car boot at Haven Woods, thinking it was safe and Izzy said that she'd have done exactly the same, which made me feel better. 'But what a pain for you. And on top of everything else. Just hang on a mo and I'll get your key. I think it's in the odds and sods drawer in the bureau …' Her bare feet salsa'd off then salsa'd back again. 'Here you are,' she said. 'And let me know if you need a bit of cash to tide you over while the bank sorts out a new card.'

I thanked her for the offer and asked if she'd read the *Messenger*, which she hadn't, so I told her about Matt Pearson's literary concoction.

'That's why I was in the woods in the first place – hiding from all the tittle tattlers. They descended on the shop like a pack of greedy vultures looking for easy pickings.'

Izzy's lived-in face tightened in fury. 'If I see that nasty little hack again, I swear I'll poke his eyes out and shove them up his nostrils. And if he had any balls I'd do much the same with those.' Her eyes glinted dangerously, and right then I believed her capable of anything.

I left Izzy to calm herself down with some more yoga moves and forced my weary legs to carry me the few steps to Corner Cottage, where I opened the front door and was instantly hit by a strong sense that something was wrong. An unfamiliar smell lingered in the air: a faint, stale whiff of cigarettes.

I didn't know anyone who smoked.

Certainly not anyone who had access to my house.

A bad feeling oozed over me like cold gloop.

Thinking fast, I remembered that along with my house keys, my driving licence had also been in the purse. And it had my address on it. Whoever stole my handbag could have let themselves into my house.

*In fact, they could be in here right now.*

Taking no chances, I made a swift about-turn and tore back round to Izzy's.

**6**

From the safety of Plum Cottage, I called the police and asked for Detective Inspector Pitts. When I was put through, I explained that someone had stolen my handbag, containing my house keys, earlier that morning and let themselves into my cottage. He asked if anything was missing, or had been damaged, which stopped me in my tracks.

'I don't know.'

It dawned on me how foolish it was to report a break-in when all I had to go on was the smell of stale cigarettes lingering in the air and a strong sense that something was wrong.

'What do you mean, you don't know? You must have seen something that gave you the impression that you've had an intruder?'

I admitted that I hadn't seen anything wrong, but explained about the smell and that I was acting on my senses.

'Ah, I see,' said the detective. There was a pause. I could hear him chewing, then swallowing. 'A case of that strange phenomenon known as women's intuition, is it?' He gave a small grunt. 'All right. I'll be along as soon as I've finished my sandwich.'

Twenty minutes later he pulled up in his unmarked car wearing a blank face. 'Miss Jarvis,' he said with a curt nod, getting out and striding towards Corner Cottage. 'Wait here while I take a look.' He wasn't gone long. 'All clear,' he said, reappearing at the open front door. 'You better come in and tell me if anything's missing.'

The first thing I noticed when I entered my home again was that the whiff of stale cigarettes was masked

by the overpowering scent of Detective Inspector Pitts'
aftershave. It smelt cheap and tawdry and reminded me
of toilet cleaner.

He walked behind as I examined each room,
checking my possessions, but everything was exactly as
I'd left it and I had to admit that nothing had been
taken.

'But I really do think someone's been in here,' I
said, knowing that candle making had bestowed me a
good nose and I hadn't imagined the cigarette smell.

'Mint, Miss Jarvis?' the detective offered, holding
out a packet of Trebor. I declined. He shrugged, popped
one in his mouth and said, in between sucks, 'Understandable
to be on tenterhooks at the moment … I know I'd be a
bit on edge if someone was killed … at the bottom of
my garden.'

'It's not the best of situations,' I said, guard sliding
into place to heed the solicitor's warning.

'Thought any more about that note in Mr
Ashmere's pocket?'

'Yes I have. Lots. And I don't know him. Nor do
I know why he had my name and address, or how he
got hold of it.'

'How strange … But don't you worry, I'll get my
head round it.' The detective looked at his watch and
then at me. The smallest of smirks played on his lips.

Once again, I stood by my front door, willing him
to leave, relief building with every step he took towards
it. But when he drew level, Detective Inspector Pitts
stopped, stared past me, down the length of Summer
Lane and said,

'It's funny you got in touch today of all days …'
He broke off and squinted.

I sought what had caught his attention. In the

distance, a van was crawling up the uneven road, creating a dust storm.

'… because I was going to give you a call …' The detective turned and faced me. 'To let you know that we'd like to conduct a full search of your property.'

I gasped. 'What on earth for?'

He looked at me as though I was stupid. 'We might find something that will give us a clearer picture of what happened on Saturday night.' He reached into his trouser pocket, pulled out another Trebor and popped it in his mouth.

Once again, I hugged the door frame for support. 'But I've already told you I was here on my own. No one came round … '

The detective held up a hand and shut me down. 'Are you *absolutely* sure that Robert Ashmere didn't enter your property, at any point?'

I was sure about the house, but not the garden.

'You see, I need to know *exactly* where Mr Ashmere went that night. And because of the proximity of your property to the spot where he died, and the fact that you have a gate leading directly onto the footpath, and because of the note in his possession, we need to investigate the area thoroughly – inside your house as well as out.'

'And if I refuse?' I said, trying to stand tall on buckled knees.

He didn't need to answer. I already knew what was coming.

He patted his breast pocket. 'I have a search warrant.'

A cauldron of hot emotion inside me surged in to a rapid boil.

'Do you want to see it?' He was unaffected by my

obvious shock.

I tried to keep my voice level. 'I need to make a phone call. In private. You'll have to wait outside.' I indicated to the door.

Detective Inspector Pitts stepped through the porch and made his way over to the grey Ford transit that had drawn up in the driveway. A man and woman got out and started pulling on white suits, gloves and masks. I heard the detective greet his colleagues and start giving them the low-down. Shutting them out, I immediately rang Brian Rotherford who advised that the police had the right to search my property as long as it was done lawfully.

'Basically, Jennifer, if you refuse entry they could charge you with obstruction. I know this is a difficult position to be in, but because Mr Ashmere had that note, a magistrate would deem it as reasonable grounds to issue a warrant. I know this isn't what you want to hear, but you're going to have to grin and bear it. But be careful what you say. If the detective starts asking you any more questions, you are perfectly within your rights to request legal advice, and I advise you to do just that. I'm in court for the rest of the afternoon, but call my office if you need to. I'll let my partner know the situation and he'll be able to help.'

Riddled with angst at the thought of the police rifling through Corner Cottage, I made a frantic dash upstairs to the bathroom, where I hung my head over the loo and dry-retched. It took a few moments for the queasiness to subside then I splashed cold water over my face and sat on the bathroom floor, back against the wall with a damp flannel across my temple, wondering if the police would find any sign of the dead man.

Outside, the scrunch of stones indicated another

vehicle making its way up Summer Lane. I discarded the flannel and slunk across the landing to investigate. Looking through the leaded pane of my study window I saw the roof of a white van with blue lights on top pull into frame. The side door opened and a handful of officers in black combats, T-shirts and baseball caps jumped out. At any other time, I might have thought I'd stumbled on to the set of a TV drama, except the lump of dread in my gut reminded me that this wasn't a fantasy – it was happening to me, right here and now.

As Detective Inspector Pitts moved across the lawn, into view, I stood back, and in doing so, out of the corner of my eye, noticed a flashing red light on my ancient photocopier. Examining the machine, I discovered it was low on toner. That didn't bother me. It was the fact that the copier was switched on in the first place that did, because I hadn't used it in weeks. But the more I considered it, the more convinced I was that Ethan had, without telling me, and had forgotten to switch it off.

An abrupt knock on the front door swung my attention back to the police.

I didn't rush to open it.

The officers filed round the side of the house, into the back garden, while Detective Inspector Pitts and the couple in white boiler suits came inside, walking straight past into my home as though I were invisible.

Izzy called across the neat laurel hedge that separated our front gardens. 'Jennifer, what's going on? Has anything been stolen?'

Weak legs carried me over. 'No. There's nothing missing.'

'Oh,' she said, leaning over the foliage barrier, trying to get a look at what was happening inside. 'I assumed the arrival of the forensics meant they were looking for evidence of an intruder?'

'No,' I said in a dull voice. 'They're looking for evidence of Robert Ashmere. Detective Inspector Pitts had it planned all along. He's got a search warrant and everything.'

'Oh dear,' said Izzy, frowning. 'You've got your malaria face on again. You better come in for a sit down and cuppa. Or something stronger? A scotch perhaps?' She beckoned me to join her. 'Come on, I've got some Talisker left. A little dram of that will pack a good punch – you can taste the sea air in it.' Izzy looked back at Corner Cottage. 'I won't offer the detective one, seeing as he's causing all the trouble.' She made a quick V sign from behind the safety of the hedge.

Grateful for her offer, I followed her into her kitchen and sipped at the drink she thrust in my hand. As the fiery liquid slipped down my throat, the phone in my back pocket bleeped. It was a text from my mother, who was wondering where on earth I'd got too. Keen to avoid another barrage of questions, I invented a migraine and messaged back, asking if she would hold the fort for the rest of the day. I received, a simple 'OK' in return, followed by another text telling me that a man called Oliver Harper had stopped by the shop again and wanted me to give him a call. With all that was going on, I decided he wasn't urgent and would wait. Instead, I messaged Ethan, suggesting we stay at his place. I didn't mention the search, because I knew his day was back-to-back with operations and consultations and I didn't want to distract him with any more bad news.

Izzy was right. The dram was just the job. With colour branding my cheeks and scotch courage powering through my veins, I readied myself for another spell of police torment and returned home. From the kitchen I could keep an eye on most of the downstairs living space and the back garden, so I made it my base and sat at the scrubbed pine table, closely observing all the comings and goings. I couldn't see Detective Inspector Pitts, but the flush of the toilet and unmelodic whistling soon indicated his whereabouts. The idea of him using my bathroom like a public convenience really peeved me. He made no apology as he wandered into the kitchen and instead simply said, rather unnecessarily:

'Ah, you're back again.'

I ignored him.

The police force must cultivate thick skins, because he sat at the table, said, 'It's dry in here,' and eyed up the kettle.

The scotch incited a hot retort, 'This isn't a hotel,' and I felt both pleased for cutting him down, and worried about rubbing him up the wrong way.

One of the baseball-capped search team stuck his head into the kitchen and with a hopeful grin said, 'It's a bit parched round here.'

Chair legs scraped against quarry tiles and I growled under my breath as I set about making a large pot of tea, deliberately giving the detective a mug with a big chip on the rim. As he sipped, he made a note of my most recent visitors so they could be matched to any prints found. I made sure he knew about the latest unwanted one.

'A reporter from the *Messenger* came round yesterday,' I said, watching his reaction.

Detective Inspector Pitts was slow to look up from his notebook. 'Pearson? Doorstep you, did he? Desperate for a sniff of a story, that one.'

'He seems very well informed.'

The policeman returned to his notebook. 'Yes, he does, doesn't he? I've no idea where he got his information. Cause you a spot of bother?'

'I live in a small town and I own a small business. Being linked to a murder investigation isn't doing much for my reputation or my bank balance.'

His eyes lifted again and met mine. 'Let's hope we get to the bottom of it quickly then.'

Someone coughed by the back door.

'Ah, I'm wanted outside.' He went to attend to his team.

I stood at the kitchen window and watched the detective stride down the garden path. He stopped to talk to one of the officers, who was pointing at the gate onto the footpath and talking in an animated fashion.

*Have they found something?*

The idea of more evidence linking me to Robert Ashmere made me quake.

Detective Inspector Pitts came back carrying my flip flops. 'I assume these are yours?'

'Well, they're not the dog's.'

His hard stare thwarted my scotch daring. I dry-gulped, regretting Izzy's generous measure.

'When did you last wear them?'

'Yesterday.'

'Did you wear them on Saturday?'

'Yes. I wore them all weekend. It was baking hot.'

The policeman handed the shoes to the forensic team. 'Bag them up.'

My muscles turned to jelly. 'Is there something wrong?'

'I'd like to have them checked over. And also your vacuum cleaner.'

I located the cleaner in a cupboard under the

stairs, then excused myself and hid in the bathroom until I felt calmer and back in control.

It was late afternoon by the time the convoy of police vehicles drove off. The detective had, of course, given nothing away when I'd asked how the search had gone.

'We'll be in touch,' he'd said, before thanking me for my cooperation.

I assumed by that he meant the stream of tea and coffee I'd felt obliged to make all afternoon. There'd been no offer of biscuits.

The surfaces in my cottage were veiled in fingerprint powder. As I had no vacuum I couldn't clean up. The place looked, felt and smelt alien and I didn't want to be there. I packed an overnight bag, called on Izzy to tell her I would be at Ethan's for the night, then, feeling like a refugee, plodded into town.

My car was ready and waiting for me at the garage, new window intact and a spotless interior. They'd polished the outside too, for free, and the Mini sparkled like a topaz nugget. The simple gesture touched a chord and I very nearly hugged old Bill, the mechanic, for the chink of light he'd provided in all the darkness.

I parked outside Ethan's house, a handsome Victorian end of terrace with large bay windows and a cheery red front door. Letting myself in, I headed straight for the fridge and the bottle of Chablis I knew I would find chilling on the top shelf. Glass and bottle accompanied me onto the outside deck, where I settled into a recliner, slugged at the wine and tried to focus all my attention on the stunning views of the Chiltern Hills. Dense, ancient woodlands disguised a steep scarp slope, providing a striking backdrop of green and silver hues.

Against a boundless, cloudless sky, the ridge provided more drama than Broadway, but nature's splendour, and the wine, failed to calm my fears, or stop flip flops and vacuum cleaners from joining the pandemonium in my head.

My heart lifted at the sound of movement from inside the house. Ethan and Digby appeared, Ethan kissing me on the cheek before disappearing upstairs for a shower and Digby showering my legs with licks before bombing down the garden to bark at next door's tomcat, who was twice the size of the terrier and totally nonplussed. By the time Ethan returned, skin smelling as zesty as a lime and thick salt-and-pepper hair slicked back with damp, emphasizing his Roman nose and giving him the look of a rugged Richard Gere, I'd drunk two large glasses of Chablis on top of Izzy's dram, and no lunch, and was feeling light-headed.

'Drowning my sorrows,' I said as he looked at my empty glass and the half-empty bottle.

He sat down and poured a glass for himself. 'Lisa told me about your car and the handbag,' he said, yawning and rubbing tired eyes. The blue purple bruise that had encased one in a planetary ring had faded to a greenish yellow smudge and was almost unnoticeable. 'Sounds like you've had another miserable day.' The glug of wine he devoured told me he'd had a pretty tough one too. 'I would have called, but I was tied up in surgery. We lost a dog on the table.' The rim of the glass touched his lips again. A second glug. 'But tomorrow's another day.'

I wished I had the same ability to detach myself from death.

As we polished off the rest of the bottle I told him the handbag was a mere kick in the teeth compared to the rest of my day, likening the police search to a Viking pillage. Then, when I shared my suspicions that I'd had an intruder as a result of the stolen bag and keys his practical head snapped on and he pointed out that I ought to get the locks changed, just to be on the safe side. We migrated to the kitchen. Ethan quickly arranged for a locksmith to come out the next day, then, while he scoured the kitchen units for something simple for supper, he said,

'Your detective turned up at the practice this morning, which caused a bit of a stir. He wanted to know where I was at the weekend.'

I scowled. 'I've already told him you were in Wales. Doesn't that man believe anything I say?'

'Ah, come on, he's just doing his job.'

Pasta twirls clattered into a pan.

'Well, he's not much good at it.' I said sourly. 'He and his merry men are so possessed by Robert Ashmere they don't seem to care that someone very much alive and kicking has let themself into my house.'

Ethan abandoned the pasta and gathered me into a hug. 'Jen, I think catching a murderer is just a bit more important to him than investigating the smell of cigarettes. And he did come and check it out for you.'

'Only because he wanted to do his own search.'

'But nothing was missing.'

'No,' I sighed into his chest. 'Everything was exactly as I'd left it. Except for the photocopier, which you'd forgotten to switch off.'

Ethan gave me a squeeze. 'Hey Jarvis, don't blame me. I haven't touched your copier. You must have left it on.'

I pulled away. 'I haven't used it for weeks. It must have been you.'

But Ethan was adamant. 'I've never used it. I wouldn't know how – it's prehistoric.'

'Are you sure?'

'Course I am.'

'Well, if you didn't and I didn't, then who the bloody hell did?'

7

Ethan did his best to temper my alarm. 'Jen, if someone has been poking about your house, the police search will pick it up and then they'll have to take you seriously, won't they? And the locksmith's coming tomorrow, so please stop worrying.'

'But what if someone comes back tonight? They could empty the whole house while I'm here with you.'

I wanted to go home to rescue my jewellery, laptop and some photographs, but we'd both had too much to drink to drive and so I spent the evening twitching as though repeatedly jabbed with hot needles, unable to eat the supper Ethan prepared, or sleep through the night. As I lay in bed, Ethan's warm body snoring gently beside me, Robert, the police detective and a faceless prowler kept trespassing into my head, looming out of dark corners and making me sweat.

I was still clammy when I drove up Summer Lane the following morning, wheels thudding in potholes, heart knocking on ribs, wondering what the hell I would find behind my own front door. A glance in the rear mirror reassured me that Ethan was still following behind. If he was at all concerned, he didn't show it, and smiled and waved when he noticed my eye connect with the reflector.

'Come on then,' he said as we stood outside. 'Let's check it over.' He went first, opening the door with my spare key and sticking his head round. I heard him inhale. 'No cigarette smells today.'

We checked every room, the garage and the garden and concluded that no one was in my house. Nor was there any fresh sign that the intruder had returned. My jewellery was safely tucked away in a box on my dressing table and the few gadgets I own were untouched. Satisfied that I was safe, Ethan headed off to work leaving me to clean up the mess the forensic duo had left behind. Fingerprint powder coated the place like icing sugar, and without a vacuum cleaner to hand the task seemed mammoth, so I wandered round to Izzy's to ask if I could borrow hers.

'Course you can,' she said, coming to the door in a floor-length shimmering gold kimono-style bathrobe. 'Give me a mo and I'll slip into something more suitable and give you a hand, if you like?'

A few minutes later, Izzy arrived at Corner Cottage practically attired in a pair of faded denim dungarees with turn-ups, a battered pair of espadrilles, silver mane held back with a red and white paisley bandana. Armed with an assortment of cleaning paraphernalia, it didn't take long for the two of us to get the place spic and span and smelling like home again. We finished just as the locksmith turned up, and once he'd been put to work we sat in the garden with a pot of tea and a pile of buttery toast.

I told Izzy about the coincidence of the photocopier and my strong conviction that someone had been in my house.

'Have you told the Detective Inspector?' she said, dunking a heaped spoon of sugar into her teacup and whipping with a vigorous wrist.

'Not about the copier, no. He wouldn't class it as evidence. He didn't believe me about the cigarette smell. He doesn't believe anything much I say.' My mouth felt dry as I said: 'He took away my flip flops as well as the vacuum. I was wearing them the last time I used the footpath. I expect he wants to match them with some prints they've found.' I tried to sound matter-of-fact about it.

Izzy's antennae pricked up. 'This really is dreadful for you, isn't it?'

I nodded and shrugged simultaneously.

Her face softened. 'Look, I'm sure it's only a matter of time before the police have a breakthrough. They have to investigate every lead – I've seen it on the telly. And they must have their work cut out in this case, what with so many people using the footpath. It must be a colossal job trying to match people to footprints. That's if they found many.'

'What do you mean?'

'Didn't you say there was a horrendous storm that night?'

'Yes. It lashed down.'

Izzy crunched her way through a toast triangle, brushing crumbs from her lap down to a grateful Digby. 'Well, the rain might have washed a lot of evidence away. That must be why they haven't arrested anyone yet.'

Topping up the teacups I revealed that Ethan had become the latest police interrogation target. 'Detective Inspector Pitts turned up at the vet practice, completely out of the blue, wanting to know where he was on Saturday night.'

'Oh, I'm not surprised,' said Izzy, helping herself to more sugar. 'I think the police automatically look for an angry boyfriend, or husband, as a potential suspect. I read it on the Internet. You'd be amazed at how many murders are crimes of passion. I suppose, because of the note, the police might think this Robert fellow was an ex-boyfriend, or that you were having an affair with him, or something equally ridiculous, and that Ethan found out about it and had it out with him on the footpath in a jealous rage. I bet that corker of a black eye of his raised a question or two.'

'But he was in Wales. And he fell off his mountain bike.'

'I know that and you know that, but the police don't know that, do they? Well, not for sure.'

'I can't believe we're sitting here discussing Ethan, of all people, as a potential suspect,' I huffed. 'He definitely didn't do it. I know he didn't.'

'Course he's got nothing to do with it,' Izzy agreed. 'Wouldn't harm a fly that one. That's why he's a vet. He likes fixing things, not breaking them.'

'I just wish the police would believe what I've told them. And stop turning up unannounced trying to catch people off-guard.' All the talk of the police made me perspire. I reached in my pocket for a tissue and blotted my damp forehead.

'Yes, that detective's very persistent, isn't he?' said Izzy. 'Clutching at straws I think. He must be under a lot of pressure to get this horrid business all bagged up. Has he found out why this Robert chap had your name and address with him yet?'

'No. Or if he has, he hasn't told me.' I paused to mull over an idea that had occurred to me during my solitary walk in Haven Woods. 'Actually, Izzy … I want to talk to you about that.'

'Go on,' she said, interest written over her face in capital letters.

'I've been thinking that I might try to find out myself.'

Her eyes gleamed. 'You mean carry on from our Internet search? I thought you got cold feet along with your slapped wrists after the phone call to his studio?'

'I did. But I can't stop thinking about him. I need

to know who he was, and why he was coming to see me. I need to prove that I didn't know him.'

*So that the police will leave me alone.*

'And what if you find out that you do – know him I mean?' Izzy said.

'I really hope that's not the case,' I replied, trying to keep my voice steady.

'Well, I'm not surprised,' said Izzy. 'If I were in your shoes, I'd have been driven round the bend by the whole darn affair. And I wouldn't be able to rest until I got to the bottom of it either. Quite the mystery, isn't it?'

'So you'll help me?'

Static excitement fizzed from her every pore. 'Love to!' she said with gusto. 'Let's make another brew and go over what we know.'

Over the sound of a boiling kettle, I relayed back what little information I had on the dead man. Izzy leant against the Welsh dresser with her eyes half closed, lids fluttering as though in a clairvoyant trance.

'So,' she said, rousing suddenly. 'We know his name. We know he was a photographer. We know he was from Oxford. We know from the photo you were shown he was married. And we know that for some reason he was coming to see you on Saturday night.'

'Not much, is it?'

Izzy retracted back into her trance, cheeks and temple flinching as a flurry of thoughts pulsed through her mind. Then she became very still, except for her lips, which murmured, 'The *Messenger* … the piece in the *Messenger* … ' Popping back to life, she said, 'Have you got a copy? No? I'll nip home and fetch mine. I got one in the end. Wanted to read what that toad of a man had concocted. Bear with …' My neighbour salsa'd off, paisley bandana askew, returning with the newspaper tucked jauntily under one arm. She spread it out on the kitchen table and scanned the text. I couldn't bring myself to read it again and became very busy making the tea. 'Here we go,' Izzy said, tap dancing on the spot. 'It says he was forty-four years old … and that his mother is called Iris …' Izzy ran a forefinger over the print, pushing her face closer and closer to the black and white sheet. 'Darn it. Should have bought my specs with me.' Then, 'Ah ha! She lives in Bicester.' As I handed her a cup I was greeted with a sunbeam smile. 'I bet that's where the funeral will be held, which, my dear, will be the perfect foil for you to do some digging, if you'll pardon the pun.'

I digested the idea with all the enthusiasm of a vegetarian faced with a plate of carpaccio.

'You might spot someone you know – one of his friends – and remember how you knew him. Or you could speak to his mother,' Izzy pressed. 'Oh, go on, it's the perfect opportunity.'

'But I'm useless at small talk. I'll say all the wrong things – I know I will. Why don't you go? You'd be much better than me.'

Izzy snorted. 'Don't be ridiculous. It has to be you. You have to see if you recognise anyone.'

I weighed up the suggestion as Izzy huffed and pouted at me, hands on hips.

'Have you got any better ideas?' she persisted with a cocked eyebrow.

'No.'

'Then do it. You'll be fine. We can work on the small talk before you go.' She clapped her hands and looked pleased with herself. 'Now all we need to do is find out when and where it is. I'll ask around.'

The locksmith interrupted us with a soft knock on the kitchen door. I swapped a hefty cheque for a new set of house keys and an enormous sense of relief that no uninvited visitors would be sneaking round my cottage again.

'I suppose I ought to get back to the shop,' I said. 'Mum doesn't like being left on her own. And she's going out to lunch again today.'

Izzy looked up from reading her newspaper horoscope. 'Good to hear she's getting out a bit more. She must miss your father. I think about Archie every day.' A dreamy, far-away look became her.

'Actually,' I said, gathering up the empty cups, 'I think she may have found herself a replacement.'

'Really?' Izzy discarded the newspaper. 'I wouldn't have predicted that in a million years. Who?'

'His name is Spencer Lewis.'

Izzy's face dropped ever so slightly. 'Oh. How nice.'

'You know him?'

'I know *of* him,' she said, doubt coating her words.

I sighed. 'Okay, what have you heard?'

'That he's a bit of a womaniser.' Then, seeing my crestfallen face, she soothed, 'Perhaps they're just good friends?'

Recalling my mother's rapturous smile and trills of laughter I thought otherwise, at least on her part, and when I turned up at the shop half an hour later and found Spencer leaning over the serving counter, murmuring in a low voice, causing my mother to blush, I found it hard to quash the desire to confront him there and then. Arms linked, they strolled off for their lunch, chitchatting away. I watched through the shop window and hoped Izzy was right, that it wasn't anything serious and would fizzle out as swiftly as it had seemed to ignite.

While they were gone I busied myself making candles – it was the only thing that seemed to ease my mind – and when the shop bell jangled a flash of resentment shot through me, even though it was a loyal customer. I undid my apron and went out to assist, trying to emulate some of my mother's superior selling techniques. Then, leading the woman over to the serving counter to pay for her choices, I opened the till and did a double take.

'What the …?'

Instead of the usual float, plus a few cash transactions, it was stuffed to the brim with twenty pound notes. As soon as the customer left, I counted up the money and locked it in the safe, wondering what on earth my mother had done to improve our fortunes.

On her return, glowing brighter than any candle in the shop, she informed me she'd had a very busy morning. 'The best ever!' She grabbed her duster and set off waltzing round the floor, tickling feathers over the display cabinets. 'Bizarrely,' she called as she worked, 'this hot weather's turned into a blessing for us. It's all the flies and mozzies. The citronella candles have been selling like hot cakes these last few days – you need to make some more – and today I sold a hamper gift set – the luxury one with the three-piece brass votive holders – to Babs Piper for her daughter's birthday. And then … ' She gave a theatrical pause and twirled the duster like a show girl with a baton, '… and then that man, Oliver Harper, stopped by again and bought one of everything!'

'One of everything?'

'One of everything! And he came in a chauffeur-driven car. And he paid in cash.' She exuded smugness.

'Why on earth would he do that?'

'Pay in cash?'

'No, why would he buy one of everything?'

My mother shrugged and started dusting and dancing again. 'I don't know. He wouldn't talk to me.' Her tone had a slight sting to it. 'I told him I'm in charge when you're away, but he was very insistent that it's you he needs to see. He left his card again. It's on your desk.'

Oliver Harper certainly knew how to make an impact.

'I'll phone him right now,' I said, escaping to the workshop and firmly shutting the door.

The conversation was brief and when I returned to the shop a few minutes later my mother was all over me like a second skin.

'Well?' she demanded.

'I'm meeting him for lunch. In London. Next week.'

'What does he want?'

'He wouldn't say. All I could find out is that he owns a chain of bespoke tailors and has a business proposal he wants to put to me.'

As my mother took an intake of breath I prepared myself for the train of questions I knew would stream from her mouth.

'What sort of proposal? And what's tailoring got to do with our candle shop? Is he on Savile Row? Where are you meeting him?'

I had no answers, except for the one about the lunch venue, and she went on and on about Oliver Harper for the rest of the afternoon. While her constant speculating got on my nerves, she at least distracted me from Robert Ashmere, who continued to goad my conscience, and Detective Inspector Pitts, who had me wound as tight as a coiled spring. And for that I was immensely thankful.

8

I'd heard nothing more from the police for nearly a week and wasn't sure which was worse – the scrutiny or the silence. In the meantime, my mother found out that my house had been searched.

'I don't know why you have to be so secretive, Jennifer,' she said, throwing bruised looks over her shoulder each time she passed.

My reasoning – that I didn't want to cause any more worry – failed to pacify her.

'Are you sure you don't know this Robert Ashmere?' she asked time and time again. 'The police seem convinced you do.'

Every now and then I caught her studying me with a blend of puzzlement and worry daubed all over her features like crude face paint. Sometimes her stare carried a feeling of confusion, as though she was trying to read a book whose words were in the wrong order. In a more serious moment I found her on my laptop, trawling the Internet for information on miscarriages of justice, and torturing herself reading stories about innocent people imprisoned. I tried to concentrate on candle making and not be distracted by my own anxious thoughts, or catch my mother's mounting hysteria and fixation with the penal system.

When the detective did reappear, he turned up unannounced at the shop. On hearing his muffled monotone I dropped the jug of melted wax I was pouring into moulds and made a mess on the granite surface. The connecting door opened with a light, ghostly creak.

'That policeman's here,' hissed my mother. 'He wants to see you. He says it's very important.'

My chest tightened. Through a bronchial crackle, I said, 'Just give me a minute to clean up.'

I scrambled about for a cloth, mopped up at motorway speed, then stood still, trying to draw deep breaths into my shrunken airways. It was like trying to suck a gobstopper through a straw. Then I pasted on a cheery smile, opened the door and invited him in.

Detective Inspector Pitts strode into the workshop sporting a concrete veneer, a strong sense of purpose and reeking of cheap aftershave. 'Miss Jarvis,' he said officiously.

I immediately blushed at his choice of salutation. Every time I was in his presence I wondered if he'd found me out, if he knew I wasn't *Miss* Jarvis at all.

'I'm here in connection with the murder of Robert Ashmere.'

I sat down. Suddenly.

'There have been some developments I thought you should know about. Yesterday we arrested and charged a man in connection with Mr Ashmere's death.'

Blood rushed into my ears like a tsunami. All the light in the room condensed into a white speck before flooding back and blinding me.

'Who?' I said hoarsely.

A crack of mistrust fractured the policeman's masonry front, but he answered the question.

'Strictly off the record, it was a local man – a Mr Nick Low.'

I remembered my mother having an unfortunate experience with Nick, when she'd told him to pick up the litter he'd dropped on the pavement. She'd been subjected to a torrent of verbal abuse and left quite shaken by the incident. The demise of good manners and rise of anti-social behaviour had become her pet subject for quite some time.

'He's denying it, of course,' the detective said. 'He says he found Mr Ashmere lying on the footpath and didn't realise he was dead, but thought he was drunk. But he's been inconsistent all along and was found in possession of some cash with traces of the victim's prints on, and also his mobile phone.'

A small wheezy, 'Oh,' was all I could muster.

'And we've numerous witnesses who've said that Mr Low had been drinking heavily. He was thrown out of The Fox and Hounds for being argumentative and threatening a bartender. Our view is that he tried to mug Mr Ashmere on the footpath, but the victim stood his ground, hence the argument you overheard and then the fight, the result of which was Mr Ashmere collapsing and hitting his head on a fallen tree trunk. He suffered a fracture to the back of his skull.'

I immediately heard the sound of bone cracking on wood and pictured the man lying limbs askew, on the footpath, life seeping out of him into a bloody puddle.

'How horrible.' I willed the image to disappear. Looking at the floor I spied a pool of wax that had dripped from the worktop and dried into a glossy disc. I focused on that as I said, 'So it was an accident? He died because he fell and hit his head, not because he was murdered?'

'The investigation is a criminal one,' the policeman informed me. 'Nick Low has been charged with manslaughter.'

I felt hollow, like an empty shell, and when I spoke I could hear myself talking as though there were another me in the room. 'What about the other man? Did you get him too?'

'There were no others.'

'Oh. Are you sure?'

'We can only deal with the facts. You said in your statement that you don't know how many people you heard, because the noise was drowned out by your dog barking ...'

He was right. I didn't know for certain.

'... and Nick Low has admitted he was alone on the footpath with Mr Ashmere.' A satisfied smile chipped into the detective's hard-set jaw.

'What about the note? Did you find out why he had my name and address with him?'

Detective Inspector Pitts pulled the plug on his smile. 'No. We didn't,' he said, slowly, 'which is a shame, because I'd really like to get to the bottom of that one.' His cold, grey eyes zoomed in on my face, like a surveillance camera tracking its target.

I caught another waft of pungent aftershave. 'And what about my intruder? Did you find out who had been in my house?'

'There were no unidentified fingerprints, or any other evidence on your property.'

'But what about the cigarette smell?'

'You must have imagined it.' The detective's tight lips said *case closed* while his hard stare dared me to challenge him.

'I see,' I heard myself say. 'Well, thanks for keeping me informed. I'm glad it's all been resolved.'

The detective nodded, and, having done his duty, turned and strode off without another word.

The moment the shop doorbell jangled my mother burst into the workshop. 'What did he want? Is everything all right? He hasn't been asking more questions has he?' Her cheeks puffed and blew as she caught her breath.

'He's arrested someone,' I said, visibly shaking.

'So what did he say? Did he tell you who did it? Did he give you any clue?'

'He said it was Nick Low.'

A toxic combination of shock, remorse and relief knotted in my gut like severe indigestion as I told her the police theory about the mugging gone wrong.

My mother looked like she'd swallowed raw sewage. 'I've always said Nick Low was trouble,' she spat and spluttered. 'I wish more people would listen to me. They should have banged him up years ago. Imagine killing someone for a wallet and mobile phone.' Then her utter disgust switched to sheer joy, and for a fraction of a second I thought she was going to hug me. 'Oh, Jennifer, this is marvellous news!' But instead she scurried off into the shop to call Spencer.

Ethan was over the moon when I rang him.

'That's brilliant! Fantastic! Thank God for that. We should celebrate – tonight. I'll take you to the Peking for dinner, my shout. Pick you up at eight.'

The door between the shop and my workspace was ajar. I could hear my mother chatting to Spencer on the phone and wondered how long it would be before the whole town knew that Nick Low had been nailed. Unable to face another barrage of questions from the local grapevine, I went out and asked if she would mind me taking the rest of the afternoon off.

'Of course not, darling,' she said, hand over the mouthpiece and eyeing me up and down. 'You look exhausted. A face like that's no good for business – except at Halloween. Go and have a little lie down. I can manage perfectly well without you, go on – go.' Her attention switched back to Spencer. 'Yes, Jennifer's going home. I think it's all got a bit much for her … Yes, it's the shock … and the relief … Yes, such a relief for us all …'

Dismissed, I fumbled with Digby's lead, stepped outside and stood on the pavement sucking in a bucket load of warm, acrid air until I felt bloated. Feet away, a line of cars came to a standstill at a bleeping red traffic light, hot engines ticking over, exhausts spewing fumes. My own car was parked across the street in a bay by the clock tower, but I decided that in my current state I wasn't fit to drive. Instead, I headed towards the town square.

It was market day and folk were out in force, the sedate pace of country life traded for a vibrant buzz. Glazed in sunshine, Ridgelow looked easy on the eye, had its own heartbeat and was alive with spirit. The cobblestone square was organised chaos, a rainbow of stalls housing local producers selling their wares to natives and tourists alike: fruit and veg; meat and cheese; bread and homemade chutneys. One of the most popular stops was the local brewery stand, which was offering free tastings. Happy shoppers downed their nip of beer whilst listening to an amateur brass band blasting out a haphazard rendition of *When the Saints go Marching in.*

Lost in my own world, I weaved through the throngs, dipping under patterned bunting and towing Digby past the burger van, struggling to make sense of the unexpected development. It was hard to take in. One minute I was a suspect in a murder investigation being scrutinised by the police, hounded by the press and analysed by the local grapevine, then in the next, I was in the clear. Just like that.

On autopilot I made for home, oblivious that my well-trained feet were carrying me toward Beckett Close and the entrance to the footpath. I trudged steadily through Ridgelow's back streets, crammed full of Victorian terraced cottages – some shabby, some chic – and colourfully painted mews houses, many buried under swathes of wisteria and clematis. But the pretty picture was spoiled by the mass of parked cars snaked bumper to bumper along the roadside, and the further I walked from the centre of the town, the more modern the dwellings became. Victorian charm turned to tree-lined avenues of smart 1930s detached suburbia, which morphed into a small housing estate of boxy 1960s pebble-dashed semis and bungalows with neat lawns and sensible family saloons parked on slim tarmac strips.

I came to an abrupt halt in front of two indistinguishable chalet bungalows. A small signpost quietly announced the public footpath, pointing down a narrow opening set between the houses. A tangle of trees and shrubs edged either side of the dirt track, which disappeared round a tight bend a few metres ahead. The police presence had gone: the cordon had been removed, and this time the only audience was an elderly man meticulously trimming his box hedging in a garden opposite.

Digby strained against his lead, eager to stretch his legs and explore. I steadied myself against a lamp post, wishing I'd walked the long way round. Digby started to whine. I unclipped him and he rocketed up the shady trail, disappearing round the corner. I coaxed my feet forward and followed the dog, aware that a band of cold was grazing the back of my bare legs. Stopping, I glanced over my shoulder. Of course there was nothing there. But that didn't stop my skin erupting in volcano pimples, or a ribbon of fear winding round my heart and tightening like corset lacing. I forced myself on, acutely aware that each step I took was leading me closer to the spot where Robert had died, right at the bottom of my garden. I wondered what I would find, what trace of him might lie in wait.

Despite my fears, the footpath was peaceful and serene. Bathed in warm sunshine, delicate shards of light seeped through gaps in the overhanging trees, decorating the pathway with gold baubles. Birds and their song filled the sky, unconducted, but coming together in beautiful chorus. The mechanical rumble of tractors and balers, combined with the sweet smell of freshly cut meadow grass, hung in the hot summer air. It was picture postcard-perfect.

Then I discovered the kaleidoscope flower carpet.

Waves of floral tributes covered the ground in hues of pale pink, baby blue, primrose yellow and startling white, all encasing a centrepiece laid in a spot disturbingly close to my garden gate – a large tied sheaf of crimson roses propped up against a tree trunk. Suddenly, I was ambushed by more snapshot memories gathered on a humid, dark night.

*The smell of blood.*

*A piercing scream.*

*The crack of a skull against wood.*

I stiffened at the light pad of footsteps, then as the figure came into view, let out a long breath and relaxed again, having recognised the large straw sun hat and wicker basket.

'Yoo-hoo!' Izzy called, spying me too. She came over, put her basket on the ground and mopped her brow with a bright saffron linen bell sleeve. 'Phew,' she said. 'Still mighty warm, isn't it?' Then admiring the petal floor covering said, 'Wow, this is quite something.

It's spectacular.' She reached into her basket and pulled out a bunch of mixed freesias. 'When I popped to the market I heard talk of people putting tributes down. Apparently there's a view that we shouldn't let the incident go unmarked, just because the man wasn't local. Quite right, so I bought these. I thought they were rather lovely.' She laid the flowers on the ground alongside a bunch of lilies, then tiptoed through the display, crouching down to read some of the messages. Moving along, her hand came to rest on a small plain white card tucked between the stems of the centrepiece sheaf of roses. She scanned the words, then closed her eyes and dipped her head.

'What is it?' I said in a low voice after a long moment of still.

'His mother.' Izzy rolled herself upright as though getting out of one of her yoga moves. 'I heard she'd been here. And look what else she's left behind.' She held out an earthy hand, its cracks and crevices lightly stained with dirt. 'Another photo. Of Robert.'

I wanted to look, and yet I didn't. But Izzy was excited at the find and hopped out of the carpet of flowers to thrust the picture at me. Once again, the dead man stared back, but thankfully this time the accusing look in his eyes was concealed by wrap-around sunglasses. He was sitting astride a mountain bike, tanned and relaxed. In the background was the rugged summit of a snow-capped peak. I knew enough from Ethan to recognise the gear of a hardcore biker when I saw one; off-road cycle shoes; ultralight helmet; wick-away jersey and stretch shorts.

Izzy was thinking the same. 'He looks just like your Ethan in all that Lycra. I've never been keen on men in tights, but these mountain bikers manage to carry it off. Mind you, a pair of baggy shorts over the top of their what-nots does help with the overall impression.' She took the photo, stepped carefully through the tributes and replaced it between the rose stems, then, returning, sized me up in an instant. 'You're very quiet today. And pale again. Something on your mind?' Blue-violet eyes blinked at me from under the floppy rim of her sun hat and she cocked her head this way and that, like a wise old owl. When I didn't reply she prompted, 'Have you heard anything more from the police?' Her smile was soft and encouraging. But as the corners of her mouth curled, the lines mapping her face deepened into canyons of concern. With a flick of the head and swing of a bell sleeve she indicated to the nearby wooden bench, a favourite night time haunt for Ridgelow's teenagers. 'Come on, let's take a pew.'

Calling Digby into view, I joined her on the graffitied perch and emptied myself of the news.

'Detective Inspector Pitts came to the shop this morning. He told me they've arrested and charged someone.'

Izzy clapped her hands together and drew them to her chin in a victory clasp. 'Oh my word! How marvellous! You must be so relieved?'

'Yes,' I said, looking at the ground and drawing patterns in the dirt with the toe of my plimsoll.

Beside me Izzy fizzed like a bottle of just-opened champagne. 'Did he say who did it?'

'Nick Low.'

'Nick Low?' Izzy bristled and the victory clasp became a white-knuckle clench in her lap. 'He ransacked my Help for Heroes charity box at the baker's last year. Horrid little creep. Do you know what happened?'

'The police think it was a mugging gone wrong.

They think Robert stood his ground, hence the shouting I heard, and that Nick beat him up and then stole his money and phone.' The hollow feeling returned as I added, 'Apparently Robert hit his head on a fallen tree trunk. That's how he died. The tree killed him.'

My neighbour immediately scanned the footpath, her straw hat generating a waft of warm air as her head swayed from left to right. 'I suspect the police have removed it,' she said lightly. 'And what about the note? Have the police worked out why Robert was coming to see you?'

'No,' I said gloomily. 'And Detective Inspector Pitts didn't look too pleased about it either.'

'I shouldn't think he would be. He'll want every single detail sewn up in a nice neat package, ready to deliver to the judge. Instead he's got a very untidy loose end. Must be driving him mad. Much worse than any elusive crossword answer. But at least he's solved the important question – who did it.'

'Yes. At least he's done that.' My foot traced another random shape on the dusty ground.

'I have to say you don't sound too thrilled about it, Jennifer,' said Izzy. 'I would have thought you'd be cock-a-hoop now it's all over.'

I raised a small smile at the old-fashioned phrase. 'Well, I'm certainly glad the police won't be on my case anymore, and I suppose it's not going to be much of a surprise to people that Nick Low is involved, but …' I stared at the sea of flowers trying to make sense of my feelings.

'Hmmm …' From under her sun hat, Izzy gave me a shrewd look. 'He may be dead, but this Robert Ashmere fellow has got right under your skin, hasn't he? You still want to know the connection, don't you?'

The words gushed out. 'I can't help it. I can't stop thinking about him. I need to know why he was coming to see me. More to the point, I need to know that I *don't* know him, that he was a stranger and I didn't leave someone I know to die out here.'

Izzy pulled a crosspatch face. 'Oh, Jennifer. I do wish you would stop blaming yourself. Even if you had called the police when you heard them fighting, from what you've said it's unlikely they could have saved him.'

I didn't reply and focused on swallowing away the lump that had balled in my throat.

Izzy filled the silence. 'Well, at least now you're off the hook you can poke around without that policeman questioning your every move. And,' she said, perking up, 'we've already learnt something new today.' I looked at her, confused, and she prompted, 'the photo in the roses. It tells us that Robert was an outdoorsy type and that he enjoyed mountain biking, something you can use as a talking point when you go to the funeral, which by the way, is being held the day after tomorrow. You are going to go, aren't you?'

'Of course I am,' I said, my insides suddenly all aflutter as nerves jostled in anticipation at the thought of meeting people Robert knew and maybe finding some answers.

'Good. That's settled. And while you're there, why don't you try to offload some of the guilt you're obviously still feeling, pay your last respects to the man and find a way to forgive yourself, because, from what I can see, you, my dear, are being a much bigger demon to yourself than Robert Ashmere ever will be.'

9

I got so caught up in the news that the police had charged someone with Robert's death that I forgot about the meeting I'd arranged with Oliver Harper. My mother reminded me an hour before I was due to catch the train and I had to rush home to change.

I was feeling a little hung-over after my night out with Ethan. He'd booked a table at our favourite Chinese restaurant and we'd celebrated in fine style, stuffing ourselves with crispy duck and king prawns and consuming far too much wine. Then we walked home sharing bad jokes and Ethan had told me how good it was to hear me laugh again. As we approached Corner Cottage, his arm draped around my shoulders and mine round his waist, our footsteps slowed and the conversation got serious.

'You know, Jen, if ever you feel uncomfortable here, after what's happened, you can always come and live with me.' Through the darkness I could hear his hesitation. 'I'm not trying to push you into anything. I know you love this place, but I want you to know that I'm serious ... about *us.*'

His words made me tingle and then crumple inwardly as pictures of my deeply regrettable wedding day exploded like fireworks in my mind. Blood burst into my cheeks at the same time and I was glad of the cover of night.

'I'm not asking you to rush in and make a decision right now or anything,' he said. 'I just want you to know how I feel.'

I leant up and kissed him on the cheek. His skin was hot too. 'Thank you. How about we let things calm down a bit then talk about it again?'

Ethan agreed and we called it a night.

I thought about his suggestion as I sat on the train to London. In fact, I'd thought of nothing else since he'd said those words. A warm glow had attached itself to my heart, but my head was all over the place. Moving in was one thing, but I couldn't stop worrying about the next step in the commitment conversation, when Ethan might dare to take it even further. I knew something had to be done before the situation got even more out of hand, but for now, I tried not to fret and instead turned my thoughts to lunch and my meeting with the mysterious Oliver Harper.

We had arranged to meet in a restaurant on Marylebone High Street. I walked the short distance from the station, treating myself to a bit of window shopping, wincing at the prices in the boutiques. Studying my reflection in a pristine pane, I frowned at my conservative navy blue trouser suit, a leftover from my corporate marketing days, but it was the only suit I owned and so it had to do.

On reaching the address I'd been given, I stood outside, flummoxed. It was a fishmonger. I checked the neighbouring stores to make sure there wasn't somewhere else I was supposed to be, then noticed people walking straight past the vast displays of fresh fish, through a nondescript doorway at the rear. Following on, trying not to inhale the stench, I found myself in a small, lively restaurant. Having been given my name, a waiter showed me to a table where I ordered a bottle of mineral water and slugged at my glass, trying to rehydrate myself from the previous night's boozing.

The fish restaurant was a popular place filled by an eclectic bunch of people talking over each other. The walls were painted in bright bold colours and covered in chalk menus. I studied them as I waited, trying to decide what I might have, even though I was still stuffed from the Chinese. I had plenty of time to choose. Oliver Harper arrived a full twenty minutes late, without apology. Younger than I'd expected and impeccably dressed in a beautiful tobacco linen suit and vivid pink shirt, unbuttoned a little too low, he clasped my hand between both of his in a firm grip.

'Jennifer, how very lovely to meet you.'

He was a handsome man, but (in my opinion) with something of the old-fashioned dandy about him. His eyes were deep amber and his skin smooth and tanned. His hazelnut hair was rich and full, and swept down towards his shoulders in long rock and roll layers. The spicy scent of his aftershave was unequivocally masculine and my nose picked out base notes of patchouli and cedar wood. I noticed Chanel cufflinks at his wrists and an impressive Swiss timepiece discreetly tucked under a double cuff. His manicured nails made me very aware of my own functional hands with their scraggy tips. Feeling bland and unpolished in comparison I wondered again why on earth he wanted to meet me.

'Ah, you've ordered water. I'd prefer something a little stronger, if you don't mind?' His Etonian accent was as sharp as his tailoring. Before I could object to the suggestion of alcohol, he summoned the waiter and requested a bottle of Laurent-Perrier.

'So, Oliver,' I said, as the waiter presented me with a crystal flute and made a song and dance of cascading bubbles into the glass, with one hand clasping the champagne bottle and the other tucked behind his back. 'Are you going to keep me in suspense much longer? I feel like a child at Christmas – dying to know what's about to be unveiled.'

He laughed, revealing immaculate Hollywood teeth. 'Let's order first, then get down to business, shall we?'

Oliver was obviously a regular and didn't refer to the menu. He ordered half a dozen oysters followed by crab. Oysters make me gag, so I selected a fish cocktail and Dover sole before he could order on my behalf. He looked like the sort who would.

Lolling in his chair, Oliver openly inspected me. 'I appreciate you making this trip in to town,' he said. 'I live in your neck of the woods too, but work brings me here in the week.' He gave a lazy smile, as though he had all the time in the world. 'I thought this would be a nice place to get to know each other better.'

I eyed him cautiously, wondering exactly what he had in mind.

Oliver saw the look on my face. 'Don't worry. I'm not going to eat you. I'm recently married – happily.' He flashed a gold band at me.

It at least broke the ice, and I made myself laugh it off with him.

'Why don't you tell me about yourself.' He took a long sip of champagne, eyes travelling over me again, long lashes languidly sweeping up and down, but pupils shining like black pebbles at the bottom of a deep, clear stream, dark and intense.

'Well, I've been running JJ Candles for three years,' I said, racking my brain for something to say. 'Before that I did a degree in Business Management, then worked in marketing … '

Oliver put down his glass, raked a tanned hand through precision-cut layers and leant in across the table. His amber eyes hooked on mine. 'No. I mean tell me about *you*. Who are you? What makes you tick? What gets you out of bed in the morning?' He stabbed a plump green olive from a bowl on the table with a wooden cocktail stick, wolfed it down and sat back. 'I like to know about the people I do business with, to get a sense of the real person beneath all the gloss and sheen.'

I had to hold back a snort of laughter. 'That's err … interesting, Oliver,' I replied. 'But as you've yet to tell me what sort of business we're here to discuss, I'm really not sure what to say, other than what you see is what you get. There's no polish, gloss or sheen. I get out of bed every morning to make candles and sell them. You've seen what I do. What really interests me right now is why *you're* so interested in me and my shop.'

Oliver smirked. 'There's more to you than meets the eye,' he said, spearing another plump olive. 'I've read all about you, in the *Sunday Post*. Pretty impressive stuff, winning an enterprise award like that. They're known as the Rural Oscars, you know. You've obviously got talent and a nose for business.'

I shrugged off his flattery. 'Not sure about that – a nose for candles, yes, but the business has been an organic thing. I'm just doing what I love, and so far it's working.'

'And what about financing? You must have a backer?'

'Yes. My father.'

'Is he a partner?'

'No. He's dead.'

Oliver took another gulp of champagne and recovered quickly. 'I'm sorry to hear that.'

'He was the catalyst and financier for JJ's,' I said, touched by sadness. It was over three years since he died, but his loss was still raw. 'He left me some money to set myself up.'

'So it's just you who makes the decisions?'

'Yes. My mother helps in the shop, but on a voluntary basis. It's my business.'

I suddenly realised that I was revealing far too much to someone I knew little of, and who so far had deftly evaded every question I'd asked of him. I checked myself and was about to press Oliver again about his motive when the starters arrived. Then, as I tucked into the food, I was distracted by the sight of Oliver throwing back his head and swallowing his oysters with the flair of a sword swallower entertaining a baying crowd in a Marrakech market.

He caught my stare. 'How's your fish cocktail?'

'Delicious,' I said, thinking that if Oliver and his proposition turned out to be a complete waste of time, at least the food was good. 'But I still have no idea why you've asked me here.'

'All in good time,' he said, lifting a final oyster shell to his lips and gulping the salty morsel straight down.

Both Oliver and the fish cocktail suddenly lost their appeal. I pushed my unfinished plate away wondering why the hell I'd taken time out of my day to traipse into London to meet a man who was proving to be as elusive as a yeti in a snowstorm. But as I thought about making an excuse to leave the next course arrived. I got a fragrant waft of lemon and parsley butter as a plate of Dover sole was placed in front of me, and decided that if Oliver was wasting my time he could do it at his own expense, then debated ordering another bottle of champagne whilst regretting not choosing the Nova Scotia Lobster, and scallops to start.

But the Dover sole was divine. Oliver, who had

ordered a whole crab on a bed of salad leaves, was happy too. His eyes lit up as the waiter delivered the dish to the table and I noticed him unconsciously lick his lips. He asked for an extra napkin, then picked up his surgically styled cutlery and tucked in. I watched out of the corner of my eye as he dissected the hard shell and uncovered the prize within. His full attention was given over to the crab. He cracked open the claws, scrapped out the soft white meat and put it carefully to one side. He did the same with the legs, then slit open the main shell with a knife, discarding small pieces of bone and cartilage before scooping out the rich brown meat with a small spatula. I was fascinated and yet repulsed. When the job was done, he meticulously cleaned his sticky, tanned hands in a finger bowl and dried them on his napkin, before spooning the delicate crab meat onto a hunk of bread, adding a blob of mayonnaise and a sprinkle of paprika and devouring it. He quickly finished the remaining meat, dabbed his mouth and lolled in his chair with a satisfied smile.

I pitied his new wife. And the crab.

Finishing my meal, I ordered a coffee, then said: 'Oliver, I have to leave soon. You have ten more minutes of my time to tell me why you've asked me to come all the way into London when I have a business to run. What exactly do you want?'

'I'd like to buy JJ Candles.'

He might as well have given me an electric shock.

'I'll offer you a good price for both the building and the business. How does £350,000 sound?' Oliver couldn't have been more causal about it if he'd offered to buy a packet of peanuts.

'You haven't seen any figures,' I said, knowing it was a very generous offer. I own the freehold to the shop and there's also a flat above, which I rent out, but even so, I was sure it was £30,000 over market value.

'I know enough.'

It was a fantastic opportunity, but JJ's was too important to let go.

'My business isn't for sale.'

'So name your price.'

'I'm sorry, but JJ's isn't for sale.'

'Don't you want to think it over?'

'No. Thank you.'

'Why don't you sleep on it? I'll come up to Ridgelow in a few days and we can finalise the deal.'

His Hollywood smile failed to dazzle me.

'No need. I've made up my mind. JJ's isn't for sale. I'm sorry if I've wasted your time, I certainly didn't intend to.'

I offered to take care of the lunch bill to make amends.

'I'll deal with it,' he said. 'Are you really sure?'

I told him again, firmly, that I was extremely sure. JJ Candles wasn't for sale.

Oliver's amber eyes glazed over and the atmosphere became artic. I thanked him for his time, made a swift exit and headed up Marylebone High Street at a Nordic walking pace. As I waited on the platform for my train, a prickle of apprehension wormed its way into my head and I instinctively knew I would hear from Oliver again. I added this unpalatable thought to the growing litter pile in my mind and headed for my train.

After London's constant traffic noise and suffocating fumes it was a relief to step out into fresh air at Ridgelow. Back in the shop, I found my mother and Spencer Lewis chatting over the serving counter.

Spencer straightened up as I came in and shook

my hand. 'Good to see you again, Jennifer.'

'We were just talking about you, weren't we?' my mother purred. 'I didn't realise Oliver Harper is a friend of Spencer's.'

Spencer corrected her gently, 'More an acquaintance really, Mary.'

'How did it go?' she asked.

I kept my voice level. 'It was a bit strange. We had a lovely meal, he asked me all sorts of questions then right at the end told me he wants to buy the shop.'

'What?' My mother paled into an alabaster statue.

'I turned him down, of course.'

'How much was he offering?' said Spencer, reaching for his silk handkerchief and trumpet-blowing his nose.

I waited for him to finish then said calmly, '£350,000.'

My mother hit the stool behind the counter with a thud as her legs gave way. 'That's a very generous offer.'

Pound signs spun in Spencer's eyes. 'Very generous. I'd say it was easily forty grand above current market value.'

I was enjoying their reaction and added, 'He told me to name my price, but I said that JJ's wasn't for sale.'

'Jennifer,' my mother croaked, fanning herself with a magazine she'd retrieved from the side of the till. 'I know you've been under a lot of strain lately, but don't make a snap decision. Why don't you think it over?' I saw her exchange a glance with Spencer.

'Mum, we've worked hard to build this business and I love it. It's everything I dreamed of. And there's more to life than money.'

'You're a braver person than I am,' Spencer warned. 'Oliver's used to getting what he wants. If he's serious about this shop, he won't give up easily, and I'm afraid he can be quite devious.'

'He didn't come across like that,' I fibbed, just to disagree with him. 'He seemed decent enough.'

'Well, as they say, appearances can be deceiving,' Spencer said. 'I happen to know that Oliver's business approach isn't always pleasant, or even legal for that matter. What I don't understand is why he'd be willing to pay so much for this place. I know it's a central location, but it's not the best shop on the parade, and from what your mother's told me, the flat upstairs is on the smallish size and needs a bit of updating.'

I was irritated by his dismissive tone, and with my mother for discussing my affairs. A knife-sharp retort clung to the tip of my tongue, but after counting to ten in my head, I was able to calm down, check myself and swallow it.

Spencer ploughed on. 'I don't get it. If he wants to open a store here, which is my guess, why is he set on your shop? There's an empty retail space at the top of the High Street that would be far more suitable and just the ticket for what he needs.'

'The offer wasn't only for the property,' I pushed back. 'He wants the whole thing as a going concern.'

Sensing the tension between us my mother changed the subject. 'Izzy popped in earlier. She said you're going to Robert Ashmere's funeral tomorrow. I told her I didn't know anything about it.' Miffed, she sucked in her cheeks and gave a little sniff.

'Oh, yes, I am. Sorry, I meant to mention it to you earlier, but forgot. Do you mind holding the fort again? I know I've been asking you a lot lately.'

'It's fine. I think it's a good idea. You're still very uptight, Jennifer. Hopefully you can use it to close the door on this dreadful business once and for all.'

'That's what I thought.'

I felt mean lying to her again. Well, it wasn't lying exactly, just not giving her the full story, but I didn't want her to know that Robert Ashmere was still very much alive and kicking to me and that I was still on his trail.

She wouldn't understand.

10

Picking up the latest edition of the *Chiltern Messenger* from the newsagents, my eyes darted straight to the front page. The headline – 'Footpath Murder Cracked'– evoked a huge sigh of relief. With a lighter heart I returned to the shop and handed the newspaper to my mother.

'Thank goodness for that,' she said, poring over the print. 'At least everyone will know the truth now.' Then, scanning me, said, 'Why aren't you in black?' It was the second outing for my navy suit that week, and, like me, it looked tired and crumpled. 'You must wear black to a funeral. Especially such a tragic one.'

'This'll be fine,' I said, brushing the material on my thighs as though the palms of my hands were iron plates and might erase the creases. 'The rules aren't as strict anymore.'

'If you say so,' she sniffed.

The shop doorbell jangled. Shirley Langham, chief gossip, stepped inside brandishing a copy of the *Messenger.* I immediately bade my mother goodbye, shot out the door and made for the car.

During the half-hour drive to Bicester, I silenced the radio and rehearsed what I might say to people. Izzy had suggested a few conversation starters and had also recommended I arrive early to chat to friends and family before the ceremony, but having missed a turn I got lost and arrived with only a few minutes to spare.

Hurrying up the path through manicured grounds, past sunken gravestones and cracked tombs, my low heels clacked against asphalt. I entered the ancient church and with a dipped, respectful head, snuck into a pew near the back. The other mourners were also taking their seats. After a furtive look round I noticed a lone woman sitting behind a stone pillar. Her features were partially concealed by Jackie O dark glasses and a black silk scarf draped over blonde hair, but she looked very much like the woman in the wedding photo – Robert's wife.

The cavernous building filled with sound as the opening piano solo of the *Ave Maria* resonated off the stone walls. When the rich voice of a female mezzo-soprano joined in my whole body tingled. The church doors swung open and the funeral procession made its way down the aisle. Two elderly women walked slowly behind, arms linked. One was weeping, the other was more composed and stared straight ahead, but her free arm gently patted that of her companion. As the coffin passed, a band of cold moved through me and I couldn't stop thinking that it wasn't an empty box at all, and pictured Robert's dead body inside.

The service was satisfactorily short. There were two hymns and the Minister made much of the sense of tragedy surrounding the untimely death. After the Lord's Prayer, the procession solemnly made its way to the churchyard and the gaping hole that was to be Robert's grave. I tagged on the end of the line of mourners and stood back, watching people gather round as the coffin was lowered. I didn't recognise anyone, other than the woman in the wedding photo, who instead of joining the family and friends around the grave, stood some distance away, partly obscured by an oak tree.

The priest scattered handfuls of reddish-brown earth over the coffin and the two elderly women who had led the procession stepped forward and took turns to drop red roses into the dark hole. I couldn't watch.

Instead, I walked over to view the row of floral arrangements lined up on the pathway waiting to be moved once the grave was filled in.

The group began to disperse. The elderly woman who had been weeping broke away from the gathering and stooped towards me, wasted legs clad in black denier, arthritis and grief hindering her every step.

'I don't think we've met,' she said, her voice barely a whisper, and holding out a delicate hand gloved in translucent skin and patterned with age spots. 'I'm Iris Ashmere, Robert's mother. Thank you for coming.' Her face was birdlike, tearstained and full of exhaustion.

'Jennifer,' I said, treating her hand as though it were made of murano glass. 'And I'm so sorry about what happened to your son, truly sorry.'

The woman's eyes filled with tears and she brushed them away with shaky fingers. 'Do excuse me. I thought I'd bear up better than this.' She took a moment to muster some strength and locate her handkerchief from a pocket. Having dabbed at her eyes, she said quietly, 'How did you know Robert? Were you a friend of his?'

I shifted my weight from foot to foot as I tried to find the right words. 'Actually, I didn't know him. He … he died behind my house and, well, I feel terrible about what happened and wanted to come and pay my respects.'

Recognition flashed across the woman's face. 'Jennifer? As in Jarvis?' Her voice had risen and she clutched at my arm. 'You're the one Robert was going to see that night. He had your name and address with him, didn't he?' Iris' grip was unexpectedly firm. 'But if you didn't know him, why was he coming to see you?'

'I don't know,' I said. Her fingers were digging

into my flesh, but I took the pain, acutely aware that her own suffering was immense.

Her voice dropped back to a shaky half-whisper. 'You heard it, didn't you? You heard the fight?'

My head was heavy when I nodded and my words loaded with regret when I said, 'It happened so quickly … If I could turn back the clock, I would …' For a moment I thought I was going to break.

Iris could see I was battling with myself and released her grip. 'Oh, it's no good blaming yourself. It won't bring him back.'

A fellow-mourner came over and expressed his condolences, giving me time to restore my crumbling veneer.

After a brief word with the man, Iris stooped round again and said, 'I'd like to know what happened. I've heard from the police, but I'd like to hear it from you.' Her desperate hand was back on my forearm. 'You were there,' she pleaded. 'Please come back to the house and talk to me.'

I hadn't the heart to refuse, and consoled myself with the thought that it would be a good opportunity to find out more about Robert and see if I could find out the connection between us. She gave me her address and some rough directions, and twenty minutes later I found myself outside a bland-looking 1970s semi. Iris hadn't arrived, but I was let in and shown into the sitting room. The doorbell continued to ring, but as people trooped in there was no sign of Robert's wife.

I wandered over to the fireplace and studied the photographs displayed in tarnished silver frames, to see if I recognised anyone, but didn't. A large print of Robert had pride of place in the centre. His eyes followed me round the room.

Iris eventually arrived and came over with her sister, Felicity. 'This is Jennifer Jarvis, the woman Robert was going to see,' she explained, before moving off to greet another mourner.

Felicity shook my hand. She was a sturdier version of her sister in both appearance and disposition. 'Thank you for coming,' she said through a polite smile. 'I know Iris will appreciate talking to you about what happened. We've been over and over it with the police, but it would be helpful to hear from someone who was actually there. Let's find somewhere a bit more private.' She ushered me into a small study. 'I'll fetch Iris.' As she shut the door the temperature in the room dropped. I sat like a stone statue on a hard, compact sofa, listening to my short, sharp breaths cutting into the silence.

*Did he grow up in this house?*

Something touched my arm and I jumped up with a shriek, skin crawling as I brushed the feeling away. Whipping round I saw a spider disappear down the arm of the sofa, scurry across the carpet and take refuge in a dusty nook.

I'd just replaced all the cushions, after checking that no more surprises lurked beneath, when the two sisters returned. Iris sat next to me. Felicity pulled up a spare chair. I told them my account of what happened and they listened carefully to every word. When I described Robert's cry, Iris flinched and drew a hand to her heart. Silent tears streamed on to her sunken cheeks.

'It's exactly what the police said,' Felicity confirmed when I'd finished.

'But why was Robert coming to see you?' Iris asked again, reaching into a box of Kleenex her sister had provided and dabbing her face with a tissue.

'I really don't know,' I said. 'That's why I came

here today, to see if I recognised anyone, and to pay my respects of course.'

'What about this Nick Low? Do you know him?' said Felicity.

'No. But I know *of* him. He's got a bad reputation in Ridgelow. He's always caught up in some sort of trouble.'

'He's an animal,' Iris spat. 'He should hang for what he did to my son.' She shook so violently that I actually listened for the rattle of frail bones.

Felicity got up from her seat and put her arm round her sister's hunched shoulders.

'Why don't you go and lie down for a while?' she soothed. 'I can deal with the buffet. Go on. People will understand.' Iris reluctantly agreed, and once she'd left the room, Felicity went over to a teak bureau and took out a tumbler and decanter. 'Sherry?'

I declined, mentioning I had to drive.

She poured one for herself. 'Iris isn't coping well,' she said. 'But who would? No one expects to bury their child.' She joined me on the sofa, obviously appreciating my keen ear. 'It was such a shock. I mean, Robert was no angel, although Iris would have you believe otherwise, but he didn't deserve to die.' She paused to sip her drink. 'It would have been his forty-fifth birthday next week. He didn't even reach forty-five. His life was snuffed out, and for what? For a poxy phone and a bit of pocket money?'

While it was hard to hear her pour her heart out I knew I had to keep her talking, to try and find out as much as I could.

'What was he like?' I dared to ask.

She sighed. 'A rogue. A lovable rogue. He could be a real charmer when he wanted, but he was always a bit of a rebel and liked to play by his own rules. Iris adored him. To be honest she spoiled him. She was incredibly proud of our Robert. No one in our family has ever really achieved much, but he got through university and landed himself a decent job in electronics. He ended up as a director of the company.'

This titbit surprised me. 'Oh? I thought he was a photographer?'

'He was. But that came later – out of the blue. He suddenly announced he was fed up with the rat race and was going to set up his own photographic studio. But it was a mistake. He didn't ever make any money from it, not like he did in electronics.'

'What about his wife?'

Felicity pulled a mulish face. 'Erica? They split up a while ago.'

'That's a shame. They looked very happy at their wedding.'

Felicity looked confused.

'The police showed me a photo of them, a wedding photo, to see if I recognised Robert,' I explained.

'We all knew it wouldn't last,' said Felicity. 'Erica was too young, and too strong-minded for Robert. Oh, the arguments they had, always clashing those two. I don't know exactly what happened in the end. All Robert would tell us was that she'd moved to Milton Keynes to start her own business – designing websites, I think.'

'She was at the funeral.'

Felicity arched an eyebrow. 'Yes, I noticed. Thankfully Iris didn't. She's never forgiven Erica for leaving. Robert went downhill after they split.'

'What do you mean, downhill?'

'He let himself go – started looking shabby and

unshaven. Iris wouldn't see him for days on end, then he'd turn up on the doorstep asking for money.' Felicity suddenly checked herself. 'But you don't want to hear about our family problems.' She downed the remnants of her sherry and stood up. 'I've been waffling on for far too long. The other guests will be expecting a bite to eat by now. I better see to it. Thanks very much for coming, and for talking to Iris.'

I was openly dismissed, which suited me fine. I'd found out more than I'd dared to hope, but being in Robert's mother's house gave me the creeps.

Pleased that it hadn't been a wasted trip, I drove back to Ridgelow, mind buzzing. I already had ideas about my next move, but wanted to discuss them with Izzy. We'd arranged to go out for dinner that evening, so I could update her on what I'd found out.

I arrived at the shop just as my mother was locking up for the day.

'How did it go love?' she said, slipping bare arms into a fuchsia pink, three-quarter-sleeve jacket. Then, smearing on some lipstick, she puckered at me like a goldfish, waiting for my reply.

'Fine. It was all fine,' I said wearily.

'Good,' she said, not really listening. 'I'm meeting Spencer for a drink. Why don't you and Ethan come along?'

*A double date? With my mother and Spencer?*

'Sorry. I've made plans to go out with Izzy.'

My mother's newly painted glossy lips formed a perfect O. 'Do you two often go out together?'

'Not really. I think she was being kind and thought I'd be too tired to cook after the funeral.'

'Ask her along. We haven't caught up properly for ages. It'll be nice.'

'Won't Spencer mind us hijacking his date with you?' I said, desperately searching for a get-out clause.

My mother glared. 'It's not a date. We're just friends.'

There was no way I could get out of it without being subjected to a barrage of questions or seeming rude.

'All right, I'll ask her. I've just got a few things to do here first. Where are you going?'

She told me the name of the pub and left, locking up the shop at the front while I shut myself in the workshop, away from passing prying eyes, and caught up on some work.

Everything was in pretty good shape. The latest Internet orders were packed and ready for posting and my mother had left me a list of stock that was getting low. The surfaces in the workshop were clear and all my equipment was clean and set up ready for more candle-making action. I made a mental note to thank my mother for all that she'd done to keep the ship afloat when I saw her later.

Perched on the tidy surface of my desk, I called Izzy and apologised for the change of plan. She was disappointed that she wouldn't get to hear about the funeral, but this was outweighed by her chance to observe Spencer Lewis in action. I also rang Ethan who said he would come as soon as he could.

My stomach rumbled and I realised I hadn't eaten anything since breakfast. I ambled into the kitchen and finished off a packet of ginger biscuits. Two dirty cups and a teaspoon sat in the sink. I washed them up to save my mother a job in the morning. There was nothing urgent left to do, so I scooped up my newly purchased handbag and the dog's lead, crossed the room and flicked off the lights.

There was a loud bang, like a crack of thunder. Digby sprung out of his basket and started barking. I dropped the bag and lead and froze.

*What the hell was that?*

At first I thought a fuse had blown, but when I flicked the switch the lights worked perfectly.

'Quiet, Digby,' I hushed, flapping my arm at him in a waving motion to catch his attention.

The dog obeyed and fell silent. He padded over and stood at my feet, eyes watching my face, but ears trained on the wider environment, and when someone called out he started barking all over again, looking at me as though to say, *you see?*

'Jen? Jen? Are you in there?' The voice was male and muffled.

I opened the connecting door to the shop and gasped. The front window had been smashed. An intricate web of delicate fractures and cracks trailed across the pane completely distorting the view of the High Street. A face peered through the still intact window of the shop door. It was Dave Mulligan and his son, the local butchers.

'Hang on a minute,' I called, grabbing my keys.

My legs felt like jelly as I crossed the shop floor and unlocked the front door, taking care not to let the window cave in.

'Are you okay?' said Dave again, short of breath. 'We 'eard a bang and when Paul went to have a look he saw the window. Cor! Right state, innit?'

'I was out the back, in the workshop. I thought a fuse had blown.' I went outside and stood in front of the shop to survey the damage. 'How the hell did that happen?'

Dave and Paul joined me, shaking their heads and tutting. 'We didn't see nothin', we just 'eard it,' Dave said.

The shop became an instant curiosity. Cars and passers-by slowed to rubberneck at the mess.

'Wait up – wots that?' said Paul, nipping inside. He came out with an object pinched between a thumb and forefinger. 'Ere's the little critter.' It was a small grey stone, the diameter of a ten pence piece and the same size as a hole at the centre of the splintered glass. 'Musta been flipped up by a car. Go hell of a speed along 'ere some of them.'

'Bloody lunatics,' agreed Dave. 'You'll have to get this sorted. Wanna hand? I've got a number for a bloke who does glass repairs.'

A bus rumbled past. I cringed as the window sagged under the vibrations. 'Thanks Dave, you're a star.'

The glazier was prompt and efficient and quickly fitted a new pane. I sat in the shop watching his progress, wondering how much it was going to cost and hoping my insurance would cover it. The whole job was completed in just over an hour. I vacuumed up the remaining fragments of glass then went on to the pub, wishing I'd had the strength to decline my mother's invitation so I could have enjoyed a long soak in the bath.

Digby and I were the last to arrive. My mother had commandeered a trestle table in the corner and Izzy was holding court with a story from her days as a croupier at a Las Vegas casino, making Ethan roar with laughter. Spencer was sitting next to my mother, who had applied even more makeup since leaving the shop. He offered to buy me a drink.

'You're late, Jennifer,' complained my mother as I sat down.

'Sorry. I had to deal with another broken window.'

A sympathetic murmur rolled round the table.

'Again?' My mother shook her head and gave a loud, exasperated sigh. 'You're really not having much luck lately. Have the garage sorted it?'

'It wasn't the car. It was the shop. The front window got smashed in.'

From his position at the bar, Spencer spun round. His ruddy face drained of colour.

'How on earth did that happen?' my mother exclaimed.

'Stone chipping. Paul, the butcher, found it. It'd cut straight through the glass like a bullet. Good job you'd left for the day, Mum, otherwise you might have been seriously hurt. Anyway, it's all sorted, but we'll have to redo the display in the morning.'

Spencer returned with a glass of white wine. As he put it down he leant over and mouthed, 'Oliver Harper.'

I made a face that said *what are you on about?*

'Oliver Harper,' he repeated, just audibly. 'I told you he's a loose cannon.' He raised both eyebrows at me as he sat next to my mother.

I couldn't believe Oliver would do something so petty, just because he hadn't got his own way. But the prickle of apprehension I'd been left with after the London lunch returned, and I couldn't help worrying that, if Spencer was right and it wasn't an accident, Oliver Harper might have more devious tricks up his sleeve to try and get his greedy tanned hands on my beloved candle shop.

11

Izzy was desperate to know what I'd found out at the funeral, and I was just as keen to tell her. I gave her a lift back from the pub and she questioned me all the way home, but there was only so much I could tell her in a short space of time, so I suggested meeting for lunch the following day.

'I'm not sure I can wait till then,' she complained as I dropped her off outside Plum Cottage. 'The suspense might kill me.' She shut up as Ethan pulled up behind, but before she walked off, turned and gave a conspiratorial wink.

We met in a restaurant in Redbury, a neighbouring town. The Mulberry Bush was a traditional stone-built pub, but inside the space had been stripped back and extended to create a vast modern eating area. It was dominated by people in suits. I wandered in, scanning the dining room, looking for a silver mane decorated with a glamorous scarf or comb, and spotted Izzy at the back, standing out like a peacock against the muted blacks, greys and navy blues of the business world.

'I'm not sure I like this place,' she said as I sat down. 'It's full of yuppies booming into phones or fiddling with those new touch-pad tablet thingys.'

'The food's good,' I reassured her, 'and I wanted to get out of Ridgelow so Mum doesn't find out what I'm up to. She'll only worry and try to interfere.'

'She means well,' sighed Izzy, peering over the half-glasses perched on the end of her nose. 'I see what you mean about the food. They've even got an ostrich burger – very exotic.'

We gave our order to the waitress, Izzy, of course, choosing the ostrich.

'So, did you recognise anyone yesterday?' she said, leaning in.

'No, I didn't.'

'And you're still absolutely sure you don't know Robert Ashmere?'

'Positive.'

'So what did you find out?'

I told her about meeting Iris and being invited back to the house.

'She has a sister – Felicity. And when Iris went for a lie down she told me about Robert and his wife – Erica,' I informed her. 'They're not together anymore.'

'Really?' said Izzy, breaking up a hunk of sourdough and dipping it into a ramekin of oil and balsamic.

'Apparently they used to argue a lot and she left him and went to live in Milton Keynes.'

'Go on,' she urged, swirling the bread to catch more of the sweet vinegar.

'The other interesting titbit she gave me was that before he became a photographer he was a company director – something to do with electronics.'

Izzy mumbled something, but her mouth was full. Swallowing she said, 'What else?'

'Felicity said that when Robert and Erica split up, he went downhill. He stopped looking after himself and started borrowing money from Iris.'

'Must have got himself in some sort of trouble – probably in debt.'

'Or maybe he was depressed about losing his wife?'

'Maybe. What do you know about her?'

'Not much. She's younger than Robert and quite strong-willed – so Felicity said. Oh, I know – she runs a business designing websites. She was at the funeral, but kept well out of the way and I didn't get a chance to talk to her. Do you think I should try and track her down?'

'Yes – good idea,' agreed Izzy. 'Now, there's something else I've been mulling over – mountain bikes. Robert was into mountain bikes, just like your Ethan. Maybe it's Ethan who knows him? Maybe Robert was coming to see him and not you?'

I digested her suggestion along with a piece of crusty bread.

*Is that it? Is Ethan the link?*

'But it was my name and address on the note, not his,' I said through chews. 'And Ethan was away that night, in Wales.' But it occurred to me that, to my knowledge, he had never seen a picture of Robert Ashmere.

'Ah ha!' Izzy exclaimed when I mentioned it. 'Why don't you show Ethan the photo on the website and see if he recognises him. The answer could be as simple as that.' She paused and pulled her brow into a deep-pleated frown. 'There's one thing that's been really niggling me. Why was Robert on the footpath in the first place? He knew you live on Summer Lane, so why was he at the back of the house?'

It was a question that I often churned over. 'I don't know. Maybe he was up to something dodgy?'

'That's what I think. The question is – what?'

As she pondered this, I glanced up at the back wall of the restaurant, which was covered in mirrored tiles. Even though I had my back to the other diners I could see their reflections. My eyes grazed the room then reversed back again to land on two familiar faces dining together.

Izzy spotted my double take. 'What is it? What's up?'

'Don't be obvious, but look straight ahead, then over to the left, to the table by the window.'

Izzy found the correct spot. 'Spencer Lewis,' she murmured.

'Not just Spencer, that's Oliver Harper with him.'

Izzy blinked over her half-glasses. 'The man you went to see? The one who wants to buy your shop?'

'The very same.' I watched their reflection. They laughed together. Spencer's guffaw travelled across the restaurant.

'Is that a good thing, or a bad thing?' said Izzy.

'I don't know, but it's definitely odd.'

'How so?'

'Spencer gave me the distinct impression that Oliver isn't to be trusted and that I should be careful. Then last night in the pub he implied that Oliver had something to do with my smashed shop window.'

'Oh, I see,' Izzy purred. 'And yet here they are having lunch and a grand old time from what I can see. They must be celebrating something – that's champagne they're quaffing.'

'That's normal for Oliver. He's a bit flash. And I suspect Spencer might be that way inclined too, or at least he would like to be.'

'He didn't offer to buy any bubbly last night,' Izzy sniffed. 'They must be good friends to go to that expense.'

'That's what's odd. Spencer said they were acquaintances.'

'Oh. People normally use that description when they don't like the person, or don't really want to be associated with them. But those two look very friendly.'

At that moment our food arrived and Izzy's ostrich burger became the star of the show. By the time we'd finished the meal and I looked back into the mirrored tiles, the table by the window was empty. But outside we came across Spencer sitting at a trestle table in the garden, puffing on a cigarette. He had his back to us and didn't notice us walking past.

'Don't forget to let me know what Ethan says about Robert,' Izzy reminded me as she got into her car.

We drove off separately, Izzy to Summer Lane and me back to the shop where my pursuit of Robert Ashmere continued. The instant my mother left for the day, I opened my Internet browser and began searching for Erica.

I started with an online telephone directory, but she wasn't listed. Next, I explored Google, but no match came up. Finally, I looked up all the companies based in Milton Keynes that had anything to do with web design and painstakingly trawled through each of their websites in the hope of finding something that would lead me to Erica. My single-mindedness eventually paid off, and an hour later, up she popped as the point of contact for Big Bottle Design, with a telephone number, email and location address. The sense of elation that accompanied the discovery was fleeting and was soon replaced by uncertainty as I contemplated my next course of action.

*Shall I pick up the phone, send an email, or just turn up?*

Emailing or telephoning would be the polite thing to do and would take less courage on my part, but Erica might ignore the message, or refuse to talk and hang up, whereas meeting face to face would be more personal and harder for her to turn me away. I decided to sleep on it and see how I felt in the morning.

My next job was Ethan.

I headed home to prepare his favourite meal. He came bounding into the kitchen full of puppy-dog exuberance.

'Ah brilliant – you're cooking Thai! I could smell it as soon as I got out of the Jeep.'

After he'd demolished a loaded plate, I broached the subject of Robert.

'Course I don't know him,' he said, yawning and gently patting his full belly. 'I'd have told you if I did.'

'But you haven't actually seen what he looked like, so how can you be sure?'

'Because I don't know anyone with that name,' he said, swigging from his bottle of beer.

'What if he had a different name?'

'Why would he have a different name?'

'Some of your friends have nicknames, don't they? Like Curly and Bungle, and I don't even know Porky's real name.'

'Ed Bacon,' said Ethan.

'Look, the reason I'm asking is because Robert was into mountain biking and I was wondering if it was you who knew him instead of me.'

He got up and went to the fridge. 'Sorry, Jen, you've lost me.' His head disappeared inside in search of another beer.

'I saw a photo of him on a mountain bike and wondered if that was the connection, that you knew Robert, but by a different name, and that he was coming to see you?'

He reappeared looking peeved. At first I thought he'd run out of cold beers, but it was me that had riled him by pushing the wrong buttons.

'This is stupid.' He slammed the fridge door. 'The whole point of you going to the funeral was to move on from all this. It's not healthy to keep digging it up.' He stalked off into the sitting room.

I was loath to upset him further, but couldn't let it

go and went straight to the study. Having logged on to my laptop, I brought up Robert's website and shouted for Ethan.

'Just have a quick look,' I pleaded, 'and if you don't know him I'll shut up about it.'

'Is that a promise?' he called back. His tone was calmer, but I detected a hint of frustration.

'Yes, I promise,' I said as I crossed my fingers.

He came into the study and I held my breath and watched as he stared at the screen. His expression was completely blank.

'Nope,' he said, finally. 'I've never seen him before in my life. Can we drop this now, please?'

Disappointed, I followed him downstairs. We didn't discuss Robert Ashmere anymore and switched to talking about Digby, who was due to be neutered and microchipped the following week. Ethan described, in rather too much detail, what he needed to do to my poor little dog to make sure he couldn't play his part in producing any unwanted offspring. I listened to his detached description of incisions and stitching, wondering if he and Lisa ever got squeamish. Later on we watched a DVD, but I couldn't concentrate and sat thinking about Erica Ashmere. I wanted to go to Milton Keynes as soon as possible, but my mother had booked a day off, so there wasn't anyone to help manage the shop. Glumly, I stared through the TV screen before the obvious solution came to mind.

*Izzy.*

I slipped into the kitchen and sent a text message telling her that Ethan didn't know Robert, but that I'd located Erica and wanted to visit her on Monday – if she could staff JJ's? Izzy replied almost immediately, agreeing, and so my clandestine plan was laid. Curling back up on the sofa next to Ethan, I felt bad that, despite his plea for me to drop it, I couldn't, and wouldn't. Robert Ashmere had too strong a hold over me.

Monday was a long time coming. All weekend I had to hide the stew of excitement and anticipation bubbling in my stomach from Ethan. I got to the shop nice and early, and, paying homage to my absent mother, wrote out a list of instructions for Izzy so she would know exactly how to work the till and lock up correctly. She came bustling in a little late, but full of joy about playing shop.

'Don't worry about a thing. Digby and I will be just fine, won't we, little fellow,' she cooed, bending over and petting the dog. 'I've brought the crossword and a Sudoku book in case it's a bit quiet.'

'Help yourself to tea and coffee,' I told her. 'There's some chocolate hobnobs in the jar and a bit of lemon drizzle cake if you get peckish. Mum made it.'

'Super-duper,' she said, surveying her new empire from behind the mahogany counter and giving a regal wave. 'I feel ever so important.' She wiggled herself onto the stool and looked at the till. 'Do I need to know what *all* these buttons do? There's an awful lot of them.'

I ran through the basics and gave her the cash register keys and my list of instructions.

'Have you thought about what you're going to say to Erica when you meet her?' Izzy said.

'Not really. I'll just see what comes out.'

'Why don't you take a bunch of flowers and play the sympathy card for the grieving widow? It might warm her up.'

'Good idea.'

The drive to Milton Keynes was easier than

expected, because a new bypass had opened. Finding Erica's address wasn't so straightforward. I got very confused by the American-style road system with its horizontal and vertical numbers. All the main routes looked the same to me. Eventually I righted myself and turned into a street of modern red and brown brick houses.

*She must work from home.*

Pulling up in front of a detached house set back from the road, I sat in the car, nerves getting the better of me.

*Come on, Jen, you haven't driven all this way to get cold feet.*

I gathered up the bouquet of chrysanthemums I'd bought at a petrol station and approached the front door. Reminding myself of the opening line I had been practising on the journey, I took a deep breath and rang the bell. No one answered, so I tried again. Still there was no response, or any sign of life. Disappointed, I turned back towards the car, but was struck by a sudden observation. All the downstairs curtains were drawn, yet it was nearly midday. I wondered if Erica was ill and in bed and hoped I hadn't disturbed her. Then as I walked away I heard a thick groan, like an animal in pain. The noise was muffled, but it came from inside the house. I raced back to the front door, bent down, opened the letterbox and peered in. The view was obstructed by a floor-length curtain.

'Hello, is anyone there?' I called.

There was another groan, then a faint, weak voice, a woman's voice, pleaded, 'Help me … please …'

I rattled the handle. The door was locked.

I bent back down to the letterbox. 'I can't get in. Are you hurt?'

Silence.

I dropped the flowers and ran round the side of the house. A six-foot wooden fence shielded the garden, but the side gate was unlocked and ajar. I pushed through it and onwards, tracking the contours of the building round to the rear, and then stopped dead, heart hammering like a drill. The back door, leading straight into the kitchen, was wide open. Inside, glass and pottery lay in smashed pieces. Cutlery had been strewn all over the work surfaces. Tins of food and dried pasta littered the floor.

I turned a full circle and scanned the garden. It was well maintained with no obvious places to hide. And as far as I could see it was empty. I faced the door again, wanting to go in and help, but common sense and a bad feeling in my bones told me to get the hell out of there. The voice called out again, loaded with desperation, and I had to do something. As I stepped into the kitchen my insides seemed to gather together and congregate round my hammering heart. Arming myself with a kitchen knife that had been discarded on the worktop, I inched into a small, square hall. On the right was a staircase. In front was a closed door. Trying to ignore a sudden urge to pee, I reached forward and turned the handle, and as the door swung open, let out a bloodcurdling scream.

In the middle of the room was a wooden chair.

Tied to the chair was a hunched figure.

A figure with a hood over its head.

I hurtled in, ripped off the covering and came face to face with Erica Ashmere.

12

Erica's hands and legs were bound together with layers of tough gaffer tape. I used the knife to saw through the sticky, tight restraint, trying not to cut her shaking wrists and ankles. Once freed, she seemed too frightened to move and slumped on the chair, body heaving, tears, makeup and snot streaming down her face.

'It's all right. You're going to be all right,' I hushed. I had no idea if she heard me.

My own body was working overtime. Everything seemed to either be pumping at a hundred miles an hour or shaking at a point off the Richter scale. My fingers were trembling so much that it was difficult to punch 999 into my phone and the emergency operator struggled to hear what I said because my train of thought was muddled. As I waited for the police and ambulance to arrive, I crouched by the poor woman, trying to reassure her through soothing sounds and small talk, but Erica had zoned out and stared into space as though tranquilised.

My brain flitted between willing the ambulance to get a move on and wondering what had happened to her. Like the kitchen, the sitting room had been ransacked. Whoever was responsible had done a thorough job of ruining her home. I prayed that being strapped to a chair and half-suffocated while her house was trashed was the only torture Erica had endured and that nothing even more sinister had happened.

In the distance, the jarring howl of sirens filled the air. At the screech of tyres, I ran into the hall, pulled the curtain away from the front door and shouted, 'She's in here,' as I fumbled with the lock. On the other side of the textured glass pane, I heard the static fizz and crackle of a radio and a man shouting orders. As I swung open the front door, three police officers trooped in, all fired-up and with hands on batons. 'There – in there,' I breathed heavily, pointing. They stormed in and quickly assessed the situation, one giving a running commentary into the radio. Two paramedics pushed past and began talking to Erica in loud voices, asking her questions she couldn't answer. I sat on the bottom of the stairs and explained to one of the officers what I had found, pointing to the hood and gaffer tape on the floor by the wooden chair.

The paramedics carried Erica past on a stretcher. She caught my eye and made a tiny sound, then she was gone, on her way to hospital. I declined medical help, telling the female police officer who had taken me under her wing that I would be fine in a few minutes, even though my breathing was erratic and I had the shivers. Someone wrapped a foil blanket round my shoulders and offered me a drink of water from a plastic bottle. I hadn't realised how dry my mouth was – my tongue felt like leather – and I sipped gratefully.

An imposing man with a shock of white hair came into the house to a chorus of politely deferential '*Sirs.*' He gave a curt nod to the officers and went through to the sitting room where he was briefed on the discovery and shown the hood.

'Mrs Jarvis?' he said, coming over to my stair perch.

I was too tired by all the drama to correct him.

'Detective Superintendent Wallace.' He told me he needed to ask some questions and I wilted like a soggy salad at the thought of another police interrogation.

Explaining why I was at Erica's house in the first place proved awkward.

'So, you don't actually know Mrs Ashmere?' he said, towering over me, suspicion and curiosity carved in his expert eyes.

'No. I just wanted to talk to her about her late husband, to see if I could work out why he had the note with my name and address on it.'

The Superintendent weighed me up and must have decided I was harmless, as he said, 'Lucky for Mrs Ashmere that you came along when you did. You'll need to make a statement.'

As a team of forensics swarmed over the house, the female officer took me outside, sat me in the back of a patrol car and wrote up my account. Then, feeling rehydrated and stronger, and having been given the all-clear to leave, I got into my Mini and drove back to Ridgelow worrying for poor Erica and wondering how I could find out more about her dead husband. The shop was already shut up when I cruised down the High Street, so I carried on to Summer Lane and went round to Izzy's to collect Digby.

'Did you see her?' she said ushering me in, then noticing my battle-worn condition, cried, 'What is it? What's wrong? Have you had an accident or something?'

'Not me – Erica. I found her tied to a chair in the middle of her sitting room with a hood over her head.'

Izzy's face dropped like a brick in water. 'Holy moly, what on earth happened?'

'I don't know. But the house had been completely trashed.'

Izzy took my elbow, guided me into the kitchen and helped me onto a stool at the breakfast bar.

'I'll fetch you a stiff drink,' she said. 'You look like you need one.' She came back with two large tumblers of scotch, obviously needing one too, hopped up beside me and listened as I filled her in. 'The poor woman,' she said through a grimace. 'Was she badly hurt?'

'I don't know. She'd completely shut down from the shock and couldn't speak.'

'Lucky you didn't arrive any earlier and catch them in the act. That could have been very nasty.' We were silent for a long moment. Then Izzy said, 'It's a bit peculiar, don't you think?'

I gave a dry laugh. 'Which bit? Everything that's happened lately is pretty peculiar.'

'I mean the fact that Robert was killed and then soon after his estranged wife gets robbed. Bit of a coincidence isn't it?'

'You think the two crimes are connected?'

'I don't know. It just seems rather … peculiar.'

'But the police said Robert's death was a random attack,' I quickly reminded her. 'And Nick Low's in custody. There's no way he could have had anything to do with it.'

'Perhaps she was just unfortunate then.'

But I could see she didn't believe it. Behind blue-violet eyes, a keen mind ticked over at high speed.

'What are you going to do now? Erica was our one link to Robert,' Izzy said eventually.

'I'll call the hospital in a couple of days and find out how she's doing. We'll just have to wait until she's up to talking, I suppose.'

'And what about Ethan? He's absolutely sure he doesn't know Robert?'

'Positive.'

'Are you?'

'What sort of a question is that? Of course I'm sure. Ethan's got no reason to hide anything.'

Izzy gave an apologetic smile. 'That's not what I was implying. I meant that perhaps Ethan just hasn't made the connection.'

'He doesn't know him,' I said firmly. 'I could tell. There wasn't even a flicker of recognition and he's getting fed up with the whole thing. He thinks I should leave well alone.'

'Oh dear. What did he say about you going to see Erica?'

'He doesn't know.'

She raised her eyebrows. 'Ah.'

I reddened. 'I didn't lie to him.'

'Oh no, I wasn't suggesting anything of the kind. More a case of not mentioning it, was it?'

My silence answered the question.

'And are you going to tell him?' she persisted.

'I'll have to, in case the police turn up wanting to talk to me about it.'

'Yes, you're a bit stuck now, and it's probably for the best. These things often start out as little white lies, and then before you know it, they've escalated into a case of full-blown deception, which is probably how Ethan might see it, bearing in mind he's made it quite clear he doesn't approve.'

'He'll be all right,' I said, trying to convince myself.

'I'm sure he will,' agreed Izzy. 'Top up?' she suggested, raising her glass.

I declined and said that I ought to be going.

'Cheery-bye, then. And good luck with Ethan.'

'I'm not seeing him tonight. He's out with friends. It'll keep until tomorrow.'

Izzy looked at me knowingly.

'Don't worry, I'll tell him,' I insisted, but without enthusiasm.

Back at Corner Cottage I had a long soak in the bath, before crawling into bed. For the first time in ages

I slept deeply for a few hours before Robert was able to bother me. But when he came in the early hours he was back with a vengeance, not in his usual guise of a floating, brooding face and piercing cries, but in a horrid nightmare.

I dreamt I was sitting in the back row of an old-fashioned theatre. The room was opulent, sumptuously upholstered in crimson velvet: on the seats, on the ceiling, on the walls and on the stage, where drape after drape of heavy curtain hung in scalloped rows, framing a stark white projection screen. Up in a velvet heaven, corner spots streamed puddles of light onto thick, crimson pile, creating a subtle pink glow. All the other seats were unoccupied. The orchestra pit was deserted. There were no breaks in the walls. No way in and no way out.

The lights began to dim, and as pink faded to black the mechanical whir of a projector cut through the silence. A flickering movie countdown appeared on the screen. 10 … 9 … 8 … The curtains slowly closed, only to open again, revealing a picture that assaulted my senses. The detail was sculpting knife-sharp. The colours were Disney with a nuclear glow. The sound was crisper than surround. Sucked into this intensified cinematic world I watched the young woman on the screen pull up in a topaz blue Mini and check her reflection in the sun-visor mirror, hand rising to the back of her head to smooth dark-blonde dishevelled locks. Gathering up a bunch of chrysanthemums, she walked up a garden path to a sound track of birdsong and distant motorway drone. The camera tracked the woman from behind and it wasn't until she rang the doorbell and turned to pan the street that I recognised the face as my own and the house as Erica's.

The film crawled into slow motion capturing my short sprint through her well-kept garden like an Olympic replay, then resumed at normal speed as I saw myself face the open kitchen door, my gulping breaths dueting at full volume with the ebb of my own heartbeat.

It was dark inside. The me in the film picked up a torch and switched on a yellow beam. Creeping forwards, glass and debris cracked underfoot, the noise rising from tiny tinkles into echoing crunches of cave-like proportions. Gripping the velvet sides of my cinema seat, I saw myself edge towards the sitting room, flashlight bobbing with each step, beam coming to rest on the hooded outline sitting in the wooden chair.

'Hello, Erica,' I heard myself whisper as I drew back the hood.

But instead of lighting up shining golden locks and emerald eyes, the torch exposed a horror-film face, bruised, bloated and blistered. Fluid oozed from a swollen nose and a thin trail of blood seeped from a gashed scalp.

*Robert.*

In the cinema, I wanted to scream like a banshee, but my constricted chest made no sound. I wanted to stand and run, but my limbs were rooted to the spot. Trapped in my seat, blood pulsed round my body so violently that I wondered if my veins might burst open.

On the giant screen, Robert picked me out, his dark, brooding eyes protruding over smashed cheekbones. His gaze was arctic and crawled over every inch of my soul. He raised himself off the wooden chair, skeletal body twisted with rigor mortis, and lumbered off the stage, into the crimson velvet room. As his warped frame loomed over me, he stretched open his mouth, peeled back his top lip and exuded a deafening, spine-curdling scream, as sharp and spiky as a needle barbing flesh. It stung me all over. I could feel his breath pricking my face and tangling in my hair. It smelt putrid – dead. His grotesque face was inches from mine, my vision obscured by his swollen tongue vibrating against yellow, crooked teeth, both drenched in a thick layer of dripping saliva.

I felt something heavy in my hand.

Robert had no warning.

The torch slammed into the side of his head with such ferocity that he staggered backwards, fell over a row of velvet clad seats and crumpled to the floor, disappearing from view.

Once more, moving images sprung to life on the projection screen. I watched as a group of people in black gathered round a deep, dark hole in the ground. A haunting rendition of the *Ave Maria* rang out, reverberating round the theatre. Iris Ashmere appeared at the head of the crowd, her birdlike face screwed up and a hideous wail pouring from her core. Blood dripped from gnarled hands shredded by the thorny stems of the red roses she clutched to her heart. The camera panned down to Robert lying in his coffin. His empty eyes caught mine, and, when all sound had faded, from his open grave he watched me all night long.

# 13

The nightmare shook me up and left me low. My mother couldn't work out what was wrong. As far as she was concerned the whole murder business was well and truly over, with Nick Low publically hung out to dry for the crime and Robert Ashmere not just dead, but well and truly buried. Having failed to worm out the reason for my doom-and-gloom mood she gave me a stern lecture on how attitude was a matter of choice.

'And a smile costs nothing,' she threw in, sweeping past into the kitchen wearing another new dress.

I wondered if Spencer ever found her tiresome. If he did, he didn't show it.

To my surprise, and dismay, my mother and Spencer's relationship appeared to be blooming right under my nose. They were spending more and more time together and he had started buying her little love tokens, as I'd dared label them once in front of her: flowers, chocolates, a biography of Grace Kelly and an antique brooch. Despite this, my mother wouldn't admit they were anything more than friends.

I worked late that evening, putting off the conversation I knew I had to have with Ethan. He called to ask what time I would be home and if he needed to pick up anything for dinner. I said I'd bring a takeaway, hoping it would butter him up and take the edge off my guilty admission. It soured the taste of the curry when I told him I'd been to see Erica and the state she'd been in when I found her. He listened, chewing on a piece of lamb for so long that I wondered if it was gristle, then, when he had finally swallowed, said gruffly,

'You might have been hurt and no one would have known where you were.'

'Next time I'll tell you, so you know where I'm going.'

'Why does there have to be a next time?'

I hesitated, then thought back to the conversation with Izzy about lies getting out of hand and decided it was best to be honest with him this time.

'Because I have to get to the bottom of it. I have to know why Robert Ashmere had that note in his pocket.'

Ethan's broad shoulders sagged. 'Why? Why can't you just let it go?'

An air of tension descended and wedged itself between us.

'I don't know,' I said, willing him to understand. 'It's eating away at me. If it were you, wouldn't you want to find out?'

His face clouded over. 'No, I wouldn't, because I don't see what difference it would make. Even if you do manage to work it out, the man's still dead. You can't bring him back, or change what's happened. All you're doing is keeping the whole nightmare alive.' His fork clattered onto the table and he pushed his unfinished plate away.

I didn't like being ticked off.

Ethan saw my frown and softened a little. 'What if you never find out? What will you do then? You can't go on searching forever.' He rubbed his face with both hands then massaged the tension in his temples. 'You're not yourself at the moment. You're still … distant.' His words stung. 'I'm not telling you this because I'm complaining, or criticising. I know you've been through hell lately, but I just want the old Jen back; the one who had big ideas about the next best smell in candles; the one who got excited about going for a walk with me and

Diggers in the rain; the one who was always up for a water fight in the garden, or a pillow fight in bed.' He looked at me with an imploring smile. 'Most of all I just want you to forgive yourself, forget about what happened and move on.'

'But that's exactly what I'm trying to do,' I said in a strangled voice, crushed. 'And I will, once I know why he had my name and address with him.'

'But what if you never find out? If you can't find a way to deal with it there'll be a constant dark cloud hanging over you – hanging over us.'

We sat at the kitchen table in silence, each of us vexed with the other, the curry becoming unappetisingly cold and congealed.

Ethan eventually took my hand and looked deep into my eyes. 'We can't let this come between us. It's stupid. We've managed to get through all the accusations and scrutiny and now we're arguing over a dead man who neither of us knew.'

'I'm sorry.' I really meant it. I hated upsetting him and wished with all my heart that Robert Ashmere had never put a foot in Ridgelow, or crossed my path.

'It's okay. You're worth all the aggro.' He gave me another meaningful stare. 'But I do need to know you're safe. So if you decide to go haring off somewhere you've never been before, to see someone you don't even know, can you call and tell me?'

I had enough willpower to hold off phoning the hospital until the following morning. Having bade a worried goodbye to Digby when Ethan took him off to the vet practice for his operation, as soon as they were out of sight I dialled Milton Keynes Hospital only to be told that Erica had discharged herself the previous evening.

Given the state the place had been left in, I doubted it, but having no other clue as to her whereabouts I decided to drive back to her house in the hope that one of the neighbours would know where she was. I rang and told my mother I would be late, without giving her any explanation, then left a message on Ethan's voicemail telling him that I was going to visit Erica to make sure she was okay, hopeful that having slept on it, he might have thawed a little about the whole subject and not be too cross with me for going back so soon.

The drive seemed to take ages. I stopped off at a supermarket to buy another bunch of flowers on the premise that they would give me a plausible reason to need to know Erica's whereabouts, then found my way back to her house. The police cordon had gone and there was no obvious sign that a serious incident had even taken place.

As I sat in the car, the front door opened and a man dressed in cords, shirt and tank top in various shades of brown came out clutching a refuse sack, which he tossed into a wheelie bin. His shoulders were hunched and his walk a tired shuffle.

'Excuse me,' I called through the wound down window. 'I'm looking for Erica. Is she home?'

The man stared at me warily. 'Are you a friend of hers?'

'Sort of. I'm Jennifer Jarvis. I found Erica on Monday.'

A seed of recognition sprouted in his eyes. 'Ah. The police told us about you … I suppose you can come in.'

Inside the house a huge clean-up operation was underway. The downstairs rooms had been cleared of mess and disarray and the few things that could be salvaged were being packed into a box by an attractive woman wearing a pink gingham cleaning overall, her platinum hair swept up into a neat bun.

'Caroline, this is Jennifer Jarvis, the woman who found Erica,' said the man.

We shook hands.

'And I'm Michael. We're Erica's parents.'

'Shall I take those for you?' Caroline reached for the bouquet. 'I'll have to put them in the sink for now. All the vases have been ruined.'

Overhead, floorboards creaked.

'Erica, you've got a visitor,' Caroline called up the stairs. 'It's Jennifer Jarvis. She's bought you some lovely flowers.'

An air of vulnerability hovered round Erica, who came into the room looking pale and drawn. Her face was bare of makeup and her hair pulled in to a severe pony tail, but with her heart-shaped face, wide, green eyes and high cheekbones she was a timeless beauty, and the look of fragility made her more so.

'I'm glad you came back,' she said, in a soft, low voice, the sort that toyed with men's heart strings. 'I was going to get your phone number from the police so I could call you. Thanks so much for what you did. God knows how long I might have been left there if you hadn't turned up.'

'How are you feeling?' I asked.

'A bit up and down. Nothing a little time and a heap of therapy won't solve, I should think.' The smile she gave was weak, but still lit up her face. I imagined that at full strength Erica Ashmere would be bewitching.

'I didn't know if I'd find you here,' I said. 'The house was left in such a mess.'

'I'm not staying,' she said. 'I couldn't face it. I'm going to live with my parents for a while and put this place on the market.'

'I think I'd feel the same,' I agreed. 'Have you managed to rescue much?'

'Only a few bits and pieces.' Tears glistened, but she caught them and held her poise.

'Did they get away with anything valuable?'

Erica shook her head. 'That's the weird thing. They don't seem to have taken anything at all. They just came in and wrecked the place. I don't know what it was about.'

Erica's mother came over and put a light hand on her daughter's shoulder. 'We're out of bin bags. Dad and I are popping out to get some more. Will you be all right on your own, or do you want to come with us?'

I was quick to step in. 'I'll stay with you, if you like?'

Uncertainty flashed in Erica's eyes, but after a short moment of deliberation she agreed. 'Okay. I want to talk to you about something the police said anyway. Let's sit in the garden. I can't stand being in this room.'

We sat outside on a painted wooden bench situated in a pretty sunspot. Erica took out a packet of cigarettes and offered me one, which I declined.

'I gave up about five years ago, but it was the first thing I needed when I got out of hospital,' she admitted. 'I hope it doesn't become a habit again.' She took a long draw then blew out rapidly. 'The police told me why you turned up here, that Robert was killed behind your house ...' She quickly sucked on the cigarette again to hide her angst. '... and that he had your name and address with him on a note.'

'That's right.'

She gave me a quick, sly look up and down. 'So, Robert was going to see you that night?'

'I can only assume so, but I have no idea why. I didn't know him. I've spoken to his mother and aunt, but couldn't work out the connection, so I thought you'd be a good person to talk to.'

Erica's eyes narrowed. 'I knew I'd seen you before. You were at the funeral, weren't you? So what did Iris say? I bet she wasn't particularly nice about me?'

'Iris didn't mention you,' I replied honestly, 'but her sister, Felicity, did. She said Iris blames you for the break-up.'

Erica was incensed. Her lips pursed around the tobacco stick and she blew out a perfectly formed smoke ring. 'Iris never could see Robert for what he was.'

'Felicity said she spoiled him,' I said encouragingly.

Erica gave a dark laugh. 'That's an understatement. She always saw me as competition.'

'How did you and Robert meet?' I ventured.

'It was at a conference in Brighton. I was in my first job, fresh out of university, and Robert was a director of an electronics company. He was the guest speaker and I ended up seated next to him at dinner. We got talking, we got on, and three months later we got engaged, much to Iris' dismay.'

'Sounds romantic.'

Erica smiled. 'We had some good times ... in the early days.'

'What went wrong?'

'The usual – money, greed ...' she said, waving her cigarette in the air like a wand and leaving a trail of fine ash sprinkling down on the immaculate lawn. 'His family don't know the half of it. Iris thinks he started up his photography business because it was his lifelong ambition, that he turned his back on a successful career and all the perks that went with it to follow his dream. What she doesn't know is that her perfect son was at the centre of a fraud scandal, that he was taking bribes from company suppliers. Unfortunately for him, one of his colleagues got wind of it. The police were called and hauled him in for questioning, rode roughshod over him, but didn't have anything concrete enough to use as evidence in the end. Then Robert's boss decided he wasn't happy with some of Robert's dealings and sacked him anyway. It was bad timing because I'd just left my job to start up my business. I ended up being the sole breadwinner. Luckily, I was getting enough work to pay the bills and keep up the pretence that we were a happy couple, but I think my saving his face really riled Robert. He was jealous. He always did have a big ego … and a temper.' She bent over and forcefully stubbed out the finished cigarette on a paving slab.

'He was violent?' I said, heart pounding as memories of the fight on the footpath snaked around my mind.

Erica frowned. 'I wouldn't go that far. When he was working he was a controlled sort of person – controlling sometimes – but after he was sacked he … well, that's when the drinking started … and then the rows.'

'What did you argue about?' I said, thinking Izzy was going to love all the riveting details Erica was sharing.

'Trivial things usually, but somehow it always ended up with Robert blaming everyone else – including me – for what happened. He wouldn't accept that he'd made a mistake. It was always someone else's fault, nothing to do with the fact he'd been greedy and careless and got caught out. He thought the police had been trying to frame him, that the company had been too quick to get rid of him and that they should have given him another chance. In fairness, he did put his heart and soul into his work and he made them a hell of a lot of money over the years, but he couldn't separate what he'd achieved from what he'd done wrong.'

'What happened then?'

'Robert got it into his head that he was going to turn his hobby into a business and become a photographer. I was really pleased at first. I thought it would be good for him, well, for both of us, you know, give him a focus and hopefully bring in a bit more money. But it changed him. He started working all hours, day and night. I never knew where he was and if I asked he got defensive. When he was home it was like living with a stranger. We hardly spoke. This went on for weeks and wore me down. I finally plucked up the courage to tell him I was unhappy with the way things were between us and that I wanted out.'

'And what about Robert?'

'He wouldn't accept it was over. He hounded me. It was quite scary, to be honest. He'd turn up here unannounced, or ring up in the middle of the night, drunk and crying. Then one time he followed me and a friend and photographed us while we were out shopping and lunching, then emailed the pictures to me, just so I would know he had been watching.'

'That is seriously creepy.'

Erica shivered. 'I know. I ended up taking legal action. My solicitor sent him a letter telling him to back off and that I'd report any further harassment to the police. It seemed to do the trick. Robert finally went quiet. I heard he was in London doing paparazzi work.'

She paused for a moment and her face softened. 'But even after all that went on between us I was devastated when I found out he was dead – that he'd been murdered – I couldn't believe it. I still can't to be honest.'

Erica's parents returned and she changed the subject to the garden and all the hard work she'd put in to get it looking so manicured.

Her father staggered through the open patio window, his arms hugging a cardboard box bursting with photographs, some loose, some bundled and some in plastic sleeves.

'I'm making a start on the office,' he puffed. 'Do you feel up to sorting through these?' He placed the box on the lawn with a groan. 'Quite a few have been damaged, I'm afraid. Trodden on and what not.'

'Thanks, Dad. I'm sure I'll be able to save some of them.' Erica pulled the photos over and picked a few out. 'A whole heap of good and bad memories,' she said sadly. 'I never did get round to sorting them into albums, or scanned. They were stuffed in the cupboard waiting for a rainy day.'

'Erica,' called Caroline. 'Can you come here for a minute? I need your advice.'

As Erica and her father went inside I sat on the sun-drenched bench, enjoying the warmth on my face while I waited for her to return. I was pleased with how well the conversation had gone and wondered what I could say next to get her talking again.

At my feet sat the box of photographs. I leant down and pulled out a few, eyes idling over snaps of Erica relaxing in another, much larger, but just as well manicured, garden. Even though she was smiling her eyes looked glazed, as though she was going through the motions, and I wondered if Robert was behind the lens.

Rerunning Erica's chat, I tried to recall any snip of information that might take me closer to the reason for the note in Robert's pocket. I certainly wasn't expecting to come across the answer there and then, and because I was so lost in thought, I very nearly missed it. Nor was it anything Erica had mentioned during our conversation. Instead, a single snapshot that I just happened to pick up made the connection.

And it was something that had been right under my nose all along.

14

I must have cried out, because Erica came rushing towards me, luminous green eyes scanning the garden like a wary, territorial feline.

'What is it? What's wrong?'

I held out the photo, unable to speak.

Erica glanced at it, then back at me. 'That's my old dog, Barney,' she said.

I found my voice. 'No it's not. It's my dog, Digby. I'd know him anywhere.'

Erica gasped, then said with urgency, 'How long have you had your dog?'

'About four months.'

'Where did you get him?'

'Orchard Farm Rescue Centre,' I said breathlessly.

'You've got Barney?' Erica wilted onto the garden bench.

'You used to own Digby?'

We both stared at the photograph.

'Is that it? Is that why Robert was coming to see me? To see the dog?'

'It must be,' replied Erica. She reached for the packet of cigarettes she'd discarded earlier, and, after lighting up again, said, 'When we split up, we agreed that Barney would be better off with me, because Robert was too busy with his photography business. He didn't bother with the dog when I left, but then a couple of days before he died he turned up on my doorstep, drunk. I let him in because I didn't want him making a scene in front of the neighbours. He went charging through the house calling for Barney. When I told him the dog wasn't there he thought I meant I'd left him with a neighbour, or my parents. When he realised that I didn't actually own the dog anymore he went ballistic.'

'Robert didn't know you'd re-homed him?'

She looked down at the ground.

'But why did you get rid of Digby, I mean Barney?'

'I had to, for the dog's sake. I was working long hours and wasn't giving him the attention and exercise he needed. He started misbehaving, barking all the time and digging up my new carpets, and to be honest, he reminded me too much of Robert. The whole situation got stressful – for both of us – so I decided it would be better to re-home him to someone who could look after him properly.'

'But you didn't discuss it with Robert?'

Erica went on the defensive. 'We weren't speaking. And he'd left Barney with me. The dog was my responsibility. I did what I thought was best.'

'But Robert didn't agree?'

'No. He made that very clear. After I'd told him the dog had been re-homed, he kept going on and on about needing the number. He got quite aggressive towards me. I wanted to get rid of him, so I gave him the address and phone details for Orchard Farm and told him it was the number he needed to find Barney. I'll never forget that moment. He stared straight at me, full of contempt, then called me a … well, I can't tell you what he said.'

'What a pig,' I replied without thinking.

Erica bristled again. 'He wasn't always that bad. Losing his job was a big deal to him. It knocked his confidence. And people act strangely when they're under pressure, don't they? They do things out of character.'

'Yes, they do,' I agreed.

'But it hurts that those were the last words he said to me.' Her voice cracked, but she recovered quickly to add, 'Robert must have got your name and address from the rescue centre.'

'Surely they wouldn't give out my details, at least, not without asking my permission first?'

I decided to find out there and then and put in a call. A volunteer transferred me to the centre manager, who remembered Digby.

'Funny you should ask,' he said, 'cos a man did pay us a visit about your dog. He said he owned him and wanted him back. I told him the dog had already been re-homed and he asked where, but I explained I couldn't give out that information. He wasn't happy about it and got quite bolshy, so I asked him to leave, which he did, but that night we had a break-in. Someone smashed a window and got into the office. Nothing was stolen, in fact we found a twenty pound note in the donation tin, but ...' he broke off, sounding worried.

'But he could have come back and looked in your files?'

He gave an apologetic sigh. 'The cabinets aren't locked. We've never had to worry about anything like that before. Did he manage to find you, then?'

'Yes, I'm afraid he did.'

'I'm sorry about that, really sorry. You've still got the dog, haven't you? Legally he belongs to you. The previous owners can't take him back now.'

'Yes, Digby's fine. He's settled in really well. We all love him. I can't imagine life without him.'

'Oh good.' He sounded relieved. 'Do you want me to report the break-in to the police? We didn't call them because nothing was stolen, but if the man's been harassing you we ought to let them know.'

'I shouldn't worry about that. He's dead.'

The centre manager was taken aback. 'Oh. Well, at least he won't give you any more trouble.'

I almost laughed.

'Robert definitely paid them a visit,' I told Erica a minute later. 'It looks like that's how he got hold of my name and address.'

I didn't mention that he'd broken into the office. For some reason, I didn't want Erica's memory of her husband to be any more tarnished.

'I'm glad Barney's got such a good home,' she said.

I smiled. 'He's a lovely boy. Actually, I'd better call and see how he's doing. He's being neutered today.'

Erica grinned. 'I wanted to give him the chop years ago, but Robert took it personally and refused. He said it was unfair to cut off the dog's manhood. I made the point that the balls don't make the man, or the dog, but that only wound him up even more.'

I called the vet practice. Ethan was busy, but Lisa was free to speak and reassured me that Digby was fine – dozy, but recovering well.

While I was on the phone there was a knock at the front door. Erica went to answer it and returned accompanied by two plain clothes police officers.

'This is Jennifer Jarvis,' she announced.

One of the policemen perked up and said I was on his list of people to visit, and would I mind hanging around so he could have a chat with me once he'd spoken to Erica?

Hearing voices, Erica's parents came downstairs.

'I'll put the kettle on,' said Caroline, ushering her husband into the kitchen.

There wasn't anywhere to sit inside the house, so Erica stayed with the police in the garden while I followed her parents. The back door was open and I could just about hear Erica talking over the sound of the boiling kettle.

'I've already told you everything I can remember,' she protested, but the policemen insisted she went over it again.

I listened in.

Her voice started steady and strong. 'I was upstairs, working in my office with the radio on. At about half past nine I heard a noise in the hallway. I assumed it was the post falling to the floor, so I went downstairs to collect it. As I got to the front door, I noticed the curtain had been pulled across ...' She began to waver. 'I knew something was wrong ... but before I could think ... or do anything ... a man jumped out from behind the sitting room door and grabbed me.' There was a short pause. Then her commentary came quick and fast. 'I tried to scream, but he clamped his hand over my mouth. He told me he had a knife. Then another man came in from the kitchen. They were both wearing balaclavas. They put the hood over my head. Then they bundled me into the sitting room, pushed me onto the chair and tied me to it so I couldn't move.' Another short pause. 'Neither of them said anything. They just trashed the room around me. I was petrified, wondering if they were going to hurt me. I'm sure you can imagine some of the thoughts that ran through my mind.' The silence was filled by an embarrassed cough from one of the policemen.

Having found her imprisoned and traumatised on the chair, surrounded by devastation, I could picture everything she described and felt sick for her.

'They went through the whole house. It seemed to go on forever. The noise – I can still hear it –

splintering and crashing, all at the same time. The next thing I remember was the silence. I was so relieved they'd gone, but petrified at being left alone, hardly able to breath. God, it was so hot under that hood … I tried shouting for help, but the hood muffled the sound. I couldn't stand up. I felt so helpless, sitting there, waiting, willing someone to realise that something was wrong and come and find me. I honestly can't describe how it felt to hear Jennifer shouting through the letter box.'

'You were extremely lucky not to be harmed, Mrs Ashmere,' said one of the policemen.

'I know. But …' Erica stopped again, trying to make sense of what had happened, then her voice rose as she said, 'I don't get it. Why? Why did they do it? Why trash the place and not steal anything? Why tie me up and not lay a finger on me? What the hell was it all about?'

'Perhaps they wanted to scare you?' said one of the policemen. 'Are you sure you haven't upset anyone, or know someone who might have a grudge against you?'

'No. I don't know anyone who would want to do this to me, I really don't.' Giving in to frustration and tiredness, her tone sharpened. 'Haven't you got any idea who did it? You must have found out something by now?'

'We're still investigating.' The policeman remained calm and collected and ignored the touch of accusation Erica had tossed in their direction. 'It could simply be that you were an easy target – a woman living alone. You told us in your previous statement that the back door was unlocked, and as your property is set back from the road and not overlooked by the neighbours, it would have been quite possible for the men to enter the house, through the garden, unseen.'

'But someone must have heard what was going on, I mean they were hardly tiptoeing around the place.' Then, after thinking for a moment, she said, 'Oh. I suppose the neighbours were at work? They all seem to leave early and come home late round here. It's like a ghost town during the day.'

'We're still conducting our enquiries, but yes, your immediate neighbours were out at the time.'

'But why didn't they take anything?' Erica repeated, frustrated that the police were asking questions instead of providing answers.

'I'll have a chat with Miss Jarvis now,' said one of the officers.

I was duly summoned to the garden and asked to go over my version of events, which I did. When I got to the end of my account I added that, since then, I had found what I originally came for – the connection between myself and Robert Ashmere – and told them all about the dog. The police weren't remotely interested in the development and, as I had nothing more to add to my original statement, they left to continue their enquiries elsewhere.

Erica looked exhausted. I could see I was close to outstaying my welcome and it was time for me to make a move too. She told me that when she felt up to it she would come and visit the spot where Robert had died, to say goodbye, and to pop in and say hello to Barney. We swapped email addresses and I drove home, pleased that all my efforts had been worthwhile and anticipating congratulations from Izzy for solving what had been a very intriguing puzzle. It was an enormous relief to finally have the answer, to be able to confirm to myself that I hadn't known Robert after all. The fact he was a stranger helped me feel a little better about what had happened.

My brighter mood faded the moment I got home, opened the front door and noticed a faint smell of cigarettes lurking in my hallway. Stood still as a rock, I held my breath and listened. All was quiet, but looking towards the kitchen I saw that the French doors were ajar. I had been meticulous about security ever since the locks had been changed. I knew I had left everything secure, which meant only one thing – someone had definitely been in my house.

My first reaction was to call the police, but thinking back to Detective Inspector Pitts' sceptical face the last time I had reported an intruder I stopped and questioned myself.

*Am I imagining the cigarette smell? No.*

*Am I sure I closed and locked the door? Yes.*

*Is that reason enough to call the police and report a break-in? Not sure.*

I didn't want to make a fool of myself again, or be accused of wasting police time. Arming myself with a carving knife from the block on the worktop I slunk through Corner Cottage. The world around me seemed to slow. My stomach rolled over and over as I checked each room for signs of an intruder or missing items, fingers clenched round my weapon.

Other than the French doors and smell of cigarettes, everything downstairs was exactly as I had left it. Quietly climbing the stairs, I concentrated on slowing my breathing in an attempt to keep panic at bay. First, I checked the office – empty. Next, I inspected the spare bedroom – empty. In the bathroom, I tentatively drew back the shower curtain, blade poised, but found no intruder lurking behind.

That left my bedroom.

I stood on the landing gazing at the closed door.

I was sure I hadn't shut it.

I never did.

My hand was surprisingly steady as I reached for the handle, turning little by little, then with sudden, violent force I threw the door open and stood back, heart thrashing wildly as I waited for a reaction.

Nothing.

I stepped forward and peered in, eyes searching for a human shape under the bed, or in a dark nook or cranny. But the room was empty. There was no one in my house.

Having psyched myself up so much, I was almost disappointed. I wanted to laugh at my stupidity and over-active imagination, but my throat was so dry all I could manage was a cracked cough. As I wondered if I was going mad, my eyes rested on the oak dressing table in the corner of the room and the threatening message smeared in red lipstick across my antique mirror.

STOP PLAYING GAMES

HAND OVER THE NUMBER OR YOURS WILL BE UP

BE SMART – DON'T CALL THE POLICE

15

My phone vibrated in my back pocket, causing me to jump and drop the carving knife, narrowly missing my toes. A knot twisted in my stomach as I answered.

'Only me,' said Ethan. 'Just checking you're home before I drop Digby round. I'll be over in half an hour or so.'

'Can you come now?' My voice was tight.

'Are you okay?'

'No. Someone's been in my house again.'

I heard Ethan draw breath. 'Are you sure?'

'Yes, positive.'

'What makes you think that?'

Hurt that he was questioning me, I tried not to bite. 'Three things; firstly, I could smell cigarette smoke again when I came in; secondly, the French doors were ajar; thirdly because someone has left me a threatening message on my bedroom mirror.'

I heard Ethan gasp. 'Are you sure no one's in the house right now?'

'Yes, I've checked round. There's no one here.'

'What does the message say?'

'Something I don't understand.' I read it out loud then added, 'You'll see for yourself when you get here. Please hurry.'

As I waited for Ethan, I focused on slowing my breathing and trying to relax my muscles, which shock had turned rigid. My eyes were repeatedly drawn back to the smeared words. The thought that a stranger had let themself, or selves – I didn't know how many there were – into my house made me feel violated and quite terrified. I had no idea how he – she – they – had got in. All the locks had been changed since my handbag and keys had been stolen. What freaked me the most was that the intruder had been in my bedroom, rummaging around my personal belongings to find the lipstick before scrawling those menacing words over my lovely antique mirror. The makeshift pen had been carelessly discarded, blunted, on top of the dressing table.

No matter how many times I read the message it didn't make sense. I had no idea about a number and I certainly wasn't playing games with anyone. I glanced at the clock on the bedside table. Ten minutes had passed. It felt more like an hour. A flash of light caught my eye. I looked down and found the kitchen knife nestled in the deep-pile carpet. Reclaiming it, I gripped the stainless steel handle as though it were part of my anatomy, then heard a car pull up outside and bolted downstairs.

Ethan wore an expression of panic when he entered the cottage. Following his eye-line I found I was brandishing the shiny blade right at him.

'Sorry.' I put down my weapon and launched myself into his arms. 'Thank God you're here.'

'And thank God you're safe,' he said, hugging me and planting a quick kiss on my cheek while scanning the house over my shoulder. 'I couldn't drive as fast as I'd have liked because of Digby.'

Glancing down I found a subdued little dog staring forlornly back. Releasing myself from Ethan's clutches, I crouched by Digby and gently stroked his head. 'Did it go okay?'

'Yes, he's fine. He'll feel a bit sore and tired for a couple of days, that's all. Now, what about you? What the hell's going on?' Ethan was tense and twitchy.

I righted myself and said, 'Can't you smell it? The cigarette smoke?'

His Roman nose wrinkled as he sniffed the air. 'Yes I can. It's faint though.'

'But definitely cigarettes, right?'

Ethan agreed it was.

I led him into the kitchen and showed him the French doors.

'They were ajar, just like this,' I said, demonstrating. 'They were definitely closed and locked when I left this morning.'

Ethan studied the lock. 'There's no damage,' he said, fiddling with the handle. 'And what about this threatening message?'

'Come on, I'll show you.'

Ethan followed me upstairs – two at a time – to the bedroom, stopping dead when confronted by the red words scrawled savagely across the mirror. His eyes darted back and forth as he read and reread the message. 'What does it mean?'

'I told you I've no idea.'

Ethan slumped down on the end of the bed. He looked thrown, and started mumbling under his breath. 'Weird … Surely it can't be? No …'

I sunk into the mattress, next to him. 'Can't be what? Ethan, what are you going on about? Do you know something about this?'

He stared at the mirror. 'I'm not sure …' His forehead creased, which made him look older and more serious. 'It's just that something weird happened at the practice today, something to do with Digby. Before he had his operation, I decided to sort out his microchip, but when I examined him I found he already has a chip implanted.'

'But the rescue centre said he wasn't chipped. They told us it was something we needed to get done.'

'It would have been easy to miss. It's not been injected in the usual place between the shoulder blades.'

'What's that got to do with my mirror?'

'Well, the identification number on Digby's chip is different to the ones we use. When I checked it on the system it wasn't recognised. That in itself isn't all that unusual. It sometimes happens if the microchip is from a different manufacturer, but I rang round all the companies who store the pet microchip and owner details on their databases and none of them could match it to any records. They all said the number wasn't an official pet microchip, because their current identifications are numerical and Digby's chip is a combination of numbers and letters. I thought the best thing to do would be to give Digby a new, proper microchip, so that he's at least registered on a database against your name and address and can be traced back to you if ever he does go missing. A note has been attached to his record saying he's got a duff chip and a working chip.' He stopped and shook his head a little, as though clearing a blockage from his ears. 'Anyway, what I'm trying to say, in a very long-winded way, is that Digby has an unusual identification number and you have a message on your mirror demanding you hand over a number.'

'All roads lead to Digby,' I muttered.

Ethan gave me a curious look.

'I went to see Erica Ashmere again …' I tried to ignore the disappointment that crossed his face. 'I did leave you a message to tell you … Anyway, I found out that Robert wasn't coming to see me after all – he was coming to see the dog.' Ethan's disappointment swung to high interest. 'It turns out that Robert and Erica used to own Digby. I found a photo of him, when I was at

Erica's, and she told me she'd taken him to Orchard Farm to be re-homed, but hadn't told Robert.'

'Why on earth not?'

'They weren't speaking. Digby was living with her, so she saw it as her decision to make. She said she didn't have enough time to look after him properly and thought it best to let someone else take care of him.'

'And you turned up at Orchard Farm, fell in love with their dog and took him home to Ridgelow.'

'Exactly.'

Ethan digested the information. 'But how did Robert know where to find the dog? How did he know you'd re-homed him?'

'It looks like he did his own bit of detective work. Erica said he turned up unannounced on her doorstep a couple of days before he died. He wanted to see Barney – that's what he used to be called. He got really upset when she told him what she'd done, that the dog had been taken to the rehoming centre. She gave him the address and number for Orchard Farm and Robert paid them a visit. Apparently they refused to give out my details, but someone broke into the office that night. Nothing was stolen, but their filing cabinets were unlocked, so if it was Robert, he could quite easily have gone through their records and found my name and address.'

'Hence the note in his pocket,' Ethan concluded.

'It also explains why Digby was so wound up that night. He must have recognised Robert's voice, or smell or something.'

Ethan went quiet.

'What are you thinking?' I said, wishing I could see inside his head.

'That I don't get it. I mean, why was Robert so

keen to see the dog all of a sudden? And why, seeing as he had your address, didn't he just knock on your front door? Why was he out on the footpath in the dark?'

The thought of Robert staking me out, watching over the fence as I sat on the terrace reading my book by candlelight, Digby snoozing at my feet, made me feel sick. 'Izzy said exactly the same thing,' I said, trying to still the queasiness. 'We both thought it was suspicious and that he must have been up to no good.'

'You think he was planning to take Digby?'

'We didn't know Digby was the connection then, but it makes sense. The chap at the rescue centre said Robert kept insisting the dog was his and that he shouldn't have been re-homed. He obviously wanted him back.'

Ethan was frowning again. 'Seems like a lot of effort to go to though – going all the way to Orchard Farm, breaking in to find a name and address, then coming out to Ridgelow. All for a dog he abandoned?'

'Some people really love their pets, sometimes more than their family and friends,' I pointed out. 'Maybe he was lonely and missed the dog. I know I'd be bereft without Diggers.'

'I know people and animals form strong bonds, I see it all the time. But it doesn't seem right to me that Robert went so far out of his way just to see his old dog again. If he felt so strongly why did he leave the dog with Erica in the first place? And why wasn't Digby's microchip registered?'

Only an hour ago I'd arrived home feeling pleased with myself for finding out the reason why Robert Ashmere had my name and address on a note in his pocket. And now I was sitting there, still talking about the dead man, with more unanswered questions littering my mind, and staring at firm evidence that I'd had an intruder.

A comment Erica had made during our earlier conversation managed to work its way through all the confusion. 'I don't know if I'm trying to make things fit here,' I ventured, 'but when Robert found out Erica had re-homed the dog he kept going on about *needing the number*. Erica thought he meant the phone number for the re-homing centre, but did he mean something else?'

'Like a strange microchip number buried inside his dog?' Ethan replied.

'Can I see it, this number? Did you write it down?'

'No. I'll have to check his file. Maybe I'll take him back to the practice tomorrow and have another look at it.' He stared at the mirror again, then said, 'But Jen, forget that for a minute. Even if you are right, and Robert did mean he needed to get hold of Digby's microchip number, and that's why he turned up in Ridgelow, what we're dealing with now isn't anything to do with him. Robert's dead. He didn't break in and leave this message. Someone else did. You've got to report this to the police.' Ethan was insistent.

'But the message says not to,' I replied, indecision pulling and pushing at me. 'What if whoever wrote it finds out that's what I've done? What if they come back again while I'm here?'

'That won't happen,' Ethan said firmly. 'Because you're going to come and stay with me. You can't live here while some lunatic is trying to scare you like this. Grab some clothes and we'll go back to my place and call the police from there.'

As I packed a bag, Ethan walked round Corner Cottage and checked that all the windows and doors were locked. He even went down to the bottom of the garden to check the shed and the gate on to the footpath, and the garage at the side of the house.

'It's all secured,' he confirmed, 'but you need to get an alarm, Jen. It's the only way you're going to stop any more lowlife from breaking in, especially being so tucked away on this lane. I do worry about you being here all by yourself.' He looked at me meaningfully and opened his mouth to say something, then changed his mind and shut it again. Glancing away he said, 'I don't like this, Jen, not one little bit.'

16

'Well, well, well. Look who's finally decided to show her face.' My mother was all folded arms and pursed coral lips. 'Where on earth have you been? You said you'd be back by lunchtime. I had to call Spencer and ask him to get me a sandwich, or I'd have starved to death.'

I'd stopped off at the shop en route to Ethan's, to make sure there wasn't anything urgent to deal with.

'Where have you been?' she said again. 'You can't just ring up like that and expect me to cover for you without saying why. It's not on, Jennifer, it really isn't.' She rolled Kohl-lined eyes, gave a loud tut and pulled a cold shoulder.

I wanted to point out that managing the shop was actually her job, but with enough on my plate, didn't want to cause an argument with my mother.

'What on earth was so important that you had to abandon me yet again?' She was relishing the role of wounded victim.

'Erica Ashmere,' I said, too tired to think up an excuse.

Her voice climbed an octave. 'Erica Ashmere? The dead man's wife? What's she got to do with anything? Oh, Jennifer, why are you still going on about that horrible business? I thought you'd put an end to this silly fixation of yours.'

Feeling suitably chastised, I admitted I'd been trying to find out more about Robert, but before I could explain, she cut in sharply,

'For goodness sake, get a grip on yourself. You've got a business to run and people counting on you. It's time to stop all this nonsense.'

'It's not nonsense,' I said, sounding like a sulky

teenager and wishing I didn't.

'Not nonsense? Chasing round the countryside like Miss Marple?' The exasperation in her voice made me feel as though I were five years old and had come home covered in mud. 'I don't understand why you keep raking it up. Even the police came to a dead end – how can you work out something an entire police force couldn't?'

Cheesed off, I threw my trump card right at her. 'Actually, it turned out to be very worthwhile, because I did work it out. I know why Robert Ashmere had my name and address with him.'

She inhaled sharply. 'Really?'

'But you're right – as usual – enough of all this silliness.' It was my turn to give the cold shoulder. I turned my back and glided into the workshop.

My mother trailed behind, tight on my tail. 'Good,' she said. 'I'm pleased for you.'

I busied myself at my workbench, tidying away a pile of wick pins. 'Me too. No more loose strings,' I said, avoiding her eye.

She was at odds with herself, trying to fathom out how best to probe for more information.

I put her out of her misery. 'It was Digby.'

'What was?'

'The connection between me and Robert Ashmere. He and Erica used to own Digby. He was coming to see the dog that night, not me.'

'Well I never. What a turn-up. How on earth did you discover that?'

'It was a complete fluke. I found a photo of him. Erica told me she didn't have enough time to look after him properly, so she decided to re-home him. He used to be called Barney.'

My mother looked down her nose. 'I much prefer Digby. He looks like a Digby, speaking of which, how is the little soldier? Did the operation go all right?'

'Yes, Ethan said it went very well. He'll soon be back to his normal self. Look, I'm sorry about dumping on you again today, but I didn't want to miss the opportunity to talk to Erica.'

My mother waved her hand dismissively. 'Oh, don't worry. I coped, as I always do. And Spencer helped out.'

'That's kind of him,' I forced myself to say, wandering across to the store cupboard to check on stock levels.

'Yes. It was nice to have some cheery company for a change,' she sailed on. 'He's very interested in the shop. I was telling him that you're not keen on the accounting side of things. He said he'd be more than happy to go over the numbers and give you some advice.' My mother switched to fast-flow. 'You'll be around tomorrow, won't you? I want to leave early. Spencer's taking me to the theatre and I need to get my hair done first. I'm meeting some of his friends for the first time.'

'Sounds fun,' I called, head in the cupboard. 'Why don't you take the whole afternoon off and have a facial too? I'll treat you, as a thank you for covering for me today.'

My mother was back onside in a heartbeat. 'Oh darling, that would be lovely. And I'm so pleased you've solved the mystery, I really am. How clever of you.'

And I was glad I'd managed to shield her from the ugly reality of Erica, her ransacked house and my graffitied mirror.

Arriving at Brook Street later that afternoon, I

found Ethan's cupboards were bare. He came home soon after me and we decided to pick up some groceries from the supermarket. His protective arm wrapped around my shoulders as we walked into town didn't stop me scouring the streets, searching for shadowy figures lurking round corners and behind cars. After Ethan had rustled up a comforting macaroni cheese for supper, we spent the rest of the evening going over what we knew, trying to decide what to do for the best. I was still reluctant to call the police, but Ethan had been brooding and a combination of testosterone and indignation had taken hold.

'Who do they think they are, threatening you like this?' he said, pacing the length of the kitchen. 'You can't be left alone, Jen, not until we know exactly who, or what, we're dealing with.'

His concern was sweet, but with a business to run, also impractical, so I agreed to call him at regular intervals, whenever I was alone in the shop, so he would know I was safe.

'Haven't you got any idea who it could be?' he asked again.

Oliver Harper's face flashed through my mind as I remembered Spencer's warning of dirty tricks and pictured my smashed shop window. I shared the thought with Ethan. He immediately pressed me again to call the police. His eyes were so etched with worry that, even though a sense of misgiving rolled in my stomach, I relented.

He insisted I spoke to Detective Inspector Pitts. 'You've already got a relationship with him,' he pointed out.

I didn't know about that.

*A history, certainly, but a relationship?*

'And he knows you've been worried about an intruder.'

I located the detective's business card and rang the number on it. A police officer in a control room answered the call. I left a slightly garbled message about cigarette smoke, French doors and lipstick on a mirror, and asked for Detective Inspector Pitts to call me back, adding that I was staying with Ethan.

Another night dragged by. Once again, I tossed and turned, desperate for sleep yet afraid of the thoughts and dreams that might enter my mind when I closed my eyes. Ethan's belief that I was safe from strangers in his home was flawed. Robert Ashmere tracked me down. I woke up clammy, unsettled and wondering what on earth I could do to get rid of him. He was very persistent. I'd hoped that solving the mystery would stop his tormenting, but that obviously wasn't to be the case.

Detective Inspector Pitts rang back as I was forcing myself to try and eat some breakfast. I told him I had clear evidence that there had been an intruder in my home and we arranged to meet at Corner Cottage within the hour. He warned me not to enter the house alone, indicating that this time he was taking my concern seriously. I decided he might be human after all, then conceded, along with Ethan, that it probably helped that I was no longer a suspect in his murder case.

Ethan left for work, taking a tired, but brighter-looking Digby with him. I'd arranged to meet him at the practice as soon as I'd finished with the policeman, so we could look at the microchip number together.

I arrived at Corner Cottage before the police detective and sat in the car feeling like a stranger outside my own home. Even early bird Izzy's curtains were still drawn, and as I waited, it occurred to me that, because of the latest hullabaloo with the mirror, I'd completely forgotten to fill her in about the Digby connection. I couldn't decide whether I should tell her I'd had another intruder. I thought it might frighten her to know that someone was still breaking in to my house, only a stone's throw away from her own.

The hum of a car engine signalled the detective's arrival. He parked up behind my Mini. Getting out, he gave a curt nod, droned, 'Morning,' then offered me a mint, which I declined. Taking one for himself, he strode towards the cottage. 'Let's be having a look, then.'

I let him in, explaining that this was where I'd first smelt the cigarette smoke again. Of course, every trace had now evaporated, but I knew Ethan would back me up. We went into the kitchen. I showed him the French doors, concerned that as Ethan and I had handled them the previous day, we might have ruined any fingerprint evidence.

The detective shrugged it off. 'I doubt it, not because you touched them, but because I suspect we're dealing with someone who knows exactly what they're doing. We didn't find a single shred of evidence when we searched the place last time, although this message on the mirror is another thing altogether.' He looked quite excited about it. His cold grey eyes actually glittered. 'Let's see it then.'

He followed me upstairs to the bedroom. We both stood in front of the mirror. I watched Detective Inspector Pitts' reflection. A strange look crossed his face. He caught my eye.

'Well?' he said, sucking loudly on his mint.

My own reflection was translucent and ghostly. I

couldn't speak. The glass was perfectly clean and shiny. No smudges, smears or angry red words. The policeman waited for an explanation, his familiar, suspicious, cool persona back in place.

'Well?' he said again, looking at me through the antique glass.

I swung from being completely mute to babbling madly, frantically telling him there had definitely been a message, that Ethan had seen it too and would back me up, if only he'd give him a call, but the detective had already switched off and was having none of it. So I shut up and listened in frustrated silence to his warning that wasting police time was a serious criminal offence, and that while he appreciated I'd been through a stressful time during the murder investigation, creating scenes and dramas wasn't the way to deal with it.

When I arrived at the vet practice I burst into tears the moment I saw Ethan. He ushered me into his consultation room and gave me a bear hug. Once I'd calmed down and could talk slowly and without stuttering, I told him there was no evidence; that the mirror had been cleaned and the policeman had given me the brush-off.

Ethan was incensed. 'Give me his number and I'll call him right now and tell him I saw it too,' he said, his whole face flaming and stubbled jaw quivering with anger.

'What's the point?' I replied. 'Even if he does believe you, there's no evidence now.'

'Jen, someone keeps breaking into your house. The police need to take it seriously. They need to do something.'

'We need real proof, Ethan,' I argued.

'What, like you getting hurt, or ...' He trailed off,

spun round and thumped clenched fists against his consultation table. Shaking his head, he said, 'It's not on, Jen. It's just not on. Some fruitcake is stalking you and something needs to be done about it. I can't believe the police are being so off hand.'

'I don't know what else we can do,' I said, swamped by helplessness.

Ethan took some deep breaths and switched his brain to practical mode. 'I do,' he said. 'If they want evidence, we'll get them evidence. We'll film whoever it is. We'll set up a hidden camera. The police won't be able to ignore that, will they? And you need a burglar alarm. When we're done with Digby, I'll have a look at security and surveillance sites online. Stuff Pitts,' he added gruffly. 'He's as useless as a chocolate teapot.'

I managed to raise a wisp of a smile. My own view of Detective Inspector Pitts was much less generous.

'Come on then,' I said, forcing myself into action, 'let's have a look at this number.' I picked up Digby and placed him gently on the consulting table.

Ethan grabbed his hand scanner and ran the instrument between the dog's shoulder blades, giving a running commentary. 'See here? The chip is giving off a radio wave that's been picked up by the scanner.' As he spoke the LED display filled with digits. 'This is the new chip that I injected – a long numerical identification.' He moved the scanner round to the side of Digby's neck. Another reading showed on the small screen. 'And this is the original chip.'

Just as he'd said, it was a combination of letters as well as numbers – 9E1JP21605357622. I wrote it down.

'Another thing that makes this code unusual,' said Ethan, switching off the scanner, 'is that it's 16 digits long. The latest codes are 15 and the old codes were only 10. That makes it even more of a rogue chip.'

I don't know why I thought Digby's strange number, or code, might mean something to me, but I did, and I was disappointed. 'So what now?'

The sound of rubber soles squeaking against the tiled floor drew our attention away from the dog and his strange ID tag. The footsteps came to a halt outside the consultation room. There was a brief warning knock on the door before it swung open and glossy blonde locks framing a smiling face poked round.

'Hi Ethan, you're in early – oh, Jen, you're here too,' said Lisa. Then, noticing Digby on the table her smile faltered. 'Is something wrong?'

'No. He's fine,' Ethan replied. 'I'm just showing Jen how the microchip system works, that's all.' He pulled a cheesy smile and held it for too long.

'Oh. I'll leave you to it then,' she said, but didn't, and continued to stare at us.

To avoid her gaze, I fixated on stroking and fussing Digby while Ethan became engrossed in his computer screen.

'You're up to something,' Lisa accused. 'You were acting strangely yesterday when I came in for those worming tablets, Ethan.'

'No I wasn't,' he denied. He was a bad liar, and like the cheese smile the feigned surprise was overdone. 'I was just concentrating.'

'Don't give me that,' she pooh-poohed. 'As if Jen's interested in the fine art of microchipping. You're up to something. You both are. I can tell.' She leant a shoulder against the door frame and made it clear she wasn't going anywhere.

I looked at Ethan, willing him to say something that would put her off the scent, but he simply gave a defeatist shrug and an awkward silence descended.

I gave in first. 'Ok, you're right.' Lisa's face lifted. 'Something is going on, but we can't tell you about it right now.' Lisa's face dropped. 'Come round to Ethan's for dinner later and we'll fill you in then.'

'Sounds cryptic,' she said, mollified. 'What time do you want me?'

'Around seven?'

Happy with the invitation, and the promise of something intriguing dished up with dinner, she headed off, long blonde hair bouncing on her shoulders, rubber soles squeaking on the super-clean floor.

'We should keep this to ourselves, Jen,' Ethan warned.

I made a face. 'I didn't know what to tell her, did I? You weren't much help. At least I've bought us a bit of time to think about what to say. We don't have to give the whole story. I could just explain that I've worked out the Robert Ashmere connection.'

Ethan relaxed. 'Yes, that'll do. But that's all we say, right?'

I nodded. 'I'll invite Izzy too. She'll have been dying to know how I got on with …' I clammed up remembering Ethan had no idea Izzy had been playing detective with me. Chewing on my lip, I hoped I hadn't said anything incriminating.

'Regular pair of Miss Marples, aren't you,' Ethan said dryly, but with shining eyes.

17

I drove to work with the code in my pocket and unease in my bones. I was nervous about entering the shop on my own in case someone had left me another nasty message, or, worse, was waiting in person. Ethan provided moral support over the phone as I opened up and checked the place over. I needn't have worried. Everything was fine and work proved a welcome distraction. I was well immersed by the time my mother arrived.

'Morning, love,' she called out before launching into her first question of the day. 'What on earth did you lock yourself in for? This is Ridgelow, not the Bronx.'

I didn't rush to come up with a reply, sure that she would breeze on, which she did, wandering straight to the kitchen, calling, 'I bought a packet of stem ginger biscuits – your favourite.' She soon returned, standing behind me and watching as I typed awkwardly on the keyboard. 'Is there much to do today?'

Wondering if she was fishing for a compliment about her management skills, I continued tapping away and said, 'Just the usual,' then, because she'd been thoughtful enough to bring in the biscuits, added as a sweetener, 'You've kept things ticking over very nicely. Don't really need me anymore.'

She tinkled. 'That's sweet of you darling, but we both know I don't have your aptitude for the candles.' Unusually, she paused. 'Actually, Jennifer, there's something I want to discuss with you.'

*Sounds ominous.*

I hoped things hadn't been moving along so speedily in my mother's life that I might be about to end up with Spencer Lewis as a stepfather.

She pulled up a chair and started speaking very carefully, as though she had rehearsed each line. 'Please don't take this as criticism, because it certainly isn't intended that way.'

Automatically, my head began to sink into my neck.

'I know you've had a lot on your plate, and it's understandable why you haven't noticed, but the fact is things have become a little unloved and neglected.'

Baffled, I could only assume she was talking about our relationship.

'I thought I should point it out, so that you can get on top of it before the cracks really start to show. It won't take much effort. I've made a list of things you could do that would make a world of difference.' She pressed a piece of paper into my hand and shot me a meaningful look.

I scanned the neatly written list. It wasn't about patching up damaged relations but about improving the look of the shop. The list amounted to eight actions ranging from a full spring clean and damp treatment to a floor-to-ceiling paint job and new display units. Totting it up in my head I could see it would cost a small fortune. She'd obviously been at more of a loose end while I'd been trailing Robert Ashmere than I'd appreciated. My mother and boredom are always a dangerous combination, particularly when she has a credit card to hand and access to QVC.

I straightened my slouched shoulders in an attempt to look authoritative and said, 'Nice idea, Mum, but we can't afford it right now.' Her face fell. 'It's not a necessity, is it?' I tried to be gentle. 'It's more of a *nice to do.*'

My mother was never one to give in easily. 'But I've chosen the paint colours and everything,' she whined. 'Oh, come on, a little face lift would do the world of good.'

Thinking of my tired eyes and newly acquired facial lines, I silently agreed.

'Maybe in the New Year, if we have a good Christmas,' I said, trying to sound resolute, but with the sinking feeling that this showed every sign of becoming a battle between us. My mother had obviously put a lot of thought into it and had her heart set.

She ushered me into the shop to show me her grand ideas. 'If we move a few things around, put in some more shelving and display units here and here ...' She waved her arms as though marshalling a plane in to position, '... you could get more stock on the floor and make space for new ranges. It would be a lovely way to introduce your autumn and Christmas collections.' She made JJ Candles sounded like a retail giant. 'We could have a grand opening, invite the *Sunday Post* people back again and use it as the launch pad for your next growth phase.' I grimaced at the Spencer Lewis business jargon dripping from her coral-coated lips. 'I know we need to watch the pennies, but don't forget – you've got to spend money to make money,' she breezed, banking on her enthusiasm catching.

I gave an unconcealed, exasperated sigh. 'That's fine if you've got the money to start with, which we don't.'

'Are you sure? We've had a really good year so far. The Internet sales are up at least thirty per cent by my sums and you've been inundated with wedding and party orders this summer. Surely we can find some spare cash to tidy things up a bit?'

I tried a different tack and said that I'd look at the books to see if there was any way we could make things stretch, even though I had no intention of doing so. Stalling her was the only idea I could muster. Thankfully, the first customer of the day came in. I got on with some work behind the scenes, trying not to think too much about the dead man, break-ins, nasty messages, rogue microchips and emerging battles with my mother. When she left for the afternoon to get her hair done, I rang Ethan and told him I was on my own. He promised to call every thirty minutes to make sure I was okay.

I felt like a sitting duck behind the counter. My heart rolled over every time the doorbell jangled. Because of my frayed nerves I kept needing the loo, but didn't like to leave the shop unattended. This dilemma went on all afternoon and added to my already heightened stress levels.

I remembered to speak to Izzy and invite her to dinner, which she was very excited about.

'How lovely! I've never been to Ethan's house before. What's the occasion?'

'We've got some good news we want to share,' I said mysteriously, knowing she'd have hours of fun speculating.

The afternoon passed uneventfully. No suspicious-looking characters came in, there were no silent or dropped phone calls, and my shop window remained intact. I sat wondering if that particular incident was an unlucky accident, or if it was tied up in the growing list of strange things that had happened.

Being stuck in the shop was tedious. I wasn't as well prepared as my mother, who always had a book at the ready for the quieter moments. Having retrieved her latest reading material from under the counter I immediately discarded it again having discovered it was a whimsical historical saga and not to my taste. Sighing and wishing I was tucked away in my workshop, mixing up wax and losing myself in the scent of essential oils, I picked up a feather duster and started flicking and twirling half-heartedly around the shelves and displays. As I moved around it dawned on me that, just as my mother had claimed, three years of trading had taken their toll and the place was starting to look a little worn and shabby round the edges. The ceiling was greying and gathering dust, spider webs were draped along the cornice, while underfoot the oak floorboards were dull and scuffed and would benefit from a rub down and good oiling. I had to admire my mother's cunning placement of objects. Strategically located candle stacks hid damp patches on the walls and soft lighting drew attention away from tired paint work. Acknowledging that I had been a bit short-sighted and that I really did need to spend a bit of money improving the place, I wondered how best to manage my mother's expectations. The full-on facelift would have to be toned down into a simple make-over, and I hoped she would be prepared to sign up for a couple of Sunday's worth of hands-on decorating, rather than expect me to *get a man in*. At least the scent of the candles masked that of the damp.

True to his word, Ethan called every thirty minutes or so. He didn't speak for long, just checked I was still alive and able to move of my own free will, and got back to his patients. Thankfully his day consisted of consultations and not complicated surgery and he was able to cope with the distraction without any serious repercussions.

At five o'clock I had one final, short conversation

with him to say I was closing up, then walked along the High Street to the supermarket to pick up a few bits and pieces for dinner. It was only when the cashier had run everything through the till and I had packed it neatly into bags that I realised I'd left my replacement purse back at the shop. A queue had formed behind me and annoyed murmurings ran up and down the line. Picking up on the growing disturbance, the store manager came over to find out what the problem was and I explained that I had no means to pay. He agreed to put my bags to one side until I returned and I power-walked back to the shop, cursing under my breath at my stupidity and praying that I'd still have time to prepare dinner and shower and change before Lisa and Izzy arrived.

I knew I'd left the purse on my desk in the workshop. Rather than unlock the front of the shop and give the impression that I was still open for business, I walked up the narrow side-alley and went round to the rear, where I pulled up with a start.

The back door was wide open.

I could see it hadn't been forced, which was odd, because only my mother and I had keys, and she was at the hairdresser and I was standing outside. Someone cleared their throat. Then echoing footsteps knocked over the wooden floor.

Common sense told me to run.

Curiosity wanted to know the identity of my serial intruder.

I decided to look and then run.

Prowling round to the kitchen window I peered in. The roller blind was pulled down, but there was a three-inch gap at the bottom that I could see through. The kitchen was empty and the door onto the main corridor wide open. A figure – a man – walked past. I recognised him instantly, and although upset at what I'd seen, part of me wasn't at all surprised.

Too late, I realised my intruder was about to leave. There wasn't enough time to escape down the alley without being seen, so I crouched behind a large wheelie bin in a dark corner, wishfully thinking that if I couldn't see him it meant he couldn't see me. The back door groaned as it closed and I heard the rattle of keys turning in the lock. Then, as though he had all the time in the world, the man walked off whistling a merry tune.

I stayed in my hiding place for a long minute, just to make sure he had definitely gone, then let myself in. Scouting around, I discovered the till hadn't been tampered with and that my new purse lay exactly where I'd left it. My laptop was also switched off. I pressed a hand on the cover to see if it was warm, but it wasn't. Just like my house, nothing appeared to have been touched, moved or stolen. So it begged the obvious question:

*What the hell was Spencer Lewis doing in my workshop?*

18

I knew Spencer couldn't be trusted. I knew it. Clearly, he'd stolen my mother's keys, or made a copy of them. Either would have been easy enough for him to do. It also occurred to me that my mother's set contained a spare key to my own house, recently updated after the locksmith visit, which explained why there had never been any sign of a break-in at Corner Cottage.

I shuddered as I pictured Spencer rooting around my bedroom, his hands touching my precious belongings, then leaving that disturbing message on my mirror. I was furious with Spencer: furious at his audacity; furious at his deceitfulness; furious that he'd been taking my mother and me for fools.

I couldn't wait to tell Ethan.

Bursting through the front door in an explosion of shopping bags and temper, I hurried straight to the kitchen and said breathlessly, 'Spencer Lewis was in my workshop.'

Ethan looked up from a copy of *Country Life* and gave a small grunt that said *so what?*

'I don't mean he popped in for a cup of tea, a slice of cake and a cosy chat. I mean he was sneaking around my workshop after I left. He's the intruder.'

Now I had his full attention. The magazine was discarded in a flash. 'Are you sure?'

'Course I'm sure. I just saw him.'

'But he's your mum's boyfriend.'

'Friend,' I corrected, 'and he has access to Mum's keys and therefore my house keys.'

Ethan was silent.

Het up, I continued, 'I knew he was dodgy. He has that look about him.' I rummaged in my handbag.

Ethan put a steadying hand on my shoulder. 'What are you doing?'

'Looking for my phone. I'm going to ring the police and report him.'

His grip tightened. 'Hang on a minute. Think before you rush in. Spencer may have had a good reason for being there.'

'Like what?'

'Maybe your mum forgot something and he went to fetch it. Was he carrying anything when he left?'

'I don't know. I was hiding behind a stinking dustbin at the time so he wouldn't see me.'

'Was anything missing from the shop?'

'No.' I started to experience a slow, unpleasant sinking sensation.

'Then don't be too hasty with your accusations, Jen. If you're proved wrong your mum won't be very impressed. And neither will the police. You've got to be really sure about this.'

I rubbed my eyes. My brain felt dense, like a thick lump of playdough.

Ethan pulled me into his chest and rested his chin on top of my head. 'Look, I want to know who's causing all this trouble just as much as you do, but we need really strong evidence to back us up, or that idiot policeman is going to think you're the one who needs locking up. And Spencer's your mum's friend. I'd tread very carefully there if I were you. There'll be a big fall out if you accuse him and it turns out you're wrong.'

I knew he was right, but I wished he wasn't.

'Izzy and Lisa will be here soon and I haven't even changed,' I said wearily. 'Would you mind starting dinner while I shower, find my rational head and screw it back on again?'

I left him methodically slicing onions with surgery-steady hands.

Our guests arrived five minutes apart. Determined to make the most of the prolonged summer sun, we sat in the garden. Izzy, cool and bohemian in a long, white-fringed cotton dress was at ease with accessorising and wore layers of multi-coloured wooden beads round her neck and a stunning red-jewelled comb in her silver mane. Lisa had changed into a yellow tunic dress that emphasised her long legs and blonde hair. I felt underdressed in denim cut-offs and one of Ethan's T-shirts, but, having vacated Corner Cottage so swiftly, I hadn't had time to put much thought into my wardrobe and had simply stuffed random clothes into my overnight bag.

After a bit of chit chat and the first drink, I slipped inside to lay the dining table and check on the pasta bake. Ethan proudly took our guests off on a grand tour of his garden. I could hear Izzy's cries of rapture as they entered the vegetable patch, followed by the slip-slap of Lisa's flip flops on stone paving as boredom got the better of her.

'Thought I'd leave them to it,' she said, sauntering into the kitchen, empty wine glass in hand. 'The ins and outs of which variety of potato to grow in chalky soil don't float my boat.' She helped herself to more Chablis. 'Come on then Jarvis – when do I get to hear about what you and Ethan are up to?'

'All in good time,' I said, rinsing chicory leaves under the tap and refusing to be drawn until Ethan was around to help with any difficult questions.

'Izzy thinks you might be secretly engaged. I mean, it's been, what, nearly a year now?'

'Just over. And Izzy has a very vivid imagination.'

'And a little crush on Ethan, I think. I saw her pinch his bottom earlier.'

I laughed. 'He won't know what to make of that. He's rubbish at flirting.'

'Well, I'm pleased things are still working out between you both, even if he hasn't proposed yet.'

'To be honest, I'm not bothered,' I lied. 'I've never been the marrying kind.' I put my head down and focused on chopping a big bunch of spring onions.

'Shame, because Ethan is.' Lisa picked at a bowl of mixed nuts.

I sucked in a breath and looked back at her. 'What do you mean? Has he said something?'

'Not exactly … but he was fishing for information the other day. It was obvious he was trying to suss out what I thought you would say if he did ask.' She flipped her head back and caught a peanut in her mouth.

I took a big gulp of wine. 'He has talked about us moving in together.'

Lisa's brows shot up in perfect arcs before her eyes narrowed. 'Jennifer Jarvis, you are such a dark horse. What did you say?'

'That I'd think about it.'

'What's to think about? The man's a catch. Get in there!' Then indicating to a pile of clean clothes – which included some of my underwear – neatly folded in a laundry basket in the corner of the kitchen, she said with an overdone wink, 'Or maybe you already have?'

'It's a temporary arrangement.'

'Well, I'd get a move on if I were you,' she teased, 'before one of his admiring patients, and I mean of the human kind, get their claws stuck into him. They all think he's the bee's knees, although he hasn't got a clue. He's totally oblivious to all the come-ons. It's hysterical to watch.'

'What is?' said Ethan, en route to the fridge to get Izzy a refill.

'Nothing. Just talking about a client,' she fibbed easily.

Despite the rush, the meal went to plan, at least the food was hot and to everyone's taste. Izzy even asked for the recipe, then, as I brought out the cheese board, couldn't contain herself any longer.

'Come on, you two – out with it. What's the big secret? I'm dying to know.'

'You tell them, Jen,' said Ethan, giving me a look that clearly said, *don't say too much*. 'I'll go and make some coffee.'

Two expectant faces gazed at me.

I kept it brief. 'I've finally worked out the connection between me and Robert Ashmere.'

'Really?' Izzy looked impressed. 'So you did know him after all?'

'No. I'm not the connection – Digby is. It turns out Robert used to own him.'

'Holy smoke!' she exclaimed, clapping her hands in glee. 'I never would have got that in a million years. How on earth did you find out?'

'I went back to see Erica yesterday …'

Izzy cut in. 'Oh, the poor woman. How was she? In a bad way I should think after what happened?'

'Hang on you two, I'm getting lost,' Lisa grumbled. 'Who's Erica?'

'The dead man's wife – sorry – estranged wife,' Izzy clarified, adding sensationally, 'Jennifer went to her house the other day and found her inside, trussed up like a turkey on a chair, with a hood over her head and the whole place completely trashed to smithereens.'

'Bloody hell,' said Lisa.

I quickly set the scene to help her catch up, then went on to explain how I'd come across the photo of Digby, aka Barney, and told them about the conversation with the rehoming manager.

'And that's the connection. That's why Robert Ashmere had my name and address with him.'

'What a turn-up,' said Izzy. 'To think the answer was right under our noses all along. How funny.' She looked over at Digby who was curled up in a tight ball, gently snoring as he snoozed on the rug by the hearth. She smiled affectionately then her lips drooped slightly and a canny look illuminated her blue-violet eyes. 'It's still curious though, isn't it?' she remarked, assessing the cheese board then helping herself to a cracker and a slither of Stilton.

'What is?' Lisa and I said in unison.

'Why Robert was on the footpath. I mean, if all he wanted was to see the dog, why on earth didn't he knock on the front door, introduce himself and explain? He had the address, so why was he skulking around on the footpath late at night?'

'That's what I said,' Ethan chipped in, as he placed a loaded tray of cups, saucers, coffee cafetiere and plate of after-dinner mints on the table.

'You think he was going to steal his dog back?' said Lisa. 'That he was casing the joint?'

'The thought has sprung to mind,' I said.

'He must have really loved him to go to all that trouble then.' Lisa had avoided the cheese, but, having eyed up the plate of chocolate mints, leant over and unabashedly took three.

'I doubt it.' Ethan threw in his ten pence worth as he poured the coffee. 'He wouldn't have left the dog with Erica if he did.'

Suddenly they were all experts on Robert Ashmere.

'Perhaps he saw it as a temporary thing,' Lisa said, unwrapping one of her hoarded chocolates.

'That wasn't the impression I got,' I replied. 'And if he was that devoted he'd have visited and taken him out for walks. Erica said he never bothered. She would have known if he wanted the dog back at some point. I'm sure she wouldn't have re-homed him otherwise.'

Izzy was intrigued. 'So why go to all that trouble? Why was Digby so important to him all of a sudden?'

She and Lisa continued to speculate as Ethan and I cleared up. Then, moving into the sitting area, the conversation kept coming back to Robert Ashmere and Digby. I hadn't anticipated all their questions and probing, and, worried about tripping up, I withdrew from the conversation and listened from the sidelines.

But Izzy noticed. 'You're quiet, Jennifer. Is something the matter?'

I didn't know what to say, so I looked at Ethan, willing him to save me. But he didn't. Instead, he sighed, nestled into the sofa and surrendered.

'There's a bit more to Jen's story than we've let on,' he admitted reluctantly. 'I asked her not to say anything, not because I don't trust you both, but because I'm worried about getting you involved.' He hesitated.

'Oh, come on Ethan, get on with it.' Izzy pulled an impatient face.

'Okay, okay.' He tucked a cushion behind his back to make himself more comfortable. 'Right … How to put it …? A couple of strange things have happened. We're not sure how they're connected, or even if they are connected, but it looks like they might be.'

'Oh, stop babbling, Ethan,' Izzy chided. 'Be clear – what sort of things?'

'If we tell you, you must keep it to yourselves.' Ethan was deadly serious.

Lisa, who was sitting next to him, gave him a small thump on the side of his thigh. 'Stop being so dramatic and tell us what's going on.'

Impatient to hear what they made of it, I butted in, picturing Spencer Lewis' smarmy face as I spoke. 'Someone's threatened me. Apparently, I have something this person wants and so he broke into my house and left me a nasty message on my bedroom mirror about it.'

'Good heavens!' breathed Izzy, a hand pressed against her heart. 'What did it say?'

'Stop playing games. Hand over the number or yours will be up. Be smart – don't call the police.'

'But you have though, called the police, haven't you?' said Lisa looking worried.

'Yes, but they're not interested. That police detective came out and looked round the house, but the person who'd left the message had been back and cleaned it off and so now he thinks I'm an attention-seeking fruitcake.'

Lisa was horrified. 'What are you going to do?'

'More importantly,' Izzy interjected, one hand twiddling her beads, 'what does it mean? What number do they want?'

'We're not sure,' I said, 'but we're wondering if it's something to do with Digby. Go on Ethan, tell them what you found.'

Ethan picked up the baton. 'We were told by the rescue centre that Digby wasn't microchipped,' he said, 'so while he was in for his neutering operation I thought

I would get it done. But when I examined him, I discovered that a chip had already been implanted. I scanned it and found it was encoded with an irregular ID number. The microchips we usually see are a long sequence of numbers. Digby's chip is made up of both numbers and letters. I checked it against the records on the national database, but it didn't register, so I did a bit of digging around and it turns out the chip is a rogue one, something I've never come across before. When I saw the message on Jen's mirror, I put two and two together, although of course, it could be nothing whatsoever to do with it.'

'Then again, it could,' agreed Izzy.

'Another reason why we think it might be connected,' I added, 'is because the night Robert went to Erica's to see the dog, he kept saying, *I need the number.* Erica thought he meant the phone number for the dog rescue centre, but maybe he meant the number on Digby's microchip?'

'But Ethan said it isn't a number, it's a code,' Lisa was quick to point out.

'Oh, yes.' Izzy said. Then, 'Can I see it, this number, or code, whatever it is?'

I fetched the piece of paper and handed it to her.

She held it at arm's length, squinting. 'Can't read a damn thing without my specs,' she sighed. 'What does it say?'

I read the code aloud: '9E1JP21605357622.'

There was a silence. Izzy looked thoughtful. Lisa looked baffled. Ethan looked worried.

'Quite a puzzle,' Izzy said eventually. 'Why don't you copy it out and I'll take it home and play around with it, see if I come up with anything. It'll make a change from Sudoku puzzles and the crossword.'

Lisa was the voice of reason. 'I think we're getting carried away. We're trying to make a connection where there isn't one. It's just a duff microchip.'

'Have you ever come across anything like that before?' said Ethan.

'No. But there must be a logical explanation. Maybe it was fitted in another country?'

Ethan was doubtful, but agreed it was possible.

'The point is,' said Lisa, 'it's not easy for someone to take a microchip, programme it and then inject it into a dog.'

'The injecting part's straightforward,' Ethan argued, 'anyone can buy an implanter and scanner. And Digby's chip isn't in the normal place, which suggests it was done by someone inexperienced.'

An interesting thought sprang to my mind. I tried to interrupt – unsuccessfully. The conversation was turning into a heated debate between the two vets, both of whom I knew from experience liked to be right.

'Some microchips do move and migrate,' Lisa protested. 'I've definitely come across that before.'

Ethan's competitive streak wasn't ready to let the ball drop. 'What about the number and letter combination?'

'That's not unusual either. Some microchips do have letters and numbers.'

'Digby's too young to have one of those. They were faded out in 2000 and replaced with the numerical ones. And,' Ethan said, a tad smugly. 'Digby's code has an extra digit. It's not a standard code. I have looked into this, you know.'

'But microchips come pre-programmed,' replied Lisa hotly. 'You can't just create your own.'

I finally managed to edge my way into the debate and shut them both up with three words.

'Robert Ashmere could.'

Three pairs of eyes turned on me.

'He used to work in electronics,' I said. 'Or maybe that's just another coincidence?'

'Oh, yes,' Izzy buzzed. 'He was a director at an electronics firm. Well, well, well … ' Then remembering she wasn't supposed to know anything, she caught Ethan's eye and had the grace to blush before swiftly recovering. 'There must be a connection somewhere. There are just too many coincidences. Think about it. First, Robert says he needs *the number*. He comes looking for Digby, who is injected with a strange number, or code – whatever it is it's definitely strange. Then, just as he's a cat's whisker away from the dog, Robert is killed – seemingly a mugging gone wrong, but in light of all this, perhaps that was just a guise and there's more to it?'

'And now someone else is looking for *the number*, someone who thinks Jen has it,' finished Ethan.

'Quite,' said Izzy. 'It must be very valuable. And whoever wants it obviously doesn't know about Digby's microchip, or they'd have taken him instead of leaving a cryptic message on a mirror.'

I paled.

Ethan saw the look on my face. 'Don't worry. We'll keep a really close eye on him.'

Lisa was still unconvinced. 'Perhaps they haven't taken Digby because he just has a duff microchip and is nothing whatsoever to do with the message on the mirror. I really think you should call the police again, Jen.'

'And say what?'

'Tell them someone's threatened you.'

'I've already done that. I told you, they don't want

to know – there's no proof.'

The room was silent again until Izzy said, 'Is there anything else we should know?'

I hesitated, heeding Ethan's earlier warning about jumping to conclusions, but couldn't stop myself saying, 'Yes. I'm afraid there is.'

19

I told them I'd seen Spencer Lewis snooping around my workshop.

'He could have a good excuse,' Lisa pointed out.

'That's exactly what I said,' agreed Ethan. 'Maybe he was collecting something for Mary?'

I tried not to sound sharp. 'The point is Spencer has keys to my workshop. Whether Mum willingly gave them to him or not isn't the issue. What I'm getting at is that her set also includes a spare key to Corner Cottage, which I recently updated after the first break-in, when the locks were changed.'

'And you think Spencer used it to get into your house and leave you a nasty message on your mirror?' completed Izzy. 'I see what you're saying. Spencer holds the key – quite literally.'

'And he gives me the creeps,' I said. 'There's something about him that gets my back up.'

'I've got mixed feelings about him too,' agreed Izzy. 'He's got his fingers in a lot of pies – some of them not to my taste.' She paused. 'And I'm sorry to tell you, Jennifer, that in the past he's been detained at Her Majesty's pleasure.' My face must have been as blank as my brain at this statement because Izzy had to be blunt. 'He's done time – been inside.'

I gasped. 'Are you sure?'

'I didn't want to mention it before, but in light of what you've said I think it best I do. I'm afraid Spencer Lewis has a criminal record. I don't know all the details, but I have it on good authority that he's definitely served a prison sentence.'

'Mum's dating an ex-con?'

'Does she know?' said Lisa.

'I doubt it,' I said, still reeling from this latest revelation.

'So,' said Izzy, 'Spencer's dating your mother whilst at the same time breaking into your shop and cottage. What a piece of work he's turned out to be.'

'Theoretically it's not breaking in,' said Ethan, who had been very quiet. 'He had the keys.'

'Which he'd stolen, or copied,' I said.

'You don't know that for sure.'

'What is it with you and Spencer?' I prickled. 'Why do you keep sticking up for him?'

'I'm not.' He threw me a hurt look. 'I just want to keep sight of the facts.'

'The facts are that Spencer Lewis – a man with a criminal record – let himself into my house and left me a threatening message on my bedroom mirror; a man who had the audacity to go back again and wipe away the evidence; a man who,' I said, holding up a hand as Ethan tried to interrupt, 'as I witnessed with my very own eyes, also let himself into my shop and had a good old snoop around.'

'And don't forget the other time you thought someone had broken in, Jennifer – when your photocopier was left switched on,' Izzy prompted.

'Yes. And he smokes. I've seen him,' I said. 'Both times my house has been broken into, it reeks of smoke.'

'I'm not disagreeing with you,' said Ethan. 'It does look suspicious, but I'm just trying to think what the police would say if you rang them. We need them on our side. If we get in touch again and we end up in the wrong, they'll never take us seriously. I know you saw Spencer in your shop, but nothing was missing. And you don't have any real evidence to prove he broke into your house. Don't forget the police didn't find any sign of an intruder when they searched the place. If it was Spencer they'd have found his fingerprints or something.'

'He probably learnt all sorts of tricks of the trade when he was inside and knew how to cover his tracks,' suggested Izzy.

'But what's it all about?' Lisa said. 'I thought he genuinely likes your mum? Why would he do something like that?'

'It must be something to do with this number. He must have checked the cottage and when he didn't find anything decided to try the shop,' said Izzy.

'And he's always sticking his nose into my business,' I added. 'He even offered to do my accounts for me, seemingly out the goodness of his heart, but perhaps there's more to it?'

'Oh,' gasped Izzy. 'Of course! The other man. We've forgotten about the other man. Spencer has an accomplice.'

I immediately saw where she was heading. 'Oliver Harper.'

'Is he the man you turned down?' said Lisa, struggling to keep up. 'I mean, the man who wants to buy your shop?'

Izzy spoke in an excited rush. 'Jennifer and I saw them having lunch together recently. They were deep in conversation and looking very pally.'

'Which is another strange thing,' I said, 'because Spencer told me he couldn't be trusted. He implied that Oliver was responsible for my smashed window.'

'So the number might be connected to the shop?' said Ethan. 'Is that why Oliver's so keen to buy it?'

'But what about Digby's code?' Izzy waved the

piece of paper in the air.

'We're jumping to massive conclusions,' said Ethan. 'We need to calm down and work this through.'

But Izzy was well ablaze. 'The immediate concern is Mary. She needs to know about Spencer. I think you should go round and tell her.'

'We can't. Spencer's taken her out for the evening,' I said, as a dull pain gnawed at my gut.

Izzy's face drained of colour. 'Oh dear.'

'It's okay,' said Ethan. 'He's taken her to the theatre at Redbury.'

'Ah, *Much Ado About Nothing*. I wanted to see that myself. Oh, look, I'm probably overreacting, but given everything that's been said tonight, I'm worried about her being alone with him. Perhaps you and Jennifer could go and meet her and make up some excuse to take her home? It's just after half past nine. I should think the play will finish around ten. If you leave now you'll get there in time.'

But we didn't.

Having dropped Izzy and then Lisa home, Ethan steered his Jeep towards Redbury and motored sedately out of Ridgelow, carefully observing the speed limit.

'Come on, put your foot down,' I said, slapping his thigh.

Ethan gave me a disapproving glance. 'You know I can't risk losing my licence. The police sometimes use a speed trap along here.'

'Ethan, it's dark. They're not going to be waiting in pitch black, are they?'

He ignored me.

In the passenger seat beside him, I pushed my right foot to the floor in the frustrated hope that an imaginary throttle would accelerate us forward.

'Then let me drive,' I pleaded. 'I don't mind getting a few points on my licence if it means getting to Mum in time.'

As I spoke, we passed the national speed limit signage and Ethan rammed his foot down on the gas. The force pushed me back into the leather seat as he negotiated the road at a steady sixty miles per hour, braking only slightly round the bends. Now I was petrified by the speed, but kept quiet. The car rocketed round tight country corners, tyres hugging tarmac. If I had driven as fast we'd have ended up in the ditch. I snuck a look at Ethan's face. Always good in a crisis, he was calm and focused only on the road ahead. In no time the Jeep slowed as streetlights came in to view. I relaxed, but my thighs hurt from clenching.

Ethan swung into the brightly lit car park just as my mother's head dipped into the front passenger seat of Spencer's Jaguar. I flung off my seat belt and reached for the door handle, but before I could jump out and grab her attention, Spencer sped off in a flurry of gravel. My heart sank as I watched the tail lights disappear into the night.

'Quick, belt up,' Ethan ordered, revving the engine and whipping up more shingle as his Jeep wheel span out of the car park.

Spencer had a complete disregard for speed limits. He motored swiftly through Redbury High Street towards Ridgelow, but instead of following the main road, steered his car down a rural lane.

'Where's he going?' I cried.

'This road takes you round the back of Haven Woods,' Ethan informed me.

We were surrounded by woodland and enveloped in darkness. Spencer had to slow right down. The lane became single track and the surface was worn, not a problem for Ethan's Jeep, but difficult for a low sprung Jaguar. Ethan followed at a reasonable distance then slammed on the brakes as a deer leapt across the road, narrowly missing the near wing.

'Jeez!' he gasped. The Jeep skidded to a halt and stalled.

He quickly turned the engine over and the car roared back to life, but Spencer had disappeared. Ethan drove as fast as it was safe to do so, given the conditions of the road and the possibility of further close encounters with wildlife, but there was no sign of the Jag's tail lights.

I thumped the top of the dash. 'Where have they gone?'

'There,' said Ethan, his head twisting to the left. 'We've just passed them.'

Spencer had pulled into the entrance of a gated driveway.

'Stop then!' I cried as Ethan drove on.

'Don't be daft.'

'Ethan …' I protested.

'Jen, you can't go knocking on their bloody window. Why do you think they've pulled over?'

To my mind, there was only one reason why Spencer, a convicted criminal and serial intruder, had driven my mother down a secluded country lane, late at night, and the thought put the fear of God in me.

Ethan had a smirk on his face. 'I hope we're still that amorous when we're in our sixties,' he said.

I digested this comment and reined in my overactive imagination. 'You mean they're … ?' I couldn't bear to think it, let alone say it. 'Oh God, keep going and pull in further up.'

There wasn't anywhere to stop on the winding lane without being seen, so we drove on, eventually coming to a T-Junction with a pub opposite. Ethan pulled in to the car park, turning the Jeep round so we faced the junction and parked up. He switched off his headlights and we waited. Nearly thirty minutes later we were still waiting. Just as I started bending Ethan's ear about going back up the lane to look for them, Spencer's Jag materialised. I was relieved to see the silhouettes of two figures in the front, still not convinced that my mother would do anything as risqué as getting frisky in a car at the side of the road.

On the outskirts of Ridgelow we were forced to drive straight past again as Spencer pulled over and Ethan didn't have time to react. Stopping in a layby, we got out and walked up the road to see what they were doing. Standing behind a parked car, we watched Spencer and my mother get out of the Jag and join a small queue beside a mobile unit.

'I don't believe it,' said Ethan, chuckling. 'He's buying her a kebab.'

'My mother doesn't eat kebabs.'

But that night she did. Spencer handed her a paper parcel of food and they sat in the Jag and shared it.

'What a charmer,' said Ethan. 'He sure knows how to treat a lady: theatre, then a drive down a dark lane, followed by a roadside kebab. I hope you've inherited your mum's discerning taste in world cuisine and sense of adventure?'

'Shall I go over and interrupt?' I said, feeling queasy, and not at the thought of the kebab.

'No. Leave them be. She's having a good time.'

'But Spencer's a crook.'

'I know, but she's not come to any harm. Why spoil her evening? Come on, let's go. We can deal with it in the morning.'

'I'd at least like to see her home safely.'

Ethan agreed. We walked back to the Jeep and were soon tailing Spencer's car again. The Jag pulled up onto my mother's drive. Ethan stopped a few metres along the road.

'What shall we do if he goes inside?' I said, craning my neck.

'Maybe call her and tell her there's an emergency?'

'Like what?'

'I don't know. You could say you've broken down somewhere and you need her to come and fetch you?'

'Ethan, she doesn't drive.'

The conversation was fruitless because Spencer didn't go inside. He walked my mother to the front door, waited until she'd found her key and let herself in, then kissed her on both cheeks and waved goodbye.

As the Jag roared past, my phone rang. I didn't recognise the number and answered with a cautious, 'Hello.'

It was Spencer. 'Why are you two following me?'

'Why were you creeping around my workshop this afternoon?' I batted back.

He sighed. 'I can explain.'

'I think you'd better.'

We arranged to meet in a nearby pub, The White Lion. It was a dingy place, full of old men with red noses and craggy, weatherbeaten faces and smelt of old chip fat and stale ale. The carpet stuck to the soles of my shoes as I walked toward Spencer, who was tucked away in a gloomy corner.

'Can I get you a drink?' he offered.

'No, but you can tell me what you were doing in my workshop.'

Ethan and I sat down. Spencer looked uneasy.

'Well?' said Ethan. 'Are you going to answer the question?'

Spencer opened his mouth, started speaking, only to falter and say, 'I think I'll just get a pint first. Are you sure I can't get you anything?'

'Delaying tactics,' I muttered as he headed off towards the bar.

He returned with a pint of something dark with a frothy head, took a big gulp leaving a trail of foam on his slug moustache.

I couldn't contain myself. 'I know you've been sneaking around my property. You're not half as clever as you think you are. What is it you're after? Why don't you just come out with it instead of trying to scare me?'

'I have no idea what you're talking about,' he said. 'If I've been a little heavy-handed about things, I apologise. I know I can be a bit of a bulldozer sometimes, but I mean no harm, none at all. I know how close you are to your mother. The last thing I want to do is come between you.'

I could smell garlic on his breath. 'Spencer, I'm not here to discuss your relationship with my mother. I want to know why you've been sneaking around my premises.'

Spencer looked both guilty and pained. 'I promised Mary I'd keep it quiet.'

'Keep what quiet?'

'It was her idea, you see?'

'No, I don't see. What was?'

He took another gulp of his ale. 'She's going to kill me for telling you. She wants it to be a big surprise.'

He shuffled in his seat. The table wobbled, slopping sticky liquid down the side of his glass. 'I was measuring up,' he revealed, 'for some new shelving and display units. Your mother's got it into her head that she wants to revamp the shop, but she knows you can't afford it. She told me this afternoon and I said I'd get some of my lads to do it as a favour, for your mother, of course.' He glowered over his pint. 'She lent me her key while she was getting her hair done. I went over and had a quick scoot around to get a better feel for the place and take some measurements. I didn't realise you'd seen me otherwise I'd have asked your mother to tell you what was going on. I know how protective you are about your workshop.'

Next to me, Ethan relaxed and sat back, obviously believing the yarn Spencer was spinning. I wasn't sure what to think. It tied up with the conversation I'd had with my mother, but what about the serial intruder in my cottage and the message on my mirror?

'Was your criminal record for breaking and entering?' I said.

'Jen –' Ethan put a warning hand over mine.

Spencer flinched. 'No, it was for dealing in stolen goods.'

'And does Mum know about it?'

He looked embarrassed. 'It was a long time ago. We all make mistakes. We all do things we're not proud of, or come to regret.'

I made myself ignore this point.

'Does my mother know you've got a criminal record?' I said again.

'Yes and no. She doesn't know the details, but I have told her that I got in a spot of bother with the law a long time ago, when I was young, stupid and arrogant.

I did a year inside and it taught me a lesson. I've been clean as a whistle ever since.'

'What about my mirror?'

'Sorry – you've lost me again.'

'Stop playing games, Spencer, that's what you told me wasn't it? And now here you are doing exactly that.'

Heads at the bar turned in our direction.

Spencer went puce, but unlike me, remained composed. 'Jennifer, you're not making sense. I'm not playing games. I've no intention of playing games. Has your mother put you up to this? Does she think I'm playing games? Is that what this is all about, because you can tell her that I'm serious, deadly serious.'

'Serious about what?' I hissed.

'Serious about her, of course. What else?' There was a pause. We eyeballed each other until Spencer said, 'I realise you're not my number one fan – you make that perfectly clear every time we meet – and I know you were very close to your father. Obviously you're going to have strong feelings about your mother getting involved with someone else, that's perfectly understandable, but you haven't really given me a chance, have you? Not from the moment we met. Now, I don't expect you to like me, but I would, for the sake of your mother, who I care for a great deal, like to think that we can at least rub along together.'

I didn't know what to say. Uncertainty crept up on me. Spencer seemed to have genuine feelings for my mother and a plausible excuse for being in my workshop. He'd also not mentioned anything about the number, even though he'd had a clear opportunity to do so.

*But then again, he has admitted he's got a dodgy past.*

'And another thing,' I accused, 'why did you say

Oliver Harper can't be trusted when you're such big pals with him?' Spencer's puce face turned deep crimson. 'I saw the two of you having a very cosy lunch together. It looked like you had a lot to talk about.'

'It was a business meeting,' he said, staring into his ale.

'I see. So, you do business with someone who doesn't always do things legally? That's what you told me, wasn't it? A man who you led me to believe was responsible for my smashed shop window?' Spencer's mouth opened and closed, but no sound came out. 'Well?'

He looked sheepish. 'I was just trying to find out why he wants your shop so badly.'

'That's none of your business,' I snapped. 'It's between me and Oliver.'

'But I was worried. I know how difficult he can be, so I met him to find out what he was up to and to warn him off.'

'Warn him off what?'

'Warn him off harassing you. I was right, you see. He, or one of his minions, did smash your window. He virtually admitted it.'

Ethan raised his eyebrows. 'Are you sure?'

Spencer nodded.

'Why would he do that?' I said.

'Because in snubbing his offer, you snubbed him.'

'But why does he want the shop so much?'

Spencer shook his head. 'He wouldn't say. Played his cards close to his chest. Anyway, I had a word with him, told him you meant what you said and that there was no chance of changing your mind. I made sure he knows how stubborn you are.'

Because Spencer actually appeared to be trying to

help me I let his dig slide.

'Hopefully there'll be no more smashed windows, or anything else.' He swallowed another glug of ale. 'And before you get all uppity about me sticking my oar in, I did it for your mother, not you. I don't want her mixed up in anything funny and I'm making it my business to watch out for her.'

'Thanks, that's really kind,' said Ethan trying to lighten the atmosphere.

'Don't worry about it. Now, about the shop revamp, can we keep it a secret from Mary? I mean, obviously she knows about it – it's her idea. What I mean is can we keep it quiet that you've found out? She wants it to be a big surprise. It wouldn't do any harm to indulge her a little, would it?'

'I suppose not,' agreed Ethan on my behalf.

Spencer relaxed. 'She's had some great ideas. She's got a real eye for interior design. And I've got a young lad who's a superb little chippy. He'll do most of the work. And I know a chap in the shop fitting trade, in Barnet. I've already asked him to ear mark me a couple of display units. All kosher of course, but they'll be second-hand, not that you'll be able to tell. The stuff people throw away these days, it's disgraceful.'

Ethan stifled a yawn. 'We'd better make a move. I've got to be up early. Thanks for your time and sorry about the confusion.'

'No harm done,' said Spencer. He put down his unfinished pint and put on his blazer. 'I'm glad we've ironed a few things out. The only bit I'm not sure about is this mirror you mentioned, Jennifer. I didn't quite get that. Is it something you want incorporated in to the shop design? I could try and persuade your mother to add one and let her think it was her idea?'

'Oh, don't worry about it,' I said. 'Give her a free rein,' then added, 'but don't let her paint it pink – anything but pink.'

Ethan and I returned to the Jeep and drove off in silence. Turning into Brook Street he parked up and killed the engine.

'Well, that's that,' he said, shrugging. 'Spencer's in the clear.'

I said nothing and stared straight ahead, into darkness.

'You do believe him, don't you?' Ethan pressed. 'He doesn't know anything about the message. What he said stacks up.'

'Oh, it stacks up,' I said. 'That's the problem.'

'I don't see why it's a problem. We've just saved your bacon. Imagine if you had gone to the police. Your mum would have gone spare.'

Through a clenched jaw I said, 'It's a problem, Ethan, because if Spencer didn't break into my house, it means someone else did. And I have no idea who.'

<h1 style="text-align:center">20</h1>

My mother was in fine fettle, humming to herself as she whipped round the shelves with her feather duster, teetering on what looked like another new pair of heels. She'd abandoned her sensible flats after the second date with Spencer.

'Morning,' she trilled as I arrived at the shop. 'Cuppa tea?'

'Actually, I'd prefer coffee today. Black, two sugars please.'

'Are you sure?' my mother said. 'You don't usually drink coffee.'

'I didn't sleep well again last night. I could do with a caffeine shot to pick me up.'

'You do look a bit peaky,' she concurred. 'I hope you're not coming down with something. Perhaps you should try a drop of lavender oil on your pillow. It works a treat. I slept like a log, but then I was quite tired after my night on the town.'

There was an expectant pause.

'Ah, of course – the theatre. Did you have a nice time?' I said dutifully.

She didn't need to utter a word. The beam that burst across my mother's face told me everything I needed to know. But true to form she gabbled on about how fabulous the production had been and gave a detailed critique of the plot, getting in a pickle with some of the character names, the most hilarious being Don Pedro, who she referred to as Dom Perignon.

'I might try and convince Spencer to take me to Sicily,' she said, misty eyed. 'It sounds beautiful.'

'I'm sure all you'd have to do is ask and your wish will be his command,' I said, half listening as I tapped out a reply to an email.

'You think so? It would be a bit serious though, wouldn't it? I mean, going on holiday with a man. Some people might think it … inappropriate?'

I wasn't sure if she was testing the water with me, or merely running it past herself.

She motored on. 'I suppose because people know Spencer's such a gentleman they'll realise it's all above board and there's no funny business going on. He has got impeccable manners and taste, you know.'

She'd ended on a note too good to miss.

'Did he take you somewhere nice for dinner?'

My mother didn't miss a beat. 'Oh yes.' She stood up and headed to the shop, talking as she walked. 'I had lamb. Delicious. Although a tad heavy on the garlic.' Talking loudly through the open doorway she said, 'We stopped off on the way home for a quick tipple with some of Spencer's friends – the Dove-Wintertons. Lovely couple. Massive pile they've got near Haven Woods – absolutely stunning. We didn't stay long. It was quite late, but they invited us over for Sunday lunch. She, Veronica, was very thin, with big hair – extensions I think. I can't imagine her tucking into a roast dinner. Perhaps she's into nouveau cuisine?'

'*Nouvelle* cuisine,' I corrected.

My mother looked blank. 'He, Laurence, on the other hand, was quite portly and balding. I think he's a bit older than she. Both completely lovely. And wealthy. Super-wealthy. Spencer said they made their money in components. I'm not quite sure what that is and didn't like to ask. Something to do with rubber hoses, I believe. Who'd have thought there'd be millions in rubber hoses?'

My embarrassment at my mother's blatant social

climbing was lessened by the relief that she hadn't been cavorting in the back of a Jaguar at the side of the road after all. For once her constant babble was a source of comfort rather than irritation, as she kept my mind occupied with Shakespearean trivia and a debate on Sicily versus Corsica as her and Spencer's first holiday destination. But I did feel on edge when she hurried off just before midday to beat the queue at the baker's, leaving me alone for a few minutes. The shop seemed a little eerie, and gave off creaks and groans I'd never noticed before. I perched on the stool behind the counter, eyes fixed on the door and hand on my phone ready to call Ethan at the first sign of trouble. But nothing out of the ordinary happened. Traffic droned past. Shoppers strolled by, but no one came in. It did occur to me that I might be putting potential customers off with my mistrustful stare. Arranging a smile, I tried to look relaxed and friendly. I couldn't afford to let business slip.

Bored, I started poking around the bits and bobs my mother stored under the counter and came across a paint colour chart stuffed inside a magazine. A syrupy, sorbet pink was circled in blue biro. Heeding my promise to Spencer, I resisted the urge to ring my preferred choice of smooth mocha and light oyster. Instead, I made a mental note to ask him to steer her towards more sophisticated neutral tones.

Now that my mother's background noise had disappeared, I couldn't help but fill the void with a mixed bag of thoughts. A nagging remorse about Robert Ashmere lingered in the background while I contemplated the fact that I now had no reason to be unfriendly towards Spencer. Then my mind came to Oliver Harper. The more I mulled him over, the more convinced I was that he must be my intruder. But why he was trying to scare me, or would go to such lengths to leave a cryptic message, was beyond me.

My phone rang. I looked at the screen and smiled. Ethan.

'How's it going?' His voice was an instant pick-me-up, and much more effective than the watery, sugary coffee my mother had been making me all morning.

'Fine. Mum's popped out to get some lunch, so I'm watching the shop, but it's all quiet.'

'Good. That's good.' He sounded relieved. 'Lisa's been on at me about going back to the police.'

'To tell them what? We can't prove anything.'

'I know, I know.' His voice was infused with frustration.

'I've been thinking,' I said. 'It must be something to do with Oliver Harper. I can't think of anyone else I've upset. And he seems really keen to get his hands on my shop. I know Spencer said he'd warned him off, but …'

'I've been wondering about him too. Shall I have a word? See what he's got to say?'

'No. I think we should wait for him to come to us. If he's half as much trouble as Spencer says then it might be best to play along with his stupid mind game.' Ethan gave a short huff, but didn't argue. I added, 'He doesn't strike me as particularly patient. He'll be in touch soon.'

'That's what I'm afraid of.'

With false bravado, I said, 'He's just a spoilt brat who's thrown his toys out of his pram because he can't have his own way.'

'It's the sort of toys he plays with that bothers me,' Ethan replied. 'Have you got your personal alarm with you?'

'In my bag,' I said. 'Oh, Mum's back, gotta go, catch you later …'

My mother came bustling in, clutching two brown paper bags. One was for me and contained a prawn mayo sandwich. I didn't have an appetite and hid it at the bottom of the waste paper basket, so she wouldn't see and ask awkward questions.

I hoped Spencer had the sense not to discuss the ominous Oliver Harper with her. She was still annoyed that I'd refused his offer without consulting her, conveniently forgetting that I was the one who actually owned the business. I didn't want her getting drawn in to any more of Oliver's dirty tricks.

Spencer certainly seemed keen. He popped in just as my mother sat down to eat her lunch. She pushed the slice of quiche to one side, dabbed her mouth with a paper napkin and made a real song and dance about his arrival. Unusually though, this time it was me he came to see, but he was polite enough not to let on to my mother.

'Is Jennifer around?' I heard him enquire.

'Yes, out the back, beavering away. No rest for the wicked. Now, sit down and I'll make you a nice cuppa.'

'How about I make you one for a change?' Spencer suggested.

I could hear my mother resisting and Spencer insisting and wondered who would win. Spencer eventually came into the workshop looking shell-shocked.

'She's a tough negotiator, that mother of yours,' he said, mopping his brow with a large, yellow silk handkerchief. 'We need to talk.' He gestured towards the kitchen.

It wasn't the best timing. I was in the middle of melting wax, but, intrigued, I wiped my hands on my apron and followed him.

Spencer looked very much at home in the galley kitchen as he filled the kettle. He knew exactly which cupboard to open for the cups and which drawer for the spoons. Over the sound of gushing water he said, 'I know why Oliver wants your shop.' There was a maddening pause as he located three Earl Grey teabags and stuffed them into the teapot. 'Actually, it's not him who wants it – it's his wife.'

*His wife? Do I know her?*

I vaguely remembered Oliver mentioning he was recently married.

'Basically, after six months of marriage she's bored playing second fiddle to her husband and living out in the sticks. She's got some silly notion in her head that she's going to build her own business empire, just like Oliver. The girl's bonkers – mad as a March hare. She's never earned a penny in her life – Daddy always took care of her. But according to my source, she's convinced she's going to be the next Jo Malone. Oliver's been looking for a business she can build up. The bad news for you is that JJ Candles is it.'

I gave an indignant huff.

Spencer poured hot water over the teabags. 'Someone told him about your shop winning an award. He did a bit of investigating, came in and bought some samples, and, well, you've become a victim of your own success. I'm told that Pandora – that's his wife – loved them. She's come over all serious about her venture into the world of business and has asked Oliver to buy your shop for her twenty-fifth birthday, which is next month.'

'Tough. I'm not selling. They'll have to look for something else.'

'And there lies the problem. Pandora's set her sights on it and Oliver won't want to lose face. In fact, he can be a bit like that little dog of yours: a real terrier. Once his teeth are stuck in he won't let go. And I've already told you his game plans aren't very sporting – smashing shop windows for instance.'

'How did you find out?'

'I have ways and means,' replied Spencer ambiguously, vigorously squishing the teabags with the back of a spoon. 'All above board though,' he was quick to add. 'Although to be completely upfront, a small bribe was involved.'

I raised an eyebrow.

He looked embarrassed. 'Nothing to worry about, just a couple of phone calls, and favours called in. You know the sort of thing … '

The conversation was interrupted by my mother, who, fed up with being left on her own, had tracked us down. 'How long, and how many people does it take to make a pot of tea?' She immediately took over. Sniffing the contents of the teapot, she pulled a face. 'Ergh! Stewed. You see, Spencer, you should have let me make it. Go on, the both of you, get out of my kitchen. I'll make a fresh pot.'

Spencer and I continued the conversation about Pandora Harper back at my desk.

'She can't seriously think she can snap her fingers and JJ's will magically appear, or that she can swan in – with no experience or training – take over and build it into some sort of global empire. There's a hell of a lot involved in candle making.' I saw Spencer glance at the pots, pans and moulds haphazardly placed on various work surfaces. 'It might not look much to the untrained eye, but I've been practising for years and I'm still learning. It's not the sort of thing you can do on a whim.'

'It is if you're stinking rich,' said Spencer. 'Oh, there's no doubt about it – she'll get bored soon enough. Oliver will end up putting in a manager to run it, or he'll sell it on again. It's easy when you've got deep, well-lined, well-tailored pockets.'

'Well, I believe in more traditional values, like ambition and hard graft. And please can you stop talking as though it's a done deal that they'll get their dirty hands on my business.'

My mother came through carrying a tea tray, delighted to find us engaged in conversation for a change, instead of the awkward silence that often descended when Spencer and I were thrust together.

'There now, Spencer, I said you should drop by more often. Jennifer doesn't mind, do you love?' she said. The shop doorbell jangled. She put down the tray and scurried out to a cry of, 'Hello Izzy – perfect timing. I've just made a brew. Come through and I'll fetch another cup.'

Izzy wandered in, peering suspiciously at Spencer. I realised I'd forgotten to tell her that he was in the clear.

'It's okay,' I mouthed.

Quick as a flash Izzy said, as my mother returned, 'Mary, do excuse me for a moment, I just need to powder my nose. Jennifer, would you mind showing me to the lav?'

Away from prying ears, I told Izzy about my mother's grand decoration plan and Spencer's involvement.

'I'm still not sure about him,' Izzy hissed back. 'What about his criminal record? Did you ask about that?'

'He said it was for handling stolen goods when he was younger. Apparently he has told Mum about it – not the exact details – but that he did something he regrets.'

'And what about his bosom buddy – Oliver Harper?'

'They're not buddies. Spencer was trying to find out why he wants my shop, and to warn him off.'

'That's big of him,' she sniffed.

'Not really. He made it clear he was doing it for Mum and not me.'

'At least the man has some balls,' she said, marginally impressed. 'And did he find out?'

'What?'

'Why Oliver wants your shop.'

'That's why he's here now. He's just been explaining. Apparently, it's for his wife.' I quickly filled her in.

'The woman sounds cuckoo,' she said. 'But at least that's filled in one of the blanks. And I may have another piece of the puzzle.' Izzy rummaged inside her beaded handbag. 'Blast, where is it? Don't tell me I've left it at home after all this. Ah ha! Here we are … ' She pulled out a slip of paper and pressed it into my palm. 'It's Digby's code,' she said, sporting a triumphant smile. 'I think I've cracked it.'

21

'Izzy's worked out the code,' I told Ethan. A sharp inhalation resonated through the earpiece of my phone. 'Well, not all of it, but she says the first part could be an address in London.'

'London? Why does she think that?'

'Part of the number looks like a postcode – E1 JP2. She's checked it out on the Royal Mail website. It comes up as Bennett Street in East London. It could be Nine Bennett Street – 9E1JP2.'

'What about the rest of it?'

'She's working on it.'

Ethan was dubious. 'Bit of a long shot.'

'At least she's come up with something. We didn't. And she's really good with puzzles.'

He gave a small grunt, which I took as agreement. 'Who lives there?'

'Hang on, I'll put you on loudspeaker and you can ask her yourself.'

Izzy and I had retreated outside and were standing by the back door away from my mother and Spencer. I fiddled with the buttons on my phone until we both could hear. Ethan repeated the question.

'No one. It's a business address,' she said. 'On the Internet it comes up as Aldgate Secretarial Services. Sounds dodgy, if you ask me.'

The lack of fact meant that Ethan was difficult to convince. 'Why would part of the code be an address?'

'Why not?' Izzy slung back.

'Seems like a long shot,' he said again.

Izzy gave an exasperated tut. 'Ethan, I've been up half the night trying to figure this out. Those wretched numbers have been doing cartwheels around my brain.

I've turned them about, chopped them up, and searched and searched for a pattern until I got eye strain, but nothing else sprang out. And,' she added confidently, 'the fact that there is a postcode that collates and a building at number nine suggests to me it's actually a rather good shot. And besides, I know we're onto something important – I can feel it in my waters.'

'I think we should check it out,' I said, my feet itching, ready to go. 'We haven't got anything else to go on. If we leave now we could be there in a couple of hours. It'd be better than sitting around here wondering if it means something or not.'

Ethan immediately quashed my zeal. 'Jen, I've back-to-back appointments all afternoon. I've got people and pets relying on me. I can't just drop everything and go traipsing off to London. And I don't think it's a good idea for you to go on your own. You don't know what you're going to find when you get there.'

'Ethan, it's a secretarial services company, not an opium den. I'll just have a look, ask some questions and see if it's relevant.'

Ethan was having none of it. 'I've got to go. I'm already running late. We'll have to talk about it again later.'

'All right,' I sulked. 'Bye.'

'That went well,' Izzy said, as I hung up.

'He's so bloody pompous sometimes.'

She smiled. 'None of us is perfect. Besides, it's only because he cares. It's nice having someone looking out for you. My Archie was good like that. Ethan really does remind me of him sometimes.' She gave a little nostalgic sigh. 'Right then, when's the next train?'

Just in case she was going a bit deaf and batty in

her old age, I said, 'Ethan doesn't want me to go, remember?'

'I know perfectly well what Ethan said. He didn't say you shouldn't go. He said that you shouldn't go on your own, which you won't be, because I'm coming too. Do you think your mother will mind if you take the rest of the afternoon off?'

Forty minutes later, Izzy and I were seated on a train en route to London Marylebone having coerced my mother into watching the shop and dog-sitting Digby again.

'It's a surprise,' I'd said when she'd asked what I was up to. 'I'll tell you later.' We'd hurried out before she could object, or delve deeper.

On the seat opposite, Izzy chatted away to herself while I worried what Ethan would say when he found out we'd gone without him. Technically Izzy was right about what he'd said, but I knew he'd be cross.

*Too late.*

I buried the thought at the back of my mind.

Arriving at Marylebone, we stopped off at a newsagent to buy a mini London A-Z map. Bennett Street was around five miles away, just off Commercial Road between Aldgate and Stepney Green. Worried about Izzy's advanced years, I headed for the taxi rank, but she insisted on using the Underground.

'It'll be quicker,' she said. 'And I love people watching. You get all sorts on the tube. Come on, it'll be fun.'

Izzy hopped on the escalator. I followed suit. At the bottom, she took charge, supporting my arm and directing me into a departing tube train. Thankfully, it wasn't rush hour and there were plenty of spare seats. We changed at the next stop – Baker Street – and took a

rickety Hammersmith and City line train all the way to
Whitechapel, where we disembarked.

'Are you sure you're okay to walk?' I said. 'It
could be a good ten minutes or so from here.'

'Course I am. Stop treating me like I'm infirm.
Now then, it's this way, I think.' Izzy strode off. I trailed
along behind trying both to walk and follow the map.

Bennett Street wasn't as far as I'd thought. After a
few twists and turns we found it, a scruffy place with a
mix of structures: mostly old warehouses and Victorian
builds that had been carved into offices and apartments.
A large, ugly 1960s purpose-built council flat complex
dominated the street. Washing hung on balconies and
industrial-size refuse bins lined the kerb beneath. The
stench of festering rubbish littered the air. We walked
past holding our noses.

Number nine was situated in a row of Dickensian
town houses. Grime concealed crumbling brickwork.
Black paint peeled from rotting sash windows. The only
smart thing about it was the shiny steel intercom plate
fastened by the front door, displaying the name, Aldgate
Secretarial Services.

'What now?' I said as we loitered outside.

The lines on Izzy's face deepened as she
contemplated the next course of action. 'As I see it
we've got two choices. We can either buzz and see if
they'll let us in, or we can go and sit in that dingy
looking greasy spoon over there and watch for a bit –
see who comes and goes.'

My earlier gusto had diminished the closer we'd
got to our destination. I readily opted for her latter
suggestion. We crossed the road and entered the cafe.
The place shrieked 'fried food' the moment I grasped
the sticky door handle. The unappetising aroma of stale

oil coated the inside of my nostrils and a thin veil of grease hung in the air. We took up a table by the window. A sweaty-faced man with a stained tea towel slung over one shoulder came out. He grunted disapprovingly at our meagre order of two cups of tea. I was now feeling a bit peckish, having discarded my prawn sandwich earlier, but the crusty debris stuck to the plastic tablecloth, along with the fatty atmosphere, put me off ordering anything edible.

We sipped at mugs of dark brown tea. Izzy added three heaped teaspoons of sugar to hers to take the edge off the bitterness. In silence, and over the rim of the mugs, we observed number nine Bennett Street, both perking up when the front door opened a few minutes later. A pencil-thin pasty girl with waist-length blue-black hair stepped outside. She tottered a few steps in skyscraper heels, then perched on a low wall. Fumbling inside her handbag, she drew out a packet, lit a cigarette and sucked and puffed hungrily before stubbing out and discarding the dog end within a couple of minutes. Standing up, the girl tottered back inside again.

'She must work there,' I said.

'State the bleedin' obvious,' Izzy replied in a cockney accent. Then, back in her native Home Counties tongue, nodded towards number nine and said, 'Look. Someone else is going in.'

A man clutching a briefcase stood in front of the door, pressed the buzzer, muttered into the intercom, then went inside.

Izzy put her mug down and rose from her Formica chair. 'Right, I'm going in. Wish me luck!'

'You can't,' I said, losing my nerve.

Izzy stuck her nose in the air. 'I can and I am. I've not come all this way to sit in a grotty little cafe and stare at a dirty front door. That girl looked friendly enough. I'll just pop across, ring the buzzer and find out what they do. You stay here. It'll look more suspicious if two of us are asking questions.'

'What are you going to say?' A ribbon of fear returned and tight laced my heart.

'Don't know yet. I'll think of something.' Izzy's blue-violet eyes glittered.

I was deeply unhappy about her going alone, but wasn't sure what I could do or say to stop her – she could be very firm at times, and fierce – so I stayed put. Through the greasy window pane I watched her march over and press the buzzer. A couple of seconds later she bent forward and spoke into the intercom, then turned, gave me a thumbs up and a grin.

She was gone for what seemed like an hour, but which actually proved to be twenty minutes. In the meantime, I ordered another mug of bitter tea, even though I didn't want one. It sat on the table growing cold as I waited for Izzy's silver mane to reappear from number nine. My heart swelled when the door opened, then deflated when the man with the briefcase stepped onto the street. He wandered over to the cafe, sat down at the table next to mine and ordered a bacon and egg butty, which pleased the sweaty cook. A more potent smell of frying fat took up residence.

The man sat in silence, reading a tabloid newspaper. The cook appeared, proudly delivering the sandwich to the table with all the pizzazz of a celebrity chef serving royalty, giving a satisfied smile and nod as his customer added a mountain of ketchup before tucking in. I inspected the man out of the corner of my eye as he munched on his snack and pored over the headlines. He didn't appear to be anything out of the ordinary, just someone going about his daily business and stopping off for a bite to eat. Eggy sauce dripped down his patterned tie. If I'd have been Izzy, I'd have had the guts to strike up a conversation and steer him on to number nine, but I wasn't and so didn't.

The minutes ticked by slowly. Still there was no sign of my neighbour. I debated going over, but worried I might ruin whatever plan had sprung to her inventive mind. I decided to give her a ten-minute deadline, at which point I would definitely go across and ring the buzzer.

Gazing out of the greasy window, eyes trained on the Victorian townhouse, I became aware of a peculiar feeling taking hold. It started with a warning tingle trickling down my spine, rapidly followed by a strong sense that someone was watching me. My attention switched to a youngish man of medium height and build standing on the opposite side of the road. I caught his eye. He turned and walked off, but not before I'd seen enough of him to think he looked familiar. As he passed number nine, Izzy rushed out, crossed his path and hurried over to the cafe. She was clutching a leaflet, holding it up like an Olympic torch.

'Bingo! This is definitely it,' she said breathlessly, plonking herself down. 'I knew we were in the right place.' She pushed the leaflet across the table.

I scanned the text. It told me that Aldgate Secretarial Services provided a wide range of business support including word processing and typing, audio transcription and telephone answering.

Izzy jabbed an earthy forefinger at a specific paragraph. 'This is what we're interested in – the mail handling services. You can use their address and have your mail sent to them and they manage it for you: you know, send it on, redirect it, or they simply keep it in a secure mailbox until you want to come and collect it.'

'Like a P.O Box you mean?' I said.

'Same principle. I found out all about it. That girl, the one with the Morticia Addams hair, was very friendly, well, bored really. It must be ever so dreary sitting in a reception area sorting mail, answering the phone and staring at the walls and dying pot plants … ' I glared at her. Izzy took the hint. 'I said I was interested to know more about their secretarial services and she took me round the whole building and explained what they do. Upstairs they've got four women who do typing and transcribing, or who go out and be a PA for the day. Then downstairs, where Michelle – that's her name – works is the mailbox section. I said I was interested in hiring a box and she showed me where they keep them. It's a room with rows and rows of steel boxes stacked against the back wall. Michelle sorts the post when it comes in and then pops the mail into the relevant box through a slit in the front. And that's where it stays, safe and sound, until the owner collects it. There's a table and chairs in the middle of the room, so you can sit and view your mail, or whatever it is you keep in the box. It's all very discreet. But here's the interesting part … ' She glanced around for earwiggers and lowered her voice. 'The door into the mailbox area is secured by a combination lock. And guess what?' She didn't wait for me to speculate. 'The number she punched in was the next part of Digby's code.'

I reeled, nearly knocking the mug of cold tea over. 'No way!'

'I kid you not.' Her blue-violet eyes seemed to dance with excitement.

'I don't believe it.'

'It was definitely 1605. I watched her carefully. She's got long painted nails and the key pad is quite small, so she had to take her time.'

I sat back. My mouth was dry. I took a moment to digest the situation and gather my thoughts. Izzy took the same time to relax and catch her breath.

'What about the rest of the code?' I said.

'Don't worry. It all fits. I was thinking about it as Michelle was talking. Heavens, she did go on. Anyway, you type in the security code – 1605 – to get access to the mailbox room. When you're inside, each mailbox has an identifying number, say from 1 – 100. It looked like there could be about 100 boxes or so in there. Now, I think Robert's box is number 35 …'

'Why? What makes you think that?'

'Because that's the next part of the code, dimwit. Do try to keep up.' She shook her head at me. 'Each box has a digital lock with a keypad. You set your own PIN number, just like you do with those little safes you find in hotel rooms. If I'm right then Robert's PIN is 7622, the last part of the code.' She sat back looking very pleased with herself. 'Goodness, I am thirsty after all that detective work.' She caught the sweaty cook's eye and ordered herself another mug of tea.

'What now?' I said, bubbling at the thought that not only did it look like we were on the right path, but actually outside the right building.

'You go in.'

'And say what?'

'Jennifer, it's very simple. I'll give you all the directions so you know where you're going. All you need to do is look business-like and confident. Just walk past the receptionist, through the security door, and find Robert's box. Open it, see what's inside and come back out again. Easy peasy.'

'What if Morticia, I mean Michelle, stops and questions me?'

'Bluff your way in. I know – say you're the new PA to Simon Cummings and you've come to collect his mail.'

'Who's Simon Cummings?'

'I don't know. I just made him up. Use your imagination.'

'What if Michelle says she's never heard of Simon Cummings? Wouldn't it be better to say I'm Robert Ashmere's PA? They must have a record of him.'

'Possibly, but he might not have used his real name. Think about it. He's gone to a lot of trouble to hide this code. I'd be amazed if he used his own name. And if he did,' she added wisely, 'it might be best not to associate with him. We don't know how far the police got on his trail. If they found out about the link to Bennett Street then they'll have been in and searched the place, and Michelle will know Robert's dead. It'll look very suspicious if you march in and say you're collecting mail for a dead man.'

'I don't know,' I said, doubt crawling all over me. 'I'm not as quick at thinking on my feet as you are.'

'Well I can't go back in, can I? Really, Jennifer, all this worrying is needless. If you look like you know what you're doing, Michelle isn't going to challenge you. She'll probably have her head stuck in a trashy gossip magazine, or be surfing the Internet. Just ring the buzzer, say you've come to collect your mail and go in. Walk straight past the reception desk on the left and stop at the second door on the right. Punch in the code – 1605 – and walk in. Find box number 35 and put in the PIN – 7622. Open the box and see what's inside.

Then come back out, thank Michelle, say cheery-bye and leave. Job done.'

My head was buzzing with all the information. I made Izzy jot down her instructions and all the numbers, on a piece of paper.

'And you're positive the code will work?' I said, wondering why on earth I just didn't say no to the whole idea.

Robert's face kept floating around my mind.

'Not positive, but pretty sure.' Izzy wasn't done coaxing. 'The worst that can happen is that box 35 won't open, but at least we'll have tried and had a nice afternoon out to boot. Where's your sense of adventure? Go on – get on with it. I'm dying to know what's inside.'

After all she'd done for me I couldn't refuse. I left the cafe and crossed the road to number nine, clutching Izzy's brief instructions. Despite its shabbily flaking black paint, the Victorian front door had stood the test of time. It towered over me like a giant tombstone. Fizzing with nerves, I turned to the steel intercom plate and pressed the buzzer. There was a crackle, then a female voice with Essex undertones droned:

'Aldgate Secretarial Services, how may I help you?'

Clearing my throat, I said, 'I've come to collect my mail.'

'Push the door,' the voice instructed.

The sound of a mechanical lock whirred behind the front door. I leant against the solid wood and found myself in a small reception area painted in a calming willow-green with an original black-and-white geometric tiled floor. Michelle sat behind a veneered reception desk. She looked up as I entered. Remembering Izzy's advice, I smiled and nodded, then walked straight past to the second door on the right.

My hand shook as I reached up to the keypad and punched in the code. '1.6.0.5.' I mouthed. I pushed my shoulder against the door. It didn't budge. 'Crap.'

Michelle looked up from her computer. 'Do you need any help?' Her voice had a rubbery twang.

'I'm fine, thanks,' I said and tried again, concentrating on steadying my hand.

This time the door opened and I stepped inside. The room matched Izzy's description to a tee. The back wall was lined with rows of small steel containers. I walked past the table and two chairs in the centre of the floor, and looked up at the metal wall. The boxes were set out in numerical order, just as she'd said. Scanning the numbers, I located box 35 on the fifth row. I glanced at the piece of paper in my hand to remind myself of the final four digits of Digby's code, then, holding my breath, carefully punched them in to the keypad.

It bleeped.

I pulled on the small round handle.

Inside were two A4-sized envelopes, one brown and hardback, the other white and padded. I drew both packages out and shut the door. My new handbag was small and slouchy and unable to conceal my newly acquired processions. I had to walk out with the envelopes tucked under my arm. Michelle looked up again as I passed, but said nothing. Her uninterested eyes slipped back to the computer screen and glazed over. Awash with relief, I sped over to the cafe. Izzy was almost beside herself when she saw my find.

'What's in them?' she squawked.

'I don't know. I haven't opened them yet.'

The cafe was empty. The briefcase man had departed and the sweaty cook was holed up in his oily kitchen. I took up the white envelope. It was unaddressed, as was the brown one.

'Robert must have stored them in the box himself,' Izzy speculated.

The thought of handling something Robert Ashmere had touched gave me the jitters. I pulled open the seal and peered inside.

'What is it?' demanded Izzy, leaning across the table and putting on her half-spectacles.

'Money,' I whispered. 'Quite a lot of it.'

'And the other one?'

I opened the board backed envelope. 'I think it's a photo.' I pulled the contents out with my fingertips. There were two images. I lay them on the table. Izzy moved chairs and sat next to me. We stared in shocked silence.

Izzy spoke first. 'Oh, Lord. That really is sickening. Very sickening indeed.'

I was too upset to say anything. The photos were like something out of a horror film, only they were clearly fact and not fiction. Two bull terrier-type dogs were locked together in a frenzied attack, both savaged and bloodied. In the first shot, the dogs were twisting up in the air, jaws on jaws. Flecks of blood flew from puncture wounds. In the other, terror flared in the eyes of one of the dogs as the other ripped into its stomach. The floor was drenched with blood. Most disturbing was the look of rapture projected from the faces of the group of men encasing the dogs in a semi-circle, as they goaded and egged them on. It was truly brutal, horrific and barbaric.

Touching such vile images sullied me deeply. The

fact they were very likely taken by Robert Ashmere increased my revulsion tenfold. From the moment I'd crossed his path the man had brought me nothing but unwanted stress and pain. Bile rose in my throat. I shoved the photos back in the envelope and escaped to the bathroom where I scrubbed my hands with soap and hot water. Feeling suitably cleansed, I returned to the table and found Izzy studying the photos again. She looked up. A strange expression had grasped her face – a mix of shock, fear and loathing. It sucked the vibrancy out of her.

'I noticed something. Something quite unbelievable,' she said quietly. 'Look at them. Look at the men.'

I did as she said. The bile in my throat returned when my eyes came to rest on two of the leering faces. Faces I knew. The first was the man who'd been watching me earlier on Bennett Street. He bore a striking resemblance to the older man he was pictured standing next to, a man I also knew, but couldn't believe was at such a scene.

Detective Inspector Pitts.

**22**

I rapidly explained to Izzy that the man standing next to the police detective in the photo had been staring at me, here, only a short time ago.

'They look quite similar, don't they?' she said. 'Definitely a family resemblance, I'd say. Oh dear. This has got rather serious, hasn't it?' Izzy slipped the photos into their envelope. 'Time to make a move.'

We hurried out of the cafe and made our way towards Commercial Road where I insisted on hailing a taxi, paranoid that we were being followed, even though there was no sign of the staring man. Even in the locked safety of a black cab I couldn't relax, and scoured the faces in passing foot crowds and vehicles.

Izzy had a vacant look.

'What are you thinking?' I said, jabbing her with my elbow.

'That we should call the police,' she said, eyes half closed.

'He is the police,' I said.

We sat in silence for the rest of the taxi journey.

It was rush hour. Long lines of people poured in and out of Marylebone Station. We sat on a bench on the platform waiting for the train, me panning the crowd for the staring man, Izzy clutching her beaded bag and its shocking contents firmly to her hip, in deep contemplation. Once on the train, she decided we should sit in First Class.

'It'll be more private,' she said.

While I vexed over the fact that we hadn't upgraded our tickets, Izzy steered me into the empty coach.

'Blackmail,' she said, sitting down and twirling a

forefinger through a loose strand of silvery hair. 'It's all about blackmail. Robert must have taken the photographs. You've got to hand it to him, it's perfect blackmail material: a respectable, highly regarded police detective taking part in an illegal dog fight, a man with a reputation, a hell of a lot to lose, and probably enough money in the bank to pay for Robert's silence.'

'But how did Robert know he's a policeman? He must have known Pitts somehow.'

'Yes … yes, he must … ' Izzy agreed. ' … I wonder how… ' She turned and stared out of the window, then said to her own reflection, 'It's all starting to make sense.'

I was still so shocked by the discovery that my brain was struggling to compute, but Izzy's was busily knitting everything together.

'Detective Inspector Pitts is your intruder,' she enlightened, 'which explains why no sign of anyone was ever found in your house. His fingerprints would have been eliminated because he was part of the police investigation team. God, what a conniving fox. And to think I was taken in. I even offered him a piece of home-baked Victoria sponge when he interviewed me. And a cup of Darjeeling. I should have reused an old teabag from the compost.'

'I'm not with you,' I said, willing my head to catch up and jump to the same page.

'He's clever, Jennifer – very clever. But not clever enough to cover his tracks completely.' She nodded to herself.

I must have looked as blank as I felt, because Izzy prompted, 'The evidence he left behind – his odour trail.'

'The cigarette smell? But I've never seen him

smoke.'

'Sucks an awful lot of mints though, doesn't he?' she said. 'And he's very heavy with the aftershave. Both are dead give-aways. People who secretly smoke often suck mints, or chew gum, and go over the top with their perfume to hide the fumes.' She looked at me pityingly. 'And I'm afraid to say that you inadvertently helped him carry out his devious actions.'

'I did?'

'Yes, you did. You see, the first time he broke into Corner Cottage – no doubt using the keys from your conveniently stolen handbag – he had a good snoop round, but failed to find what he was looking for – these photos. Then, when you came home and realised someone had been inside, you called *him* and told him your suspicions. He probably couldn't believe his luck, because this gave him a very good and timely excuse to visit you on police business and enter your property again, thus providing a perfectly legitimate reason why his own fingerprints and DNA were all over the place when your house was searched officially later that day. That's why there wasn't any trace of a stranger. It wasn't a stranger at all. It was someone you knew and trusted.'

I took my mind back to the day of the first break-in. I remembered the detective following me round every room as I checked if anything was missing. I also thought about the photocopier that had been left switched on and wondered why the policeman had tampered with it.

Izzy was gripped by the shady dealings and gory discovery. 'I do love Eureka moments!' she said with gusto. Finding her stride – a steady canter – she went on. 'Think about it – the second time he broke in he was even more devious. He left the message on your mirror to try and scare you into revealing whether you knew about *the number*, or code, as we now know it to be. By then, he was probably pretty confident that if you did contact the police, you'd ring him again, which is exactly what you did.'

I groaned. 'I left him a message saying I was staying at Ethan's. So he knew the coast was clear and could go back and clean off his artwork.'

'He must be pretty desperate to get his hands on those photographs,' Izzy said. 'They'll ruin his career. I wonder what he's up to right now.' Her remark shut us both up until Izzy said, 'He must have had something to do with Robert's murder.'

I stiffened. 'Detective Inspector Pitts? What about Nick Low? His fingerprints were on the body and he'd stolen Robert's cash. And he admitted being on the footpath that night.'

'I know. But didn't you say Nick claimed Robert was already lying on the ground when he came across him? That he thought he was passed out drunk? What if he was telling the truth? What if someone else – Detective Inspector Pitts and his sidekick – killed Robert and let Nick conveniently take the blame? There's always been a question mark around how many people were out on the footpath that night. You seemed pretty convinced that you overheard at least three voices …'

'… but Pitts insisted I was wrong.'

Izzy sat bolt upright. More strands of silvery hair escaped the clutches of her tortoiseshell clip. 'But,' she said, the pace of her narration now back to a crawl, 'if he wanted the photographs that badly, and he didn't know where they were, why kill Robert? Why kill the source? That, Jennifer, may be the point that scuppers my theory.'

'Perhaps Robert refused to hand them over and that's why they started fighting,' I said, the sounds of that awful night swimming round my head again.

*Angry voices.*

*A piercing scream.*

*The crack of a skull against wood.*

'Yes! And maybe he thought that getting rid of Robert would be the best way to get rid of the photos? My word, there's a lot involved,' Izzy murmured, rubbing her eyes then closing them.

I thought she'd fallen asleep, but a few minutes later, having allowed herself a little time to recharge, she burst back to life, blue-violet eyes large and luminous, gleaming like Ceylon sapphires in a ring of brilliant diamond white.

'Right, I've got the hang of it now,' she said. 'Here goes … Robert takes the photographs of Detective Inspector Pitts at an illegal dog fight. He keeps the evidence locked away at Aldgate Secretarial Services and stores a reminder of all the security codes needed to access the photos somewhere even a good detective wouldn't think of looking – in his dog's microchip. Meanwhile, his wife, Erica, decides she's had enough of him and leaves, taking the dog with her. Robert goes off the rails and starts drinking. Perhaps he runs out of money and decides now is the time to blackmail the policeman? Anyway, he pays Erica a visit to see the dog and access the code, but Erica has re-homed the dog without telling him. When he finds out, Robert goes up like a rocket, screaming at her that he needs *the number.* Erica, quite logically, gives him the address and number for the re-homing centre. Robert immediately makes his way there and demands they tell him where the dog is.

When they refuse, he breaks into their office, gets hold of your details, then comes to Ridgelow and susses out your house. He discovers the footpath and the fact you have a gate opening on to it.' Izzy paused for a moment. 'This is where it gets a little sketchy in places,' she excused herself. 'Let's assume that Robert decides to hang around on the footpath in the dark, with a plan to steal Digby. Now, let's also assume that Detective Inspector Pitts and his dog-fighting accomplice are there too. They have an argument that turns into a fight and Robert ends up dead. We know that bit, because you, Jennifer, were sitting in the bath listening to all the commotion, and downstairs Digby, who must have recognised Robert's voice, was barking like a loony. Later that night, if we go along with Nick Low's version of events, he's also out on the footpath and comes across Robert lying in the bushes. Being stupid, drunk, and an opportunistic slimeball, he steals the wallet and phone, thus leaving evidence linking him to the body. The next morning, Detective Inspector Pitts is out on the footpath again, this time in his official capacity investigating the suspicious death. He discovers the note with your name and address on it in Robert's pocket and wonders how you knew him. More importantly, he wonders how much you know about his sick, illegal pastime, and also if *you* have the photographs.' Izzy stopped to catch her breath before cantering on. 'He questions and questions you, over and over again, trying to find out exactly what you know. You tell him nothing, because you don't know anything, but he thinks you're lying. Now, at this point, he's in a very tricky position. Given the note in Robert's pocket and the proximity of the crime scene to your house, he knows your property will need to be thoroughly examined. He must have tied himself up in knots about this because if, as he suspected, you were safeguarding the photos somewhere in your house for Robert, then they would turn up in the police search. He couldn't let that happen. He's thinking, *I've got to get to them first.* So, he does an unofficial search before the official one, but doesn't find what he's looking for. This must have been very frustrating for him. He wants those photos badly. So, he changes tack and gets heavy-handed, leaving you a threatening message in the hope that it will scare you into revealing the whereabouts of the photos.' Her fingers drummed energetically on the plastic table between us. 'My money's on him being behind Erica's house search too. Unfortunately for her, she was still in it at the time.' She shivered. 'One thing that is clear is that he had no idea Digby was hiding the number, or he'd have just taken the dog.' Her eyes narrowed. 'And given what we've just discovered as his favourite pastime, I think Digby has had a very lucky escape.'

My heart lurched at the thought of my little dog in Pitts' corrupt clutches.

'But,' I said, dwelling on this point, 'that doesn't make sense. How did Pitts know he needed to look for *the number*? How did he know a number existed, that it was linked to the photos, but not that Digby was hiding it?'

Izzy frowned. 'Really, Jennifer, be fair. My brain has been working double overtime trying to figure this out. I can't be expected to have the answer to everything.' She turned and gazed at the lush Chilterns countryside rolling past then murmured, 'But writing that message on your mirror was a big mistake, a very big mistake indeed.'

'Go on,' I said, wondering what further revelation

her athletic mind had unearthed.

'Well, if he hadn't drawn your attention to the importance of *the number*,' she said, wiggling her forefingers in an air quote, 'Digby's strange microchip would have seemed pretty unremarkable and probably would have gone unnoticed, just a microchip injected in the wrong place. As it was, Detective Inspector Pitts' lipstick handiwork sparked Ethan's mind and got him thinking, which in turn led to you sharing the code, me cracking it, us hopping on the train and sussing out Bennett Street, you raiding Robert's mailbox and the both of us discovering a humdinger of a secret.' A serious looked flooded her face. 'When Detective Inspector Pitts broke into your house and wrote that message, Jennifer, he had no idea he was hammering nails into his own career coffin. Those words are about to come back and bite him on the bum.'

As the train slowed on its approach to Ridgelow station, I stewed on her theory and my deep misfortune in getting caught up in the murky life and death of Robert Ashmere. By cleverly bonding fact with assumption it looked as though she had brought us closer than ever to a conclusion. But there were still unanswered questions and gaps in her thinking. Perturbed, I wondered if she would actually manage to get to the bottom of the mystery and find out what really happened the night Robert Ashmere died. I sincerely hoped not.

Disembarking, we made our way across the platform bridge to the car park. Izzy's pace had slowed, clearly worn-out by the mission, but she refused my offer of a supporting arm.

'Don't fuss, Jennifer. I can manage perfectly well,' she grumbled.

'What now?' I said, opening the passenger door of my Mini for her.

Izzy hugged her beaded bag. 'Seeing as the inspector's dog-fighting partner in crime was hanging around Bennett Street, I think it wise to presume they both know we've got the photos, which means we better get a shift on: best we go straight home and get onto the police.'

'What if they don't believe us? What if Pitts has told them I'm a timewaster?'

'I've already thought of that. Have you got a scanner?'

I nodded.

'We'll scan the photos and email them to someone important – a Chief Super something. Come on, Jarvis,' she ordered, 'put your foot down.'

I drove as fast as possible down Ridgelow's High Street without being dangerous or courting attention. My heart danced when I caught sight of Corner Cottage. Izzy sniffed the air appreciatively as she got out of the car then headed, a tad unsteadily, to my front door.

'Are you sure you're up to this?' I said, worried that she wasn't as energetic as she made out and that the afternoon's jaunt had been too much. 'I can deal with it if you want to go home and put your feet up?'

'Stuff and nonsense,' she retorted with a little

snort. 'Do you really think after all this cavorting around and the brain power I've put in that I'm going to let you finish the job and take all the credit?' There was a wry smile hidden behind the indignation. 'I tell you what though, old age is getting the better of my bladder – I'm off to the lav.'

I scooted upstairs to the office, fired up my laptop and ancient photocopier-cum-scanner. The equipment gently clicked and whirred as it booted up. Everything else was quiet.

*Too quiet.*

Something was missing.

*Digby.*

Racing downstairs to the kitchen I discovered an empty dog bed next to the Aga and a tonne of bad vibes in the air.

'What on earth's the matter?' Izzy demanded, emerging from the cloakroom.

'It's Digby. Mum said she'd walk him home for me, but he's not here.'

'It's only just gone six, maybe she's working late?'

'She never works late. She's out the door at five on the dot. She should have dropped him off by now.'

'Perhaps she's gone to the pub with Spencer and taken Digby with her? She's very fond of him, the dog I mean. If you ask me, she'd have been much better off getting a loyal pooch instead of a … '

Izzy was cut off by a loud Latino ringtone. I retrieved my phone from my handbag and checked the display. The caller ID was withheld, but I sensed bad news through the airwaves. With an ache in my heart and a bad taste in my mouth, I accepted the call.

'Ah, *Miss* Jarvis,' Detective Inspector Pitts hissed theatrically. 'Missing your four legged friend?' Before I could reply, he gave a short, shady cackle. 'Don't worry, he's in safe hands, although he very nearly had my finger off. Feisty little tyke, isn't he? Definitely up for a bit of sport. I'd put money on him any day.'

His mocking words were like an ice arrow spearing my heart. 'If you hurt him … '

'Now, now. No need for threats or dramatics. This is easily sorted. You have my holiday snaps and I have your dog. It's a simple exchange, nothing more.'

The thought of the detective's illegal pastime detonated a bomb of rage inside me. 'How can you do that?' I bawled. 'How can you stand there and watch those poor creatures maul each other like that?' My mouth spewed insults like an overloaded city sewer. 'You're vile. Heinous. The absolute scum of the earth.'

'I'm not interested in what you think,' Pitts growled. 'I just want my photos. It's that simple. So let's stop pussyfooting around with pleasantries and get down to business.' He named a spot in the middle of Haven Woods as the meeting point. 'Be there in ten minutes if you want your ugly mutt back in one living, breathing piece,' he snarled, before hanging up.

'Fine,' I yelled into the dead connection, feeling far from it.

Hearing his voice through my phone had tainted it. I discarded the handset on the hall side-table and dusted my palms against my denim-clad thighs, trying to rid myself of all trace of the foul man.

Izzy's face was laundry-white and starch-stiff. 'What's going on?'

'Pitts has Digby.' Energy drained from my body, leaving me quivering.

My attention honed in on the antique French carriage clock on the mantelpiece, which seemed to be tick-tocking louder and louder and faster and faster, building up to a crescendo chime, which made both Izzy and I jump. While she clutched at her heart and swore, I was spurred into action.

'I need the photos. Give me the photos,' I demanded, shaking empty hands at her.

Izzy located her beaded bag and retrieved the brown envelope. 'Where are you going?' she wailed, as I grabbed it and took off.

'To fetch my dog,' I shouted, sprinting out of the front door. I hastily started the Mini, forgetting it was parked in gear. The car lurched forward, narrowly missing the garage door, as the engine stalled. 'Oh, come on,' I howled, smacking the dash. As I tried again, this time dipping the clutch, Izzy called from the porch and pointed to something in her hand. I couldn't hear, or see, and there wasn't time to stop. The Mini roared to life and bounced over potholes, puffing a cloud of dust in the air. The moment the tyres hit smooth tarmac, I rammed my foot on the gas and wheel-span off in the direction of Haven Woods. Glancing at the clock, I cursed under my breath every time a minute went by. More expletives were dished out to drivers who were unfortunate enough to find themselves in my path. I made the journey in record time by breaking the speed limit, and skidded to a halt in the car park. Tucking the envelope under one arm, I jogged down a narrow trail, deeper and deeper into the woods, towards what felt like the centre of the earth.

Despite my supreme effort to meet the detective's deadline, I knew it had taken me more than ten minutes to get this far. I delved for my phone to check the time again, but encountered an empty pocket. Swearing loudly, I remembered abandoning it like a hot potato back at Corner Cottage. Boiling anger cooled to icy fear as I wrestled with the fact that I was completely cut off from the rest of the world and about to meet a desperate and, quite possibly, unhinged man in a secluded spot in the woods. Common sense told me to turn back. But there was no way I was leaving Digby, no way I was leaving my beloved pet in the hands of a man with a penchant for a sordid underground sport. Having made this pledge, I dug deep and trawled up enough conviction to follow the trail into a small grassy glade encased by dense woodland and thicket. Here, I came to a standstill and looked around. In the centre stood a weatherworn obelisk, a stone monument erupting from the earth and towering over me, a good fifty feet high. Dark trees and mature scrub leant inwards, creating a spiked prison wall. The place was deserted. The winding footpath I'd travelled was the only route in and out, and I hadn't passed a soul on the way.

*Where the hell is he?*

I gave the obelisk a frustrated kick then jumped when a voice barked,

'You're late.'

There was a rustle in the undergrowth. Detective Inspector Pitts pushed his way into the glade – alone.

'Where's my dog?' I said, willing myself to be cool, calm and collected. 'I've stuck to my word,' I brandished the package, 'so where is he?'

'As I said, he's in safe hands.' Pitts glowered at me. A tic cracked in his cheek. 'You'll get him back when I'm satisfied with the contents of that envelope.'

He stepped forward.

I stepped back, matching the policeman's glower and clutching the photos behind folded arms, deep into my chest. 'No way. I want to see him first.'

Pitts gave me another filthy look, but for Digby's sake I held his gaze. He could see I meant business. The policeman put two fingers to his mouth and gave a short, sharp whistle. The crack of twigs underfoot announced the arrival of Pitts' safe pair of hands, who pushed his way through the thicket into the grass clearing with Digby trailing behind on a tatty piece of rope. It was the other man in the photos, the man who'd been hanging around on Bennett Street. Izzy was right. There was a strong resemblance between them.

*His son?*

'Keep an eye out,' Pitts ordered his sidekick.

Pitts Junior gave a single nod and planted himself at the opening of the glade.

Digby appeared unharmed, if a little confused, but was thrilled to see me and wagged his scraggy tail like a metronome set on top speed. Then he made a dive for me and was yanked back with a yelp by a cruel hand. This mean, needless act sent waves of loathing and anger pounding through my veins. I already knew I was capable of killing a man, and in that moment I also knew I would do everything possible to save my dog. Blood rushed through me, swelling my body with hate. I was overcome by an urge to somehow burst out of my own skin and unleash the wild, uninhibited version of myself that was holed up inside. It took a lot of control to rein myself in and stop me from lashing out with every limb and every ounce of strength in them. Wound as tight as a coiled spring, I kept my body in check and let my tongue loose instead.

'I know you were on the footpath with Robert the night he died,' I said through gritted teeth, balling my fists against the sides of my hips, the envelope vice-gripped in one of them. 'I heard you. I heard you arguing and I heard Robert cry out. In fact, I heard both of you.' I jutted a defiant chin at the policeman and then at Pitts Junior. 'Three voices, not two.'

'You've nothing on me,' Pitts sneered. 'The dog was barking too loudly for you to hear anything. You said so yourself. I've got it all nicely recorded and filed away in your statement.'

'Too loud to make out exact words, but I know I heard three voices. You had a fight and then Robert cried out. I heard it all.' My toes were curled up in my shoes and my shoulders were hard set. I wanted to go straight for Digby and get the hell out of there, but this time it was two against one, and I lacked a weapon and the element of surprise, so I kept the coil of anger tightly wound.

'So what? Things got out of hand. Who cares?' Pitts' grey face was slashed with pink. He screwed his face into an animal snarl, top lip curled. 'The case is closed – done and dusted – and with a big fat pat on the back for me for solving it so quickly, and for locking up Nick Low. We've been trying to nail him for years. All in all it was a very satisfactory result.'

'Except for the photos,' I said, mind whirring as I wondered if Pitts actually believed that he, or his son, had killed Robert Ashmere, or if it was a tactic to try and trip me up.

'Yes, except for the photos,' he said, the words sharp and encrusted with ice. 'So stop messing around, *Miss* Jarvis,' he hissed. 'Hand them over so we can all go home and lay the greedy scumbag to rest.'

Having wormed a confession of sorts from the vile man, and seeing no other way to get my dog back, I took a chance. Raising my arm I offered up the envelope. Pitts stepped forward and snatched it from my clenched fist. I wanted to replace the defiant look on his face with a bloodied nose.

'Now give me my dog,' I said, turning to Pitts Junior.

'Wait,' Pitts instructed him with a staccato shake of the head. He opened the envelope, checked the photographs while growling, 'This better be the lot. No copies or future surprises.'

'That's it. That's all we found,' I said. 'Now give me back my dog.'

He handed the envelope to Pitts Junior and then turned back to me, slowly looking me up and down. 'Impatient, aren't you?' he said, his sense of urgency evaporating. 'But there's something we need to straighten out first – my insurance policy.' He paused. 'Bit of a dark horse, aren't you, *Miss* Jarvis?' Again, he emphasised the *Miss* with a snake-like hiss. 'Not quite as wholesome as you'd like people to believe.'

'I don't know what you're talking about,' I snapped, but my heart was racing.

Through a mean twist of a smile he drawled, 'Really? You haven't got a little secret you'd like to share? Like your real name?'

All the mess in my head began to hum as I tried to bluff him. 'My name's Jennifer Jarvis. I am Jennifer Jarvis.'

He smirked. 'Didn't take his surname when you married him? I wonder why?'

'I don't know what you're talking about,' I lied again, feeling dizzy with all the noise between my ears and the fluttering in my chest.

'Let me prompt your memory.' A wave of déjà vu hit me as Pitts drew a piece of paper from his pocket. He unfolded it slowly, prolonging my agony and enjoying it. 'I found this when I was poking around your house.' He held the paper up to my face. It was a photocopy of a marriage certificate. My marriage certificate. 'And so I did a bit of digging.' The pleasure on his face mimicked the one captured on the revolting dog-fighting photos. 'Leeds Town Hall, wasn't it, where you got hitched? When you were a student?' He fanned my face with the paper. 'Known him long, this Julian Botha, from South Africa?' Then in a pantomime pose he stepped forward, put a hand to the side of his mouth and stage whispered, 'What was the going rate for a sham marriage back then? Two thousand? Three?'

As I prayed this was the only secret he'd uncovered, the muscles round my airways went into spasm and I struggled to catch my breath.

Pitts was unmoved. He made a show of folding the marriage certificate into perfect origami squares then put it back in his pocket. Rocking back and forth on his heels, arms behind his back, he assumed his best officious police tone and said, 'You do realise you've committed immigration fraud? A serious criminal offence?' Another pause. 'Does your boyfriend know?'

I threw him a look swept straight from the gutter and wished my eyes could actually spray daggers.

'Oh dear. Thought not. So, *Mrs* Jarvis, or *Botha*, whatever your name is, you'll be keeping your trap shut about our little meeting today and what I like to get up to in my spare time, because if you blab, so will I, and I'll have immigration crawling all over you faster than you can say 'I do' in a civic hall registry office.' Pitts looked at his sidekick. 'Give her the ugly mutt.'

Digby came bounding towards me. I grabbed at the tatty rope trailing behind him like a limp second tail and made straight for the exit.

Behind me I heard Detective Inspector Pitts crow, 'Nice doing business with you.' Then, 'Don't worry, your secret's safe with me.'

Back in the safety of my car, I crumpled and lay my forehead against the rim of the steering wheel, whole body quivering like a plate of blancmange. Hearing Julian's name spoken out loud had opened a floodgate of memories that I had locked away in a box in the darkest corner of my mind. My cheap pink suit. The cheap bottle of cava we'd guzzled. The cheap chicken and chips in a basket we'd shared in the pub.

Julian was nice enough, from what I could tell in the two meetings we had before tying the knot. He was studying pharmacy on a visa that was about to expire and was so humble and grateful that I had agreed to help him finish his studies and training. He told me all about his dream to make a home in the UK and set up his own business. After the meal we shook hands and wished each other well before heading off, in separate directions, into the sunset, the only romantic notion about the whole affair. I got on with my life, three thousand pounds richer, still Jennifer Jarvis to the rest of the world. The only evidence was a piece of paper hidden away in my filing cabinet. And it was only ever meant as a temporary arrangement. The deal was to file for divorce three years later. I'd be free of Julian and he'd apply for British citizenship. Only, when the time came and I tried to contact him, he'd disappeared and I was stuck with my married status, which wasn't a problem, until I met Ethan. And now Pitts' had uncovered the pretence and knew I was living a lie.

I brooded on the quirk of fate that had befallen me: a policeman blackmailing me, having been blackmailed himself by Robert Ashmere, a man whose path I'd had the misfortune of crossing and who had bought nothing but fear, pain and trouble into my life.

*Always back to Robert.*

I was beginning to see that I would never be able to sever the tie, that we would always be connected.

*And now Pitts.*

I consoled myself with the thought that the policeman needed my co-operation as much as I needed his, and that we had at least arrived at a strange sort of truce.

Unfortunately, there was a very important person that we'd both forgotten.

24

While Detective Inspector Pitts had gagged me, he'd overlooked Izzy. As had I.

Returning to Summer Lane, I found a shiny bronze Volvo parked outside my house. Pulling on to the drive, I caught sight of my neighbour's slightly dishevelled silver mane, nodding left and right, through the leaded window as she held court in my sitting room. The crunch of wheels on gravel drew her attention. A split second later, Izzy came rushing out.

'Thank God, you're alive,' she gasped through the open car window. Looking into the back she added with just as much feeling, 'And Digby too. I didn't know what to do when you drove off like that, so I called the police.'

My hand shook as I drew the car key from the ignition. Pitts' threatening drawl rolled against my temples.

*If you blab, so will I, and I'll have immigration crawling all over you faster than you can say 'I do.'*

Lurching out of the car, I gave a flick of the head towards the Volvo and said in a strangled voice, 'Are they here already?'

'Yes, dear. I kicked up quite a stink. I said your life was in great danger and they came straight out.' I felt dire and my face must have shown it because she immediately went on the defensive. 'Well, I thought it was. You tore off like a bat out of hell, with a face like death, to meet a ruthless, untrustworthy man, without saying where you were going. What on earth did you think I was going to do? Calmly get my knitting out of my handbag, sit by the fire and perfect the garter stitch while waiting for you to return? I tried telling you that you'd forgotten your phone, but you drove off. So, naturally, I called the police.'

'What have you told them?'

'Everything – the break-ins, the message on the mirror, the photos of the dog fight, that one of their detectives dognapped Digby …'

My head filled with thick grey fog, leaving limited room for clear thinking. It was a real effort to try and work out my next move. Then, just when despair threatened to finish me off, I was struck with a thought and snapped back into focus.

Pulling an apologetic face, I said, 'There's a big problem. I'm really sorry, but I gave the photos to Pitts.' I tried to sound dismal. 'It was the only way I could get Digby back, and without them, it's his word against ours. There's no evidence. And the police will want evidence. We know that only too well.'

Izzy's blue-violet eyes narrowed. 'Are you giving up? Just like that?'

I shrugged. 'What else can we do? He'll probably make a big deal out of the fact that I've been wasting his time with stories of imaginary intruders and that you're a barmy old lady with too much time on her hands.'

'I see,' said Izzy slowly. She looked at me – right inside me. 'Something happened, didn't it? Something happened when you saw him.'

All the time I'd been trailing Robert Ashmere, trying to work out the connection and the reason behind the strange goings on, I'd been mightily thankful for Izzy's shrewdness. Now I wished she'd give up the ghost, let it go and get back to the *Daily Telegraph* crossword and her Sudoku puzzles.

'No,' I lied. 'I handed over the photos and he gave me Digby, that's all.'

Izzy was having none of it. 'What cock and bull,' she retorted. 'He threatened you, didn't he? It's obvious he would. You must tell the police, Jennifer, you really must. They need to know everything.'

I fervently disagreed, but could hardly say so.

Izzy marched to my front door. Over her shoulder she said, 'They need to know exactly what this abominable man's capable of. We can't let him get away with it.' Then she added steelily, 'I won't let him get away with it.'

Doing my best to keep a composed front, I followed her into the sitting room and found a woman standing by my fireplace. In her forties, she had strawberry-blonde hair cut into a feathery crop and a plump figure acerbated by the severity of her dark blue uniform, which was finished off with a pair of very sensible black shoes. She moved towards me with unexpected speed and poise, hand held out confidently in front of her. The handshake was firm and business-like.

'Hilary Brookes, Deputy Chief Constable,' she informed me economically. Her face was make-up free, but an abundance of freckles gave her a youthful glow.

'I tried my hardest to get hold of the Chief Constable,' Izzy apologised, 'but he's on holiday in the South of France, or so they told me. They put me through to Hilary instead and she agreed to come straight out.'

I had no idea about police hierarchy, but assumed from the very shiny gold buttons on her uniform that Hilary Brookes was way up there when it came to ranking. This provided no comfort.

'Given the very serious nature of the allegations you're making against one of my officers, I thought it appropriate.' She appraised me in a split second. 'Mrs Wilder's given me a brief account of recent events, but perhaps you'd like to fill me in, Mrs Jarvis?'

'Miss,' I corrected automatically. 'But call me Jen.'

'How about making a nice pot of tea, Mrs Wilder, while Jen and I have a chat?' Hilary Brookes was used to giving orders and being obeyed. Izzy obediently hurried off.

'I don't know where to start,' I said. 'It's all very complicated and we haven't any evidence to prove anything.'

'Mrs Wilder said you recovered two photographs of Detective Inspector Pitts engaged in an illegal activity.'

My heart knocked against ribs. 'Sorry. There aren't any photos.'

The Deputy Chief cocked her head. 'Oh. Why would Mrs Wilder say there was?'

*Clever. Now I have to either tell the truth, or insinuate my friend is lying.*

I considered my next move in the awful mess my life had become and decided that even though I was in a real pickle, Izzy was far too good an ally to dump on.

'We did have the photos,' I admitted. 'There were two of them. But I gave them to the detective. He knew we'd found them, so he stole my dog to use as a trade-off. I met him in Haven Woods and gave him the pictures in return for Digby. He'll be long gone by now. And the first thing he'll have done is get rid of them. So there's no evidence, nothing we can use against him, nothing at all. I expect that means we don't have a case?'

The whites of Hilary's eyes were very bright. Under her watch I felt very disconcerted.

'Mrs Wilder has made some serious allegations about a member of my team,' she said. 'This isn't something I can take lightly. I'll have to investigate these claims through the correct channels and procedures, because if what you've both told me is true, then not only am I dealing with a case of severe misconduct, but of serious criminal activity.'

'You're going to talk to him about it?' I felt faint.

At that moment, Izzy rattled in with a silver tray bearing a pot of tea, my best china and a plate of custard creams.

'Shall I be mum?' she said. Without waiting for a reply she reached for the strainer and poured. Passing a cup to the Deputy Chief Constable, she breezily pressed her on progress. 'Have your boys in blue reeled him in yet, Hilary?'

The Deputy Chief smiled. 'Not yet, but I'm expecting a call very soon. Now, Mrs Wilder, Jen and I were just discussing the fact that you don't actually have any hard evidence to back up your very serious allegations.'

Izzy dropped the tea strainer on the tray with a clatter. 'Goodness. Of course. The evidence. I meant to bring it in.' She turned on a sixpence and rushed out of the sitting room.

The Deputy Chief gave me a questioning look.

I had no idea what my neighbour was up to, and inside I was quaking.

She returned with her beaded bag and pulled out the white envelope, brandishing it triumphantly in the air. 'We found this in the mailbox. It's stuffed full of cash. I thought you'd want to check it for fingerprints. You never know, your detective might have had something to do with it and left his mark.'

The Deputy Chief took the package. 'We'll certainly run some tests. Thank you.'

Izzy delved deeper into her bag. 'Now, where the hell is it?' she murmured. 'Ah ha! Here we are … ' She pulled out her own mobile phone. 'Let me see … oh, I need my specs. Hang on just a jiffy and I'll be right with you.' Her hand returned to the bag and retrieved her half-glasses, which she propped crookedly on the bridge of her nose. Peering at the handset, face full of concentration, she pressed a few buttons then grinned. 'That's it. There.' She thrust the screen into the Deputy Chief's face. 'You can see him perfectly well.'

'What is it?' I said, both fearful and intrigued.

'Detective Inspector Pitts at the dog fight,' Izzy said smugly. 'While I was spending a penny in the lav, when we got back from the station, I took copies of the photographs using my camera phone.'

'Quick thinking,' said the Deputy Chief, with more than a hint of admiration, 'taking photos of the photos. I would never have thought of that.'

'Here, let me focus in,' Izzy offered. She pressed some more buttons, squinted and said, 'There you go. There he is in all his disgusting glory.'

The Deputy Chief looked sickened by the image, but impressed with the technology. 'The clarity is very, very good indeed.'

'James Bond used this phone in *Quantum of Solace*,' Izzy boasted. 'I do like Daniel Craig as Bond, don't you?' she said to an empty space by the fireplace.

The Deputy Chief had vacated the room. The words, 'Excuse me a moment,' floated in the air, suspended in a back draft created as she closed the door.

I grabbed Izzy's phone and stole a look. The resolution quality was astonishing. I gazed at a smaller version of one of the images we'd found in the mailbox and felt elated that Izzy's sharp wit spelled the end of the police detective, and wretched, because it could also spell the end of my relationship with Ethan. Izzy could pan in on the image so closely, and with such clarity, that we could see, very disturbingly, the sensation of ecstasy erupting across Pitts' face as he witnessed the final moments of an innocent dog's gruesome death. It was horrid.

The Deputy Chief swept back in. 'I'm afraid I'm going to have to take that phone,' she said. 'And I've arranged for my best officer to come out and talk to you both. I appreciate you've had a very long day, Mrs Wilder, but do you think you could manage to go over it one more time?'

Izzy swelled with importance. 'Of course,' she said, tapping her temple with a forefinger. 'It's all stored up here – every detail.'

The rest of the evening was spent explaining and answering question after question to the top police officer – who turned out to be Detective Superintendent Wallace, the man in charge of Erica's case – and then to Ethan, who turned up expecting a conversation about postcodes and trips to London, only to find we'd been without him. Fortunately, his initial annoyance soon turned to concern when he'd heard the full story, and then to relief that Izzy had outwitted Detective Inspector Pitts by taking photos of the photos.

'Pure genius,' he'd said, clearly impressed.

While Izzy sparkled brightly, chatting animatedly to Ethan and revelling in the glory, I withdrew into silent contemplation, trying to hide the feelings of misery and helplessness that had wrapped around my soul like a heavy, ill-fitting overcoat. I knew it was only a matter of time before Pitts would use my secret wedded status against me and that I'd be answering more questions, not just from the police, but everyone around me, and most of all from Ethan.

*My life is a sham. I am a sham.*

There was only one thing for it. I had to do the right thing. I had to come clean and tell him.

*Well, about Julian.*

I decided to confess the following day, giving myself time to find the right words and hopefully minimise the fall-out. That night, I lay in bed listening to Ethan's gentle snores, thinking about how deeply I loved him and clung fiercely to the hope that, in time, his big heart would find a way to excuse my stupidity and deceit and we would be able to work things out. But a twist of fate caught me unawares. Despite my vow to open up and tell the truth, I completely lost my nerve, because Ethan got down on one knee and proposed.

25

'Will you be my wife, Jen?' Ethan whipped out a distinctive light blue box from behind his back and proudly revealed a beautiful Tiffany pear-shaped diamond ring.

Of course I said yes. It came out automatically.

My hand shook as he slid the gleaming jewel on my finger. He mistook my panic for overwhelmed joy and kissed me passionately.

I felt like crying.

Gathering me up in his arms, Ethan pulled me close and whispered, 'I love you so much, Jen.'

I was too choked with emotion – mostly despair – to reply and instead pressed my face into the crook of his neck and breathed in deeply, trying to calm myself.

'I wanted to ask you weeks ago,' he said, 'but you got so caught up in that awful murder business that there never seemed to be a good time.'

We were outside on the terrace waiting for my mother, Spencer, Izzy and Lisa to arrive for a celebratory dinner to mark the end of Detective Inspector Pitts' stalking campaign. Ethan had picked his moment beautifully. It was a glorious late summer evening. A bottle of Taittinger chilled in an ice bucket on the table while the setting sun warmed our faces. Ethan released me from his tight embrace, cracked open the bubbly and poured froth into two crystal flutes.

'To us,' he said, raising his glass.

'To us,' I repeated parrot-fashion.

We chinked glasses and I guzzled the dry fizz in three gulps.

Digby barked at a loud rap on the front door.

'I'll go,' I said, feeling claustrophobic and needing to get away.

It was my mother and Spencer.

'Hello, darling,' she cooed, kissing the air at the side of my cheek.

'Hello, Jennifer,' he boomed, shaking my hand heartily.

In the garden, my mother greeted Ethan with a full, proper smack on the lips, leaving a smudge of coral lipstick behind.

'Champagne, Mary?' he offered. 'Spencer?'

'How extravagant,' my mother gushed, 'but then I suppose we are celebrating, aren't we? To the end of all the drama?'

I wondered if Ethan was going to blab about the latest headline in my life – we hadn't had time to agree when and how we'd tell them – but my magpie mother spotted the sparkling new addition on my finger as I handed her a glass, and gave a melodramatic gasp.

'Is that what I think it is?' Grabbing my hand she pulled it up to her face for closer inspection. 'It's absolutely beautiful. Did you choose it?'

'No, Ethan did.'

'It's very classy, and very elegant.'

'It's from Tiffany,' Ethan said, delighted with my mother's reaction.

'White gold?'

'Platinum.'

My mother was in raptures. 'How romantic! A platinum diamond engagement ring from Tiffany! Oh, Jennifer, you are lucky. When did all this happen? And where? Come on, spill the beans, I want all the bended knee details.'

'There's not much to tell,' I said summoning up a smile, but inwardly cringing at the fuss she was making. 'It happened about ten minutes ago, right here.'

My mother had glassy eyes. Spencer offered her a red silk hanky.

'Congratulations,' he said, kissing me awkwardly then shaking Ethan's hand and patting him manfully on the back. 'So, when's the big day?'

'We haven't even started thinking about that,' I replied. 'I'm still getting used to the idea of being engaged.'

I was relieved when Ethan added, 'No rush,' then anxious when he said, 'we've got a lot to sort out first, like where we're going to live. No point paying for two places when we're saving for a wedding.'

'Very sensible,' my mother agreed, before motoring tactlessly on: 'I do like this little cottage and I know you've put a lot of heart and soul into the renovation, Jennifer, but murder at the bottom of the garden rather spoils the outlook, doesn't it? Probably best to move on and find somewhere new to start afresh. Actually, there's a lovely property just round the corner from me that's worth a look: detached with four bedrooms – plenty of room for a family.'

Ethan caught my look of alarm and gently manoeuvred my mother into safer waters.

'I hear that you and Spencer are going on holiday together, to Sicily?'

My mother happily changed course and, full steam ahead, began bending Ethan's ear about volcanoes, sardines, Marsala and hotels with separate bedrooms, while Spencer chipped in whenever he found a small opening in the flow.

Digby barked again as a familiar voice called, 'Yoo-hoo!'

Izzy emerged through the side gate clutching a huge bowl of strawberries and small jug of cream. 'I've bought pudding,' she said. As I relieved her of her gifts, she gave a little shriek and dropped a few of the prized strawberries on the terrace. Quick as a flash, Digby wolfed them down.

'My word, are you engaged, Jennifer?' she gasped.

I nodded dumbly.

'To Ethan? I mean, of course to Ethan, but when?'

'Earlier. When we were waiting for you all to arrive.'

'This is just too fabulous for words,' she beamed ecstatically.

More gushing ensued when Lisa arrived. 'It's gorgeous,' she said unable to hide a speck of envy as she tried my ring on for size. 'Congratulations.' Then with a wicked smile she added, 'I knew you were the marrying kind – the lady doth protest too much!'

I left Ethan holding the fort and disappeared into the kitchen under the pretence that dinner needed my attention. Methodically slicing cucumber for a Greek salad, I focused closely on the knife rather than the gleaming ring on my finger. Chopping a strong red onion gave me an excuse to shed a quick tear.

'A problem shared is a problem halved,' whispered a concerned voice in my ear.

Glancing up I found a pair of bright blue-violet, quizzical eyes staring back.

'I thought you might need a helping hand,' Izzy offered kindly. 'You looked a bit overwhelmed out there. Not surprising really. It's a big deal, isn't it? I didn't know what to think when my Archie proposed. A combination of wild excitement and utter panic is probably a good way to describe it, shortly followed by a sinking feeling that my browse round the sweet shop was most definitely over and that I'd have to sleep with the same man for the rest of my life.' Despite my black mood, Izzy coaxed a small smile from me. 'It's not that bad, you know,' she said.

'What's not?'

'Being with the same man for the rest of your life. It's actually rather lovely.'

'That's what I'm hoping,' I said, picking up my knife again and lopping at a block of feta cheese.

'Then what are you so worried about? There's obviously something bothering you. I mean, it's perfectly normal to have mixed emotions about something so important, but you don't seem to be very happy about it. You do want to marry Ethan, don't you?'

'Of course I do. I love him.'

'Then why can't you raise a genuine smile? The man you love and want to marry has just proposed and presented you with a huge sparkler the size of Gibraltar and you've got a face like a wet weekend. Come on, out with it,' she demanded.

'You really don't want to know,' I warned, desperately fighting an urge to share my woe.

'I might be able to help.' She picked up a cucumber baton and dunked it in a nearby tub of hummus.

'Unless you're going to whip out a wand and claim to be my fairy Godmother then I doubt it very much.'

'I do dabble in practical, but not in magic.' She made to leave. 'If you change your mind and need an ear to bend, or a shoulder to cry on, you know where I am.'

To her departing back I blurted, 'I really want to marry him, but I can't.'

Izzy turned very slowly. 'Why on earth not?'

'Because … because I'm already married … ' the

words came out as a hollow whisper, '… to someone else.'

There was a long silence.

Izzy eventually broke it. 'I had no idea.'

I hung my head. 'No one does. It was a while ago, when I was a student. I didn't tell anyone … ' I let out a heavy, jaded sigh, '… because I did something very stupid … I married a man for money.'

Izzy looked mildly surprised, but not shocked. 'Lots of people marry for money.'

'No, I mean I married a South African man I didn't know for money and never saw him again.'

Izzy's eyes were full moons. 'A sham marriage?'

'He was here on a student visa,' I explained, highly embarrassed. 'And I was getting in a bit of a muddle with money, so we got together for, err, mutual benefit. The deal was we'd get a divorce as soon as we could, but when I tried to get in touch he'd disappeared.'

'And now you've met Ethan, who obviously has no idea about your … colourful past. Deary me. Sometimes, Jennifer, you are very, very stupid indeed. Does anyone else know?'

'Detective Inspector Pitts. He found my marriage certificate when he was poking round the house, which is why the photocopier light was left on. He did a bit of digging and worked it out. That's why I didn't want to go to the police about him. He said if I blabbed, he'd blab right back.'

'Ah, that does rather complicate things somewhat, doesn't it?' Izzy closed her eyes for a moment and retracted into deep thought. After a few seconds she popped back to life and said reassuringly, 'I shouldn't worry about him. I doubt he'll say anything, because if he does, it'll be an admission to his crimes.'

'What do you mean?' I said, a wisp of hope stirring inside.

'For a start, he'll have to explain how he knows about it, which will mean admitting that he broke into your house and stole your marriage certificate and used the information to blackmail you, which in turn points to him dogknapping Digby and to the reason why – to get the photos – and so on. I would bet my life on it that Detective Inspector Pitts will be keeping your little secret exactly that.' On a roll, she continued, 'More importantly, what shall we do about you and Ethan? The obvious thing is for you to stall him on committing to a date until we've found your husband and got you a quickie divorce.'

'You'll help me do that?' I said, immediately feeling brighter.

'Of course! I was wondering what on earth to do with myself now that the Robert Ashmere mystery is done and dusted. This is perfect. I'll have him tracked down in no time. Hopefully we'll find he's popped his clogs and that you're officially a widow, or something that will simplify things. Come round tomorrow,' she breezed, 'and we'll get straight to it.'

Izzy's words switched my faded mood in a heartbeat. And more good news was coming my way. The messenger was Hilary Brookes, the Deputy Chief Constable, who turned up just as we finished our celebratory meal. My initial reaction to her arrival was one of panic. Since that awful night on the footpath, the sight of a police uniform made me quake. My angst was further compounded by my mother who grabbed my left wrist and held it up.

'Come on in, Ma'am, and join the party,' she said, proudly.

I wrenched my hand away and hid it under the table.

'Beautiful ring,' the Deputy Chief clocked. 'Congratulations.'

In the grip of paranoia, I prayed that Izzy was right and Detective Inspector Pitts hadn't blabbed.

*Is it illegal to get engaged when I'm still married to someone else?*

I really didn't know and waited for the police chief to whip out a pair of handcuffs, read me my rights and lead me away there and then.

'Sorry to interrupt your evening,' Hilary said, her voice smoothly sliding down into a deep, solemn tone, 'but I wanted to come in person and give you an update on our ongoing investigation into the death of Robert Ashmere, and the allegations made against Detective Inspector Pitts.' She looked at me with a serious face.

*Robert Ashmere. Robert Ashmere. Robert Ashmere.*

A megaphone inside my head blared out the dead man's name, over and over.

*Is this it? Is it time?*

Part of me wanted the whole truth to come out. I was tired of all the pretence. Living a lie was exhausting and lonely. Remorse gnawed away at me like a chronic disease. But then I pictured Ethan's face, how he might look when he found out that the woman he loved and wanted to marry was a complete sham, and my heart ached for him. I didn't want him to think badly of me. And I couldn't bear to lose him.

*Stay strong, Jen. Stay strong. Don't lose it. Not now.*

Spencer brought out an extra chair. We all shuffled up and made space at the table for the police chief.

'I don't suppose you'll accept a glass of wine while

on duty, so perhaps you'd like a cup of tea or coffee?' my mother fawned.

'Thank you, I'd love a tea. Milk and one sugar please.'

My mother scurried off to the kitchen. Hilary started to explain what the police had uncovered.

'Detective Inspector Pitts and his son, Todd, were picked up yesterday evening and taken in for questioning,' she informed us. 'He's denying all the allegations and when he was shown the photographic evidence, he claimed he was at the dog fight in an undercover capacity. Unfortunately for him, his version of events and his son's don't tie up. Todd has admitted they were on the footpath with Robert Ashmere on the fifth of July, and that they were involved in an argument, and then a fight. He said Robert had demanded £5000 from his father in return for the photos.'

Izzy clasped her hands together and shook them victoriously. 'See, I told you – blackmail.'

'It appears it wasn't the first time Robert had approached my officer and demanded money: hence the reason why his actions were so extreme,' the police chief explained. 'According to Todd, his father had already paid Robert a substantial sum a few months ago on the understanding that the photos were handed over and any electronic files were destroyed. But it appears that Robert didn't stick to his side of the bargain and made more copies, which he hid in the mailbox you discovered. He then went back for a second bite of the cherry, contacting Detective Inspector Pitts a week before his death and demanding more cash.' Hilary stopped to take a sip of the tea my mother placed in front of her.

Izzy, impatient as ever, tried to gee her up. 'And?'

The police chief wouldn't be rushed. She calmly returned her cup to the saucer in her own time. 'Detective Inspector Pitts couldn't pay. He didn't have the money. He was forced into confessing the situation to his son and asking for his help in dealing with it once and for all. They came up with a plan to meet Robert and get a bit heavy with him – give him a fright and then take the photos. But he didn't show up …'

Izzy butted in, 'Ah ha! Because he didn't have them did he? He went to Erica's to get the code to his mailbox, but Digby, or Barney, as he was back then, had been re-homed.'

'Exactly. Robert must have known he was messing in murky waters. Blackmail is a risky business, but targeting a senior police officer, a man who could easily abuse his position to check out Robert and his property, well, that's a highly dangerous strategy. It was quite ingenious of him to hide the location and security details of the photos somewhere even an experienced detective wouldn't think of looking.'

'And rather stupid of him not to keep tabs on the dog,' Izzy pointed out, quick as a flash.

'Quite,' agreed Hilary. 'Anyway, when Robert didn't show up, Todd went looking for him. He eventually found him and called his father. They tailed him to Ridgelow, onto the footpath …'

'Where he was casing Jen's joint, waiting to steal Digby,' Izzy interrupted again, with a knowing nod to everyone round the table.

Lisa topped up her wine glass. 'But how did Robert know your detective in the first place?' she said. 'How did he know that he would be at that dog fight and that he'd be able to take those pictures?'

'I don't know how he knew about the fight,' the

police chief replied, 'but I do know that Detective Inspector Pitts and Robert had crossed paths in the past, when we carried out an investigation at the electronic components company where Robert was a director …'

'Oh yes, that's right,' Izzy interjected again, fizzing with glee. 'Erica told Jennifer that Robert was involved in a fraud scandal. He was accused of taking bribes from company suppliers and ended up losing his job. She said he never got over it and was really angry with the way the police dealt with him. He thought they were trying to frame him.'

'So he went after Pitts to get revenge?' said Spencer, who'd been listening keenly.

'As I said, we don't know for sure,' repeated Hilary, 'and because Robert is dead I'm afraid we won't ever understand the true motivation behind his actions.'

'Hmm, I think you might be right though,' Izzy speculated. 'You read all the time about revenge crimes. And Erica told Jen that Robert was quite volatile and controlling. I bet when he lost his job he looked for someone to blame, so he could feel better about himself. And knowing Detective Inspector Pitts, he probably made his life an absolute misery during the fraud investigation. I bet Robert felt he had a score to settle with him.' She turned to me. 'Didn't Erica complain that Robert was out at all hours and she never knew where he was? What if he was stalking Detective Inspector Pitts and that's how he found out about his disgusting hobby?'

In the company of the policewoman, I didn't want to say anything about the dead man and simply gave Izzy a quick confirming nod.

'If it was revenge he was after, he certainly got it,

but at the cost of his own life,' said Ethan sombrely.

'There's one more piece of the puzzle missing for me,' said Izzy. 'How did Detective Inspector Pitts know *the number* existed, but not that the dog was safeguarding it?'

'Now that is something I can shed a bit of light on,' the police chief disclosed. 'Todd told us that when they were on the footpath demanding that Robert hand over the photos, he kept repeating that he would, but that he needed *the number*. We know from the post mortem that Robert had been drinking, so he probably wasn't very coherent at the time. Todd said that when they pressed him about this number, Robert kept pointing up the footpath saying he was here to get it. At the time, Detective Inspector Pitts and Todd didn't understand what he meant, but the following day when the note with Jennifer's name and address on it came to light, Detective Inspector Pitts immediately assumed that she had the photographs and was hiding them on Robert's behalf.'

'Hence the break-ins and the threatening message on the mirror,' Izzy exclaimed happily. 'See, I was right! I bet Detective Inspector Pitts was petrified the photos would turn up in the hands of his colleagues when Jennifer's house was officially searched. And I'll put good money on the fact that he and his son trashed Erica's place too when nothing turned up here.'

'What about Nick Low?' Ethan said suddenly. 'Was he framed by Detective Inspector Pitts?'

'Not entirely, no,' responded the deputy chief. 'We have strong evidence linking Nick to the deceased and the scene of the crime. He was found in possession of some money with traces of Robert's prints on and his mobile phone, but he has always maintained that he found Robert lying on the footpath. Now that we have Todd's confession about the fight, it seems that Nick was telling the truth after all, though he still committed a crime.'

My mother, who'd remained quiet for an extraordinarily long length of time, piped up, 'This is all very interesting, but have you actually charged your detective with anything, Ma'am? Have you got enough proof to lock him up and throw away the key?'

Mixed emotions swept through me like a ferocious bush fire when the police chief confirmed that both Detective Inspector Pitts and his son had been charged in connection with Robert's death.

'There's enough evidence to prove beyond reasonable doubt that they were involved and they've also been charged with an offence under the Animal Welfare act. We're still investigating any connection with the break-in at Mrs Ashmere's property and also running tests on the cash found in the mailbox. I'll let you know the outcome of these lines of enquiry when they've been formally completed.'

Izzy placed a comforting hand on my mother's forearm. 'Don't worry, Mary, I'm sure the cunning, conniving beast will get his just deserts. They say what goes around comes around, don't they?'

'I hope you're right,' my mother complained. 'He's caused us a huge amount of distress. It's been absolute hell. To think he led us to believe that Jennifer was a suspect in his murder investigation, when all along he and his son killed the man.'

Despite being in pieces inside, I managed to keep up the charade and look suitably appalled.

'Utterly disgraceful if you ask me,' she complained. 'I wonder if we can claim for damages?' She gave the police chief a sly sideways glance. 'Jennifer, I think you and I ought to talk to our solicitor in the morning. Brian Rotherford will be very interested to hear about this.'

The police chief rolled out a smooth apology. 'I really am very sorry for any distress you've been caused as result of the actions of Detective Inspector Pitts, Mrs Jarvis, and also to you, Jennifer. If you do wish to appoint a solicitor to act on your behalf, please let me know so I can ensure your case is dealt with appropriately and swiftly.'

Heat raided my body in tumultuous waves. 'Actually, Mum, I think I'd prefer to let it go,' I said, looking down at the table.

I couldn't believe I'd got away with it again. I couldn't believe someone else had been charged with Robert's death: first Nick Low and now Detective Inspector Pitts. Of course I felt a sense of regret for the policeman, I really did, but after all the trouble he'd put me through and all the games he'd played, part of me reasoned that it was okay to let him and his son take the blame for a crime that I unintentionally committed when I had the misfortune of coming across Robert Ashmere that night, on the footpath at the bottom of my garden. A night that will haunt me for as long as I walk this earth.

**26**

I can recall it like it was yesterday. Snapshot memories of the night I killed a man play like a never-ending reel of film in my mind, a train of chaotic thoughts pelting along a looped track.

*The smell of his blood.*

*His piercing scream.*

*The crack of his skull against wood.*

It all spins round my head like a carousel of hideous images, smells and sounds, transporting me back to the garden where I'm sitting on the terrace, alone, wafting the paperback I'm reading at a persistent mosquito and mopping a clammy brow with the back of my free palm. Dark has swallowed me up, but the candle beside me glows, illuminating the words I'm devouring.

Over Ridgelow's chimneys and rooftops, the dong of a church bell striking ten o'clock stirs me from the tight grip of the novel. I yawn, stretch, blow out the flickering flame and head upstairs to run a cool bath. After opening the window, I sink into scented, foamy water with a sigh. My eyes close and I lose myself dreaming of Ethan.

Loud voices rudely disturb the peace. Male voices. Out on the footpath. Eyes and ears snap open. I sit up. Water laps round my midriff. I listen. Someone is angry. They are arguing. Three people, I think, but it's hard to tell because downstairs Digby is barking, whining and howling like a banshee.

*Bloody kids*, I grumble.

The voices are rising. Shouting. A fight has broken out.

Wrenching myself from the bath, I sling on a

robe. The cotton clings to wet skin. As I make for the kitchen to quiet the dog, someone cries out. The sound is like a nasty tear in the hush of night. A chill of foreboding washes over me. I run to the phone, 999 on the tip of my fingers, but a wailing siren echoes in the distance and I think, *Good. Izzy's already called the police.*

Downstairs, Digby is spinning round by the back door like a whirling dervish. I let him out, hoping he'll scare off the noisy, brawling teenagers. The dog bombs off. Sirens and voices are replaced by incessant, sharp barks. I call for him. He ignores me.

*Little sod*, I think.

Bare feet slip into flip flops. A hand reaches for a torch. The light is dim, the battery ready to give up the ghost. I track the path with a thin ribbon of yellow. Digby is close by. He's making snuffling and yapping sounds, like he's chasing a rabbit or found something really exciting. A few more steps and I reach the bottom of the garden. The weak beam traces the wooden fence. It comes to rest on the back gate. I freeze and drop the light. It hits the path with a thud and then a fizz as the connection comes loose. All my senses switch to high alert.

Because the gate is open.

Stock still, my ears pound with the sound of my own heartbeat. Nervous fingers tighten the cord of my thin cotton robe. I quietly crouch and fumble the ground for the torch. A faint metallic smell sneaks up my nose. I stand, muscles tight and breath quick. I rattle the torch. The components reconnect and produce a trickle of yellow. I run it over the gate again. Yes, it is definitely open. Wide open. And Digby is out on the path. I can hear him snuffling around like a badger nosing for grubs.

*Come, Digby, come*, I call.

I try to sound firm, but the dog doesn't appear. A bad feeling hangs in the air like an impending superstorm, suffocating and tense. I want to turn and run back to the house. But I can't leave Digby.

So I step on to the footpath.

The beam swings left and right at ground level, looking for a ball of fur in the bushes. I detect a small movement.

*There you are*, I chide.

The torch picks out a pair of Converse canvas shoes. I half-scream, step back and pull the yellow beam upwards. It finds a face. A man's beaten, bloodied face. His eyes are wild. His mouth is open. His arms are poised. I hear a strangled moan – my own. The man lumbers closer. The reek of blood, sweat and booze reaches me before he does. His hands stretch out towards my neck. Electric adrenaline surges through me as though I've been plugged into the mains. I don't think. I just pull my arm back and up, like a golf pro, and swing with everything I have.

The torch whacks against his temple.

The man screams as he staggers and falls.

His skull cracks as it hits a tree trunk.

The silence is heavy. The stillness is hollow. I know he's gone. But I don't feel bad. I don't feel anything. Because inside I'm like him – dead.

*Come on, Digby*, I say.

I stoop to grab the dog. Flip flops slap against the soles of my feet as I lead him into the garden. The barrel bolt grates into place. Then I'm gliding through the air on anaesthetized limbs towards home.

As the storm broke, so did the enormity of what had happened, of what I had done. Thunder rumbled the heavens. Shockwaves battered every inch of my body. As the dense fog in my head began to thin, I was overcome by an intense thirst. I rushed to the sink. Water gushed into a tumbler. As I drank, the fog became a mist, then the mist began to clear and my head refilled with a series of snapshot memories that will never, ever leave me.

*The smell of his blood.*

*His piercing scream.*

*The crack of his skull against wood.*

I paced the kitchen, face in my hands, wondering what the hell to do, what to do for the best. I wished Ethan were there to help me. He would know what to do, what to do for the best.

My phone lay on the table. It kept catching my eye. I walked over. My hand hovered.

*Who should I call? Ethan? Or the police? And say what? Say that I killed a man?*

I dropped my hand and resumed pacing. Two voices emerged in my head.

*He was going to grab you. He was going to hurt you. It was an accident – self-defence. Anyone would have done the same. People will understand.* Then, *Don't be ridiculous. The man's dead. You hit him and you killed him. And you'll be sent to prison. You'll lose everything. You'll be ruined.*

I stopped at the sink and downed another glass of cold water, splashing some over my face, which felt hot and taut. Through the window I noticed the storm had passed and a flamingo-pink sky was emerging behind purple clouds.

*If you're going to own up you need to do it soon,* one of the voices told me.

*Just sit tight,* the other advised. *Say nothing. Do nothing.*

The glowing tip of the sun began inching over the horizon, dawning a new day. I sat at the table thinking, a tug of war in my mind. The higher the sun rose, the louder one voice shouted, and as the sky turned into a sea of orange and the birds began to sing, I rushed upstairs, threw on a clean pair of shorts and a T-shirt, raced back down again and opened the back door. My bare feet slipped into wet flip flops, a hand reached for the discarded torch. Calling Digby, I headed round to the front of the house and walked down Summer Lane.

The moment I dumped the torch in the canal I knew I would never tell a living soul about the man. Digby and I walked for miles that morning as I worked out what to say when the body was discovered.

I kept it simple.

I erased him.

I imagined myself back in the garden, swamped in darkness, walking down the stone path with a thin strip of yellow providing just enough light to track the ground. This time I spot the dog hovering on my side of the fence line and the gate just as I'd left it, closed and bolted. I pictured myself taking Digby by the collar and leading him back to the house, locking the back door, settling him into his basket by the Aga and heading upstairs to my own bed. I imagined this over and over again as I walked up the steep, rutted chalk path towards the top of the ridge, and by the time I reached the top the story felt real and believable and possible.

Standing on the ancient Ridgeway trail, I looked out at the world. To the left, in the distance, the cooling towers of Didcot Power Station rose from the ground, oddly beautiful in the early morning haze. To the right, I picked out the white-tipped locks of the shimmering Grand Union Canal that had swallowed my torch for breakfast. Dropping my gaze, I saw a slumbering Ridgelow nestled into dark green hillside, so quiet and still it could have been frozen in time. And somewhere in that peaceful haven, on that peaceful Sunday morning, on a peaceful public footpath lay a dead man waiting to be discovered.

I was expecting the police to knock and ask questions. It was inevitable. But I felt sick as a pig when I sat before them, the constable in her official uniform and the detective sporting a bland veneer, and even sicker when I was shown the photograph of Robert Ashmere.

But I wasn't expecting the note.

When the policeman held up that crumpled piece of paper with my name and address written on it in a smudged scrawl, my world caved in. The thought that I'd killed a random drunken man was terrible, but that he might be someone I knew? It was like being shot in the heart at point blank range and all the tiny ripped-up pieces sewn back together with barbed wire. There and then I was sucked into the dead man's world, injected with a powerful desire to know who he was and how he knew me. When guilt wasn't shaking my bones, desperation gnawed at them.

And to think all this came about because I fell head over heels in love with a scruffy little dog. Who'd have thought that doing a good deed would lead to such misery? When I re-homed Digby I didn't expect my new pet to come with that sort of baggage, such deadly connections.

Robert wound up dead.

Pitts got banged up.

And I got caught up in a horrible nightmare that will live with me day in, day out — my very own life sentence.

I will never forgive myself for killing him. He won't let me. I am now forever wedded to Robert Ashmere, another stranger, Till Death Us Do Part.